"Evasive maneuvers, pattern Zeta-nine-two!"

"Yes, Captain," answered Will Riker at the auxiliary conn controls. The regular conn officer sat dazedly on the deck beside his burned-out console, and Dr. Beverly Crusher ministered to a wound on his forearm. Everywhere on the bridge was the acrid smell of burnt and overloaded circuits, caused by high-density electromagnetic pulses sweeping the ship.

"Shields down to forty percent," reported Data at the ops console. The android spoke in a calm, business-like tone that belied the urgency of the situation.

"Target aft torpedoes on the lead Cardassian ship," ordered Picard.

"Targeting quantum torpedoes," reported Ensign Craycroft on tactical. She was a young woman with nerves of titanium, and she reminded Picard of another young woman who had manned that station ten years ago on another vessel called the *Enterprise*. It seemed like a lifetime since they had grieved the loss of Tasha Yar, because now Starfleet lost a thousand Tasha Yars every day.

"They're lined up," Riker reported urgently.

"Lower shields," ordered Picard. "Fire!"

STAR TREK
THE NEXT GENERATION®

THE
DOMINION WAR
BOOK ONE

BEHIND ENEMY LINES

A Novel by John Vornholt

POCKET BOOKS
New York   London   Toronto   Sydney   Tokyo   Singapore

An *Original* Publication of POCKET BOOKS

POCKET BOOKS, a division of Simon & Schuster Inc.
1230 Avenue of the Americas, New York, NY 10020

Copyright © 1998 by Paramount Pictures. All Rights Reserved.

STAR TREK is a Registered Trademark of Paramount Pictures.

A VIACOM COMPANY

This book is published by Pocket Books, a division of Simon & Schuster Inc., under exclusive license from Paramount Pictures.

ISBN: 0-671-02499-X

First Pocket Books printing November 1998

10 9 8 7 6 5 4 3 2 1

POCKET and colophon are registered trademarks of Simon & Schuster Inc.

Printed in the U.S.A.

For Dennis, who taught
me stealth and guile

BEHIND ENEMY LINES

Chapter One

RO LAREN LOOKED UP at the yellowing clouds, which rested uneasily upon the jagged teeth of the olive-hued mountains in the distance. She didn't see the beauty of the twilit sky or the flowering land with harvesting season upon it; all she saw were the vapor trails of shuttlecraft and small transports streaking away from the planet Galion. The former Starfleet officer knew that most of those vessels were little more than junk and had no warp drive. Where did they think they were going?

Her hands paused over the lush sprawl of tomato vines and plump red fruit in her small vegetable patch. Who would have thought she could have gotten so much pleasure from coaxing food from the ground? Emotions gripped her throat like the teeth of a vole, and she wanted to lash out with her fists. *This isn't just!* No sooner had they found a semblance of peace

1

than another war was engulfing them with its acrid
stink. Ro knew well the stench of war. Burning rubble,
bloated bodies, wretched refugee camps—those were
her childhood memories. This war was less her fight
than any of those other conflicts, yet it threatened to
dwarf them all.

She heard a door slam inside the corrugated shed
that served as their home. Ro took a deep breath and
rose from her muddy knees. Lean, hardened by
manual labor, her brown hair cropped short, she was
more striking than beautiful. Her nose ridges were
prominent, and she wore the traditional chains and
bands on her right ear, proclaiming her Bajoran
heritage in this mostly human Maquis community.
Ro wiped her hands on the apron that covered her
frayed jumpsuit, and she listened to his footsteps
creaking on the thin floor of the prefabricated shed.
Derek sounded unusually tense; he was probably
working up the nerve to face her.

The door banged open again, and she heard his
footsteps on the black volcanic gravel that served as
their soil. Only a combination of hydroponic tech-
niques, chemical fertilization, and constant irrigation
had rendered it fit for growing. Ro wasn't keen on
leaving this soil just yet—she had poured too much
sweat into it.

The human walked around the corner of the shed
and stopped when he saw her. She could tell everything she needed to know from the slouch of his
shoulders and his tired blue eyes; even his mustache
drooped wearily. He was gray-haired and many years
her senior, but he had a rakish charm that kept him
youthful. Today that charm could not disguise the
weathered, worried lines in his face. Derek had been a

freelance smuggler and weapons runner, but she had won him over to the Maquis cause. He still dealt weapons, but for his people, not profit.

She ran to him, and he wrapped his wiry arms around her slender frame. A strand of his gray hair brushed her cheek, and Derek lifted her chin and gazed at her. "They didn't take the deal," he said softly. "We have to go."

"Again?" she muttered, pulling away from him. "I've been forced to run too many times—I'm not sure I can do it again. We stood up to the Cardassians and the Federation; can't we stand up to *them?*"

He gave her a melancholy smile. "These aren't the Cardies or the Feds. This is the Dominion. We can't fight them; nobody can. The Federation, the Klingons—they're getting crushed right and left, and the Jem'Hadar warships look like they're invincible. Plus they've rebuilt the entire Cardassian fleet, and they're eager for conquest. Believe it or not, our envoys saw two ships full of Federation prisoners come in while they were docked at Tral Kliban for the negotiations."

Ro snorted derisively. "Some negotiations. What did you expect, trying to convince the Cardassians that we're *neutral?* Once an enemy of the Cardassians, always an enemy."

"Not so," answered Derek softly. "We may have failed, but the Bajorans accepted a nonaggression treaty. They *are* neutral."

"Bajor?" scoffed Ro. "I don't believe it."

He gave her a sad smile that insisted it was true. "I don't think Bajor had much choice, and the Dominion probably did it just to annoy the Cardassians, to let them know who's boss. Deep Space Nine fell, and it's all going to fall—the whole Federation. Only the

3

cloaked mines they stuck in front of the wormhole have saved them so far.

"We're small potatoes, but the Dominion *will* get around to us. Our spies say they want to clear out this sector, because they're building something big on the other side of the Badlands, near Sector 283."

"What?"

"An artificial wormhole," answered Derek with awe in his voice. "They may be using slave labor— Federation prisoners."

Ro stared at him, stunned by the implications. With an artificial wormhole deep in Cardassian space, Dominion forces could travel back and forth between the Alpha and Gamma quadrants without using the Bajoran wormhole. They could even destroy it, along with everything the Bajorans held dear.

"Some of our cells have already returned to the Federation," declared Ro. "We've got to swallow our pride and do the same thing. With the Federation's help, maybe we can defend this system instead of running."

Now it was Derek's turn to snort. "The Federation will be lucky if they can defend *Earth.* We're unimportant, forgotten. About all we can do is find some quiet place to hide until it's all over." His attempt at a smile looked more like a wince.

"So the proud Maquis just run for their lives, giving up years of struggle?" asked Ro disdainfully.

Derek kicked a black pebble. "Our envoys got one promise from the Cardassians—they'll give us time to evacuate, as long as we don't try to enter the hostilities."

Ro stared at him in disbelief. "Evacuate to *where?*

There's no running from a war like this. We can fight, or we can surrender and be at their mercy."

"Bajor's always an option," answered Derek, calmly ignoring her tirade as he often did. "Remember, Bajor is neutral. In fact, the committee is assembling a crew for you, and you're going to captain the *Orb of Peace* and take as many people as we can fit in. Traveling as Bajorans—with you in command—you stand a good chance of getting through Dominion space."

"I wasn't even at the meeting!" snapped Ro. "Who decided this for me?"

He gave her a weary smile and gripped her shoulders. "Laren, you're the only one who can pull off a mission like this. We've got to gain control of the evacuation, so we don't just have people scattering to the four winds. We'll never find each other again. The Maquis are a community, even if we keep getting chased off our land. I'll feel better knowing you're on Bajor. I'll come as soon as possible."

Ro's nose ridges compressed like a bellows. "You're not coming with me?"

"No. Someone has got to move our weapons stores, and I'm the only one who knows where everything is. I mean, we're not total pacifists, are we?" For an instant, the roguish grin was back.

She gripped him desperately, and he hugged her, his fingers digging into her flesh. When their lips met, it was a bittersweet kiss with a taste of tears. In a vegetable patch behind a corrugated shed on a little-known planet in what was formerly the Cardassian Demilitarized Zone, now the Dominion, they clung to each other. They knew it could be the last time.

"How long do we have?" she asked hoarsely.

"An hour, maybe. Your ship is en route."

"They may have to wait," said Ro, taking his arm and pulling him toward the shed.

Ro materialized in the small but elegant transporter chamber of the *Orb of Peace*. In her gray cap and jumpsuit, with a duffel bag slung over her shoulder, she looked like a common crew member. But she was the captain on this ship, as testified to by the importance of her welcoming committee. Crunched into the dimly lit chamber were three provisional admirals, two of the envoys who had returned empty-handed, and a cadre of dignitaries that spilled out into the corridor.

I might have known, thought Ro. *I'm ferrying the brass to safety, not the common folk.*

Although these men and women outranked her in the Maquis hierarchy, they looked upon her with awe. Ro was a legend to the Maquis—a reclusive figure who had deserted Starfleet to join their hopeless cause, only to become one of their greatest heroes. Time and time again, she had distinguished herself in guerrilla attacks against both the Cardassians and the Federation. Yet when the Cardassian-Klingon War brought them relative peace, she had spurned Maquis offers of higher rank. A small cell of well-trained fighters was all she had ever commanded, until now. Ro knew she was an enigma to these people, an outsider whom they both respected and feared.

"Citizen Ro," said Shin Watanabe, one of the recently returned envoys, "we are pleased that you have undertaken this mission."

Ro stepped off the transporter platform, and the sea of people parted respectfully for her.

"You know our objective," said one admiral brusquely. "Do you think we can make it to Bajor?"

With her jaw set determinedly, Ro studied the faces confronting her. Most of what she saw was fear, uncertainty, and anger, emotions she could well understand. These people were close to falling apart, and she had to make sure they held together.

"I know you're all afraid," she began, "and so am I. But we have to get one thing straight before we start this journey. I am now Captain Ro—by *your* choice—and I am in total command of this vessel. Bajor is a considerable distance, and a lot can happen between here and there. I want your promise that nobody will overrule my orders and decisions."

Watanabe laughed nervously. "Well, naturally, we will have some input and advice—"

Ro jumped back onto the transporter platform, then turned to face them. "Transport me back. I'd rather take my chances with the Cardassians than have you questioning my orders."

A female admiral charged forward. "Laren, we've known each other a long time. Don't start playing hierarchical mind games."

"We all know a ship can have only one captain," said Ro evenly. "We have no world, no homeland—only this vessel flying under a false flag. When you elected me captain, you chose to put your lives into my hands. It was your decision. If I'm in charge of this ship, then we're going to be a *crew,* not a rabble. It's that simple—take it or leave it."

The second admiral, a older man named Sharfer,

saluted her. "Aye, Captain. You have my word on it, and I'll throw anyone into the brig who argues with you."

The others stared at him in shock; then they lowered their heads in resignation, shame, and fear. Ro hadn't meant to come down on them so harshly, but it was best to settle this matter here and now. The journey would be difficult enough without endlessly debating every decision. Besides, Ro wasn't in a very charitable mood today. The good-bye with Derek had been painful.

"Admiral Sharfer," she said, "have I been assigned a first officer?"

"Not yet. For the past year, this ship has only had a maintenance crew. We've staffed it as best we could on short notice."

"Then would you be willing to serve as first officer?" asked Ro.

He nodded solemnly, and the Bajoran jumped off the platform and knifed through the crowd. She ushered Sharfer out the door into the corridor, ignoring the stares of the others. After walking past a spiral staircase that led to the lower deck, Ro got her bearings and strode toward the bridge, with the admiral walking beside her.

"What's the ship's status?" she asked Sharfer.

"As you know, the *Orb of Peace* was in bad shape when we bought her on the black market. We refitted her, leaving enough original technology to show a Bajoran warp signature."

"So she's slow," said Ro, "and underarmed."

Sharfer smiled. "Well, we boosted her armaments with six photon torpedoes, and she is capable of warp three—but she's still just a midrange transport."

"What's our complement?"

"Crew of twenty, plus eighty passengers."

Ro scowled. "They must really be crammed in."

"They are. But she was meant to carry clergy, so it didn't take much to refit her as a troop transport. There's one good thing—she has a working food replicator."

"That makes her a rarity in the Maquis fleet," said Ro dryly. "See if the replicator can make some Bajoran uniforms for the bridge crew. Are there any other Bajorans on board?"

"Only one, a junior engineer named Shon Navo."

"He's no longer an engineer. Promote him to the bridge crew—he's to be on duty every moment when I'm not, which won't be often. If we get hailed by Dominion ships, they *must* see a Bajoran in command on the bridge."

"Understood," said Sharfer.

A door slid open at their approach, and they swept onto the bridge. The small bridge of the *Orb of Peace* was more tasteful than practical. It was appointed in red with austere control consoles that looked like prayer booths, and the main viewscreen was framed with sayings of the Prophets. "The ways of the Prophets lead to peace" was the first word of advice to catch her eye. Ro hid her scowl, having never been as religious or aesthetic as most of her people.

The three-person crew, which included a young pilot at the conn, an operations officer, and a tactical officer, jumped to their feet. "Captain on the bridge!" piped one.

"At ease," she told them. "I'll learn your names as we go. First dim running lights by sixty percent. That'll help to hide the fact that most of us aren't

Bajorans." The young crew sat stiffly in their seats, and the ops officer dimmed the lights as ordered.

There was no official captain's chair on the Bajoran craft, and Ro took a seat at an auxiliary console. "Set course for Bajor."

"Direct course?" asked the conn. "No evasion?"

"Ensign, obey my orders as I give them," said Ro testily. "We're not going to be evasive—we have nothing to hide. We're a Bajoran trade delegation to the Dominion, and now we're headed home. I only wish that we had time to surgically alter everyone to look Bajoran; but we don't—so we'll have to fake it. Set course for Bajor, maximum warp."

"Yes, sir." The young blond woman worked her ornate controls. "Course laid in."

"Take us out of orbit, one-third impulse."

"Aye, sir."

Admiral Sharfer moved toward the doorway. "I'll get to work on those uniforms, and I'll have Mr. Shon assigned to the bridge."

Ro nodded. The reality of their departure from Galion had left an unexpected lump in her throat, and she didn't trust herself to say much.

"We're clear of orbit," reported the conn officer. "Warp engines on-line."

Ro pointed her finger exactly as she had seen a certain Starfleet captain do it. "Engage."

Phaser blasts from two Galor-class Cardassian warships crackled across space and rocked the sleek form of the *Enterprise*-E. The Sovereign-class vessel shuddered before it veered into a desperate dive, with the yellow, fish-shaped warships in quick pursuit.

On the bridge, Captain Jean-Luc Picard gripped the armrests of his command chair. "Evasive maneuvers, pattern Zeta-nine-two!"

"Yes, sir," answered Will Riker at the auxiliary conn controls. The regular conn officer sat dazedly on the deck beside his burned-out console, and Dr. Beverly Crusher ministered to a wound on his forearm. Everywhere on the bridge was the acrid smell of burnt and overloaded circuits, caused by high-density electromagnetic pulses sweeping the ship.

"Shields down to forty percent," reported Data at the ops console. The android spoke in a calm, businesslike tone that belied the urgency of the situation.

"Target aft torpedoes on the lead craft," ordered Picard.

"Targeting quantum torpedoes," reported Ensign Craycroft on tactical. She was a young woman with nerves of titanium, and she reminded Picard of another young woman who had manned that station ten years ago on another vessel called the *Enterprise*. It seemed like a lifetime since they had grieved the loss of Tasha Yar, because now Starfleet lost a thousand Tasha Yars every day.

"They're lined up," Riker reported urgently.

"Lower shields," ordered Picard. "Fire!"

Ensign Craycroft plied her console. "Torpedoes away!"

A brace of torpedoes shot from the tail of the *Enterprise,* and they looked like shooting stars as they streaked across the blackness of space. The torpedoes swerved into the lead Cardassian ship like hungry piranhas, and it exploded in a blaze of gas, flames, and imploding antimatter which engulfed the second ship behind it. The second ship veered off, sparkling like a Christmas tree before it went dark and began to drift. The *Enterprise* kept going, steady on course.

Riker looked back at Picard and gave him a boyish grin. "Works every time."

"It works on Cardassians in any case," said the captain cautiously. He didn't like being reduced to tricks, but when they were outnumbered by superior forces, they needed all the help they could get. The Cardassians were arrogant and eager to make a kill on big game such as the *Enterprise*. That made them careless, something the Jem'Hadar were not.

"Damage report," ordered Riker.

"There are energy fluctuations on the starboard nacelle, bridge, and decks fifteen through twenty-six," reported Data. "Plasma couplings and EPS conduits on deck seventeen require immediate repair. Recovery systems are compensating, and repair crews have been dispatched. Shields are holding steady at forty percent, and I am rerouting power from the main reactor. Five casualties reported, none serious."

Beverly Crusher rose wearily to her feet and brushed back a strand of blonde hair that had escaped from her hair band. Her lab coat was stained, and her face looked gaunt—a doctor at war. "I'm on my way to sickbay," she said.

The doctor looked down at her patient and gave him a professional smile. "Ensign Charles is stabilized, but I want him to sit still for a while. I'll send somebody for him as soon as I can. Just keep him comfortable."

Picard gave her a wan smile. "Still shorthanded down there?"

"No, I just come up here in case both you and Will

12

get knocked out, and I can finally take over. I want to be on hand when it happens."

"Good thinking," said Riker, who appreciated gallows humor more than Picard. "But we could have the computer notify you."

"I'm sure I'll know." The doctor put her head down and walked across the spacious bridge, past two empty science stations, unused since the war started. Her shoulders stiffened as she entered the turbolift, but she didn't look back.

Picard swallowed dryly. He was having a hard time adjusting to a war in which they were being overwhelmed on all fronts, in which every department was shorthanded and shell-shocked. Many of his most experienced crew members were now chief engineers, doctors, and captains on their own vessels. Only by calling in personal favors had he managed to hang on to his core staff of officers. Defeats and surrenders had taken their toll, but Starfleet could build more ships faster than they could build good crew to fly them.

"What's the fleet situation?" he asked Data.

Theoretically, they were in the middle of a major offensive against Dominion forces, but Starfleet had stopped massing their ships in close formation. The Dominion fleets simply outgunned them, and they couldn't stand toe-to-toe against them. Instead the new tactic was to spread the battle in three dimensions, so that the enemy had to break off and pursue. With good luck and a good crew, a captain might face only two or three Cardassian warships instead of one Jem'Hadar battle cruiser, and he might live to fight another hit-and-run skirmish another day.

Data shook his head. "Captain, I cannot make an accurate assessment without breaking subspace silence, although long-range scans should indicate possible hostilities." The android's fingers swiftly worked his console.

"Search for distress signals," said Picard, rubbing his eyes. "Let's go to our secondary mission—rescue."

"Setting predetermined course for secondary mission," reported Riker. "Warp three?"

"Full impulse, until we make repairs," replied the captain. "I want to coddle this ship—she's all we've got."

Riker nodded and tapped his comm badge. "Riker to Engineering. How are we doing, Geordi?"

"Fine," came a curt reply. "I know I owe you a repair crew—they're on their way. Is the war over yet?"

"Not quite," said Riker with a half smile.

Captain Picard settled back into his chair. By all rights, they had destroyed one enemy ship and had crippled another, and they should be finished for the day. But somebody out there needed help—a great many somebodies.

On the *Orb of Peace*, the bridge was not as spacious and as efficiently laid out as the circular bridge of the *Enterprise*. The dimly lit chamber reminded Ro of a small Bajoran chapel, facing the viewscreen instead of the shrine. To complete the impression, there were all those religious homilies decorating the frame around the viewscreen. However, the elegant Bajoran instrument panels lent a soothing reddish and turquoise glow to the surroundings.

Ro looked back at Shon Navo, a teenager who ought to be in school instead of fighting a war. The two of

14

them were wearing the rust-brown uniforms of Bajor, and they were wearing their most ostentatious ear apparel. As the only Bajorans on this Bajoran ship, they had to play every part. For two hours, their journey had been totally uneventful, and they were chewing up the parsecs as fast as the transport would go. Ro felt she could take a few moments to coach the boy in his duties.

"Mr. Shon," she began, "stay close to me."

"Yes, Captain," he said eagerly, as he shuffled up to her right shoulder blade. She judged him to be slightly shorter than herself.

"If anybody hails us for any reason, you are to position yourself in a similar position, very close to me. We'll go on visual and let them know we're Bajoran."

"Yes, sir."

"I will address remarks to you as if you were my first officer, and we will speak in Bajoran. They'll be able to translate it, so keep the remarks pertinent."

He cleared his throat nervously.

"Yes?"

"I . . . I don't speak Bajoran. I used to know it as a kid, I think, but I've forgotten it."

"War orphan?"

He nodded. "And my new parents took me with them to the Fellowship Colony. Boy, that was nice . . . for a while. Then the Federation betrayed us and handed us over to the Cardassians."

"Let's keep personal opinions to a minimum," said Ro. "We're going to Bajor. Despite being officially neutral, Bajorans hold the Federation in high regard. After all, the Emissary is a human."

The boy's face hardened. "Thus far, the Cardassians have killed all four of my parents and have tried to kill me several times. Anyone who appeases them is a coward."

"I'm not telling you you can't hate," said Ro. "Just keep it to yourself."

"Yes, sir."

"You might be forced to answer a hail when I'm not here. Don't delay—it looks suspicious. Simply identify yourself as the first officer and send for me. This isn't a big ship—I'll get here quickly. Time permitting, I'll teach you a few Bajoran words. You can start with—"

"Captain," said the operations officer, his back stiffening, "there's a fleet of ships passing within four parsecs of us. Two of them have dropped out of warp and are breaking off. They're headed our way."

"Where are the other ones going?" asked Ro urgently. "Plot their course."

"The two Jem'Hadar ships have gone back into warp and will catch up with us in a few minutes!" said the nervous pilot.

"We'll talk our way out of it," declared Ro. "We're lucky they're Jem'Hadar, not Cardassians. Get Admiral Sharfer to the bridge. And I want to know where the rest of that fleet is going."

"Oh, no," groaned the tactical officer. "They're . . . they're headed toward Galion! What are we going to do?"

Ro could tell she was a Maquis-trained officer, not Starfleet, and she tried to have patience with her. "First of all, get control of yourself."

"Yes, sir," responded the woman, straightening her shoulders. "Should I arm torpedoes?"

"No, don't make any aggressive moves without my command. By the way, we all have people back on Galion."

The woman smiled gratefully at her, then gulped. "Should we warn them?"

"If we send a message right now," said Ro, "we probably won't get to finish it."

Ro turned to gaze at Shon Navo. The fresh-faced Bajoran looked so innocent, even though his life had been steeped in tragedy and hatred. "Shon, I want you to be the first thing they see. Just identify our vessel, say we're Bajoran, and that you have sent for the captain. With any luck, they'll be in a hurry."

She paced behind her unfamiliar crew. "Lower the lights another ten percent. Put the ships on screen."

The viewscreen revealed two silvery shapes in the distance, dwarfed by the vastness of space. The Jem'Hadar attack ships looked unprepossessing— they were smaller than the *Orb of Peace*—but Ro knew they were tremendously swift, maneuverable, and destructive. She had never seen the Jem'Hadar, but she had heard reports of their single-minded ruthlessness and devotion to their masters, the Founders.

"They're at warp six and gaining on us," said the pilot.

"Steady as she goes," ordered Ro. "Don't come out of warp unless they force us to. Don't change speed."

On the viewscreen, the Dominion ships were larger now—two puglike fighters with twin nacelles, all spit and chrome. Ro imagined that her ship was being scanned and their warp signature was being verified. Even though she was expecting it, the sudden beep of the communications panel made her pulse quicken.

"They're hailing us," said the tactical officer with a quavering voice. "And they're demanding that we come out of warp."

"Answer the hail first." Ro motioned to Shon Navo to step in front of the viewscreen as she retreated to the shadows at the rear of the bridge.

Spine erect, trying to look like his idea of a first officer, the young Bajoran stepped into the pool of light in front of the viewscreen. He cleared his throat and nodded.

At once, the frightening aspect of a Jem'Hadar warrior appeared on the screen. His face was gnarled with prickly ridges like a cactus, and his skin was gray and lifeless. His eyes appeared to be red and vivid, yet they were darkly hooded like a lizard's eyes. A strange mechanical appendage seemed to grow out of his collarbone and hover in front of his left eye, and a tube pumped a white liquid into an orifice in the side of his neck. Behind the Jem'Hadar stood another less imposing figure. Like her, he was hovering in the shadows.

"We are the *Orb of Peace,* a Bajoran transport," said the young Bajoran in a confident yet respectful tone of voice.

"Come out of warp," ordered the Jem'Hadar in a gruff voice. "This is Dominion space."

"I'm only the first officer," answered Shon, his voice cracking. "The captain has been summoned."

"This is Dominion space," repeated the craggy face on the viewscreen.

"And we are friends of the Dominion," replied Ro, marching to the front of the bridge. Shon Navo fell into line behind her, nearly leaning on her back for support. She could feel him shivering.

"Captain Tilo at your service," she added.

"Come out of warp," ordered the Jem'Hadar.

Ro nodded to the conn and said loudly, "Full impulse. Maintain course for Bajor."

On the Dominion attack ship, the shadowy figure at the rear of the cockpit leaned over the shoulder of the pilot. This one was a different species than the Jem'Hadar, although he certainly wasn't Cardassian. He had huge ears, pale violet eyes, and an obsequious expression, like a professional politician. A Vorta, she thought, the midlevel managers of the Dominion.

"What is your business in this sector?" he asked pleasantly enough.

"We are a Bajoran trade delegation," she answered. "In the past, we have traded with many worlds in this sector, and we hope that we can continue to do so."

"We're in a state of war," answered the little man with the big ears, "as we aid our allies in their battle against the unscrupulous practices of the Federation. You might be wise to continue on your way home without further interruption."

"That is our intention," answered Ro. "Thanks to the benevolence of the Dominion."

The Vorta nodded in appreciation of the compliment, then he added, "We had noticed a large number of passengers on your vessel—most of them human."

"Carrying passengers is a sideline," answered Ro evenly, "especially on our return voyage. We are headed straight home."

"Make certain of that." The Vorta nodded to the Jem'Hadar pilot, and the screen went blank as the link ended. A moment later, they watched the two Dominion vessels zoom off into warp.

Ro scowled. "What's their course?"

"The same course we traveled," replied tactical. "They're headed toward Galion and the Maquis settlements."

"Do we resume warp speed for Bajor?" asked the helmsman, his voice quavering.

Ro gazed from the expectant faces of her young crew members to the wizened face of Admiral Sharfer. None of them ventured an opinion; none of them offered to make the decision for her. This is what she had said she wanted—total control over this vessel and the lives of a hundred people—and she had it.

Her eyes rested on the young blond woman at the tactical station: her face was tight with fear, but she kept her tears at bay. Ro knew the fear wasn't for herself but for those left behind, unaware that an enemy fleet was streaking toward them. Her moist eyes seemed to say that only an animal flees without any concern for loved ones left behind. They couldn't beat the Dominion ships to Galion, but they could try to rescue survivors.

"Alert Galion Central," she ordered. "Tell them about the Dominion fleet. Reverse course, maximum warp."

"Aye, Captain," said the conn officer with a mixture of awe and apprehension.

The boxy little transport executed a 180-degree turn and elongated into a streak of golden light before vanishing entirely.

Chapter Two

THE ONCE LUSH PLANET OF GALION floated in space like a charred tree stump, with only patches of moss left alive. The great forests and groves of olive trees were blackened swamps, and the lakes were dark with silt and mud. The cities and towns were nothing but blasted craters, still burning like hellish volcanoes. Half a million dead, at the very least. There was open weeping on the bridge of the *Orb of Peace*, and Ro said nothing to discourage it. The sight was so horrible that she almost ordered it to be taken off the viewscreen, but it demanded to be witnessed.

She walked over to the navigation console and asked softly, "Any life signs?"

The young man shook his head. "No, none, sir . . . although the extreme radiation could be affecting our sensors."

"They were so much faster than us," said Admiral

Sharfer in shock. "They got here in minutes, and it took us two hours."

Ro strode behind her crew and admonished them, "Keep scanning for life signs—target the cities." In her eyes and her heart, she knew it was hopeless. Galion was nothing but a funeral pyre, and Derek was dead, along with scores of friends and comrades.

The bridge continued to fill with passengers and their families, and the anquished cries became too great for her to bear. Ro turned to face them, holding up her hands to quiet their gasps and sobs. "You are witnesses. Without provocation, the Dominion has destroyed our homeworld, our last refuge. I submit that we are no longer innocent bystanders in this war—we're part of it."

She strode to the conn and gazed over the young man's shoulder at the readouts. "It will take four days to reach Bajor, and they could destroy us anywhere along the way. On Bajor, Shon and I could fit in, but the rest of you would have to be in hiding, right under the nose of the Cardassians on Deep Space Nine. I don't think you can hide from this war—I think you have to stand up and be counted."

She tapped her finger on the panel. "I say we cut straight across the DMZ to the Federation lines and offer them our help. We can be there in a few hours."

"Yeah, kill the lying bastards!" cried the envoy who had spent days begging the Dominion to leave the remnants of the Maquis alone.

"Our safety—" began another man.

"Safety is illusory," answered Admiral Sharfer. "The enemy has shown us that. We must return to the Federation."

"That will mean prison for a lot of us," muttered the other admiral. A resolute yet pained shadow played across her face.

"I'm higher on their list than any of you," replied Ro, "but we have to stand by the Federation, no matter the personal risk. We certainly can't depend upon the mercy of the Dominion. Are there any life signs down there?"

"No, sir," came the answer.

"Set course for Federation space, best guess," she ordered. "And turn up the lights in here."

On the viewscreen of the *Enterprise* was a heart-rending sight—a Federation starship floating in space, dark and lifeless, with several jagged rifts in her hull. The *Gallant* was a Nebula-class vessel, more compact than the *Enterprise,* with her twin nacelles located directly beneath the saucer section and a large stabilizer atop the craft. Not a light shone on the derelict vessel, and debris stretched behind it like a trail of blood.

"Life signs?" asked Captain Picard, already dreading the answer.

Data shook his head. "None, sir. There are fourteen separate breaches in the hull, and it is unlikely that any section of the ship maintained sufficient integrity to support life. The distress signal is on automatic and is fading in strength."

"It looks like they used her for target practice," muttered Riker through clenched teeth.

"Log her position," ordered Picard glumly. "Someone can tow her in later. Alert sickbay and the transporter rooms to stand down—there's no one to save here."

Data frowned at his readouts. "I am receiving two new distress signals in the same vicinity at a distance of six parsecs. One is Starfleet; the other is . . . Bajoran."

"Set course, maximum warp," ordered Picard. "With all this killing, it would be nice to save even one life today."

Within minutes, the *Enterprise* was closing in on another pocket of death and destruction in the unforgiving bleakness of space. Picard could only hope that this time they would arrive soon enough to help.

"Long-range scans show hostilities in progress," reported Data. "An Ambassador-class starship, the *Aurora,* and an unknown Bajoran transport are engaged with a Jem'Hadar cruiser."

"Shields up," ordered Picard. "As soon as we come out of warp, fire phasers and keep firing. Don't give the Jem'Hadar time to react."

"Yes, sir," snapped Ensign Craycroft on tactical. "Phasers ready."

"Coming out of warp in thirty seconds," said Riker from the auxilary console. "I thought the Bajorans were neutral."

"This war doesn't play favorites," replied Picard. "On screen."

The Jem'Hadar battle cruiser looked like a bullet with short fins and a vibrant blue glow along her hull. She was chasing the *Aurora* through a thin, purplish gas cloud, exchanging fire with the crippled ship. Above the fray, a rectangular transport fired a photon torpedo at the Jem'Hadar cruiser, rocking it slightly. But the enemy had its sights set on the bigger ship, and was ignoring everything else.

The captain tapped the comm panel on his chair.

"Sickbay and transporter rooms, stand by for casualties."

With skillful piloting, the *Enterprise* dropped out of warp matching the speed and course of the enemy, and they bombarded the cruiser with phaser fire. Suddenly, the Dominion warship was caught in a three-way cross fire, yet the single-minded Jem'Hadar continued to pound the fleeing *Aurora.* To her captain's credit, *Aurora* never stopped firing, even as a brace of torpedoes dissolved her port nacelle. The once-proud Starfleet ship fizzled like a dud firecracker before it lurched into a fatal spin.

Picard wanted to commence rescue efforts, but they were too far away to use transporters. Unless they eliminated the Jem'Hadar cruiser, they would all suffer the same fate as the *Aurora.*

"Target quantum torpedoes," he ordered. "Ready to lower shields."

"Torpedoes targeted," reported Ensign Craycroft.

"Shields down. Fire!"

Picard could only hope that the cruiser's shields had been sufficiently softened during the battle. Nobody breathed on the bridge of the *Enterprise* as the torpedoes slammed into the Jem'Hadar craft. The first two shots blistered off the enemy's shields, but the second two found their mark, chewing up the aft fins on the sleek craft. Even as explosions racked the Jem'Hadar ship, she came about and unleashed a withering blast of phaser fire that engulfed both the *Enterprise* and the plucky Bajoran transport.

As the bridge rocked, the captain hung on to the arms of his chair. "Keep firing!" he shouted.

Craycroft staggered back to her feet and pounded her console. At once, another bracket of torpedoes streaked from the saucer of the *Enterprise* into the Dominion ship. Energy rippled along the hull of the doomed cruiser, finally reaching her antimatter core, and she exploded in a violent shower of gas, flame, and debris.

"Captain," said Data. "The Bajoran craft is severely damaged. They are losing life-support."

"All transporter rooms, lock on to the Bajoran craft and begin transporting," ordered Picard. "Med teams, report to transporter rooms."

He turned to Data. "The *Aurora*—"

As if in answer to his unfinished question, the Ambassador-class starship erupted in an explosion greater than that which had claimed the Jem'Hadar ship. All of space seemed torn apart by the blast, which sent waves of sparkling confetti swirling into space.

Picard's shoulders slumped, and he turned away from the tragic sight on the viewscreen.

"No survivors," said Riker glumly.

"Log it." Picard turned back to the viewscreen, half-expecting the Bajoran transport to explode as well. But the small, unassuming vessel just hung there in space, still intact.

"Captain," said Data with a trace of puzzlement, "we have transported ninety-five wounded people off the Bajoran ship, and most of them are human."

"Human?" asked Picard. "Not Bajoran?"

"Two of them are Bajoran," replied the android.

Riker frowned. "Maybe that explains why they were fighting the Dominion."

"Is the transport salvageable?" asked Picard.

Data nodded. "Yes, sir. Except for the failure of

life-support and artificial-gravity systems, it is relatively undamaged."

"If they're civilians, they'll need their ship," suggested Riker. "She's small enough that she won't slow us down."

"Ready tractor beam," ordered Picard. "Let's be thankful that we were in time to save a few lives. Set course for the Kreel system. Maintain subspace silence."

The captain wasn't anxious to find out how the battle had fared. From what he had seen today, he hardly expected victory. No doubt they had widened the front and won a few skirmishes here and there, but he couldn't be optimistic that they had dealt a serious blow to the Dominion and Cardassian forces. They were fighting now to keep from being overrun, nothing more.

"Tractor beam locked on," reported the conn. "Course laid in."

"Maximum warp," said the captain. "Engage."

The crew of the *Enterprise* were as brave as they come, yet there was a palpable sense of relief on the bridge once they were headed back to Federation space. Picard knew they could keep fighting—there was no shortage of Dominion ships along the ragged front—but his crew was exhausted. Sickbay was full of wounded civilians, and the *Enterprise* still had damage to repair. Despite a gnawing sense of guilt over having survived when so many other brave captains and crews hadn't, Picard knew it was time to call it a day.

He was rubbing his eyes and wondering if he had the energy to get up and get himself a cup of tea, when the comm panel beeped. "Picard here," he answered wearily.

"Jean-Luc," said the familiar voice of Beverly Crusher. "I think you should come to sickbay."

"Is there a problem?"

"We've got gurneys spilling out into the corridor, but that's normal these days." She paused. "We beamed over somebody you know from the transport. I've sent for a security team."

That piqued his interest, and Picard rose to his feet. "I'll be right there. Number One, you have the bridge."

Ro Laren! Picard stared in amazement at the unconscious figure stretched out on the observation table in sickbay. As if it wasn't crowded enough, four gold-collared security officers stood guard around her table and the beds of several prominent Maquis officers. The captain never thought he would see his former lieutenant again, not in this lifetime, but here she was.

Unbidden, a host of memories came cascading back to Captain Picard. He remembered when young Ensign Ro had first come aboard the *Enterprise*-D—she was already under a cloud and barely hanging on to her Starfleet commission. With her independent attitude and spotty record, Ro had instantly earned the distrust of Will Riker and half the crew, but they needed her to infiltrate a cadre of Bajoran terrorists. She had succeeded in that difficult task as she had in so many others, until she had finally become one of his most trusted officers.

Then she had betrayed him and Starfleet.

Or was it Starfleet that had betrayed Ro? After

promoting her and training her in antiterrorist tactics, Admiral Nechayev had thrust her into a volatile situation in the Cardassian Demilitarized Zone. Perhaps it was inevitable that a renegade and underdog like Ro would sympathize with the ultimate underdogs—the Maquis. At any rate, she had refused to betray them, opting instead to betray Starfleet. Fighting Federation colonists and former comrades had been the most painful duty of Picard's career. But like so many other chapters of his life, it paled in comparison with the awful conflict that now engulfed them.

He turned to Beverly Crusher. "Will she be all right?"

"She'll recover," answered the doctor. "Another few seconds without air, and none of them would have survived. I can bring most of them back to consciousness, but do you think they'll be a security risk?"

Picard shook his head. "They were fighting the Dominion when we rescued them. I'm inclined to give them the benefit of the doubt." He turned to the security officers. "Wait outside, on alert."

After the security detail had cleared out, it was a bit easier to move in sickbay, and Picard stationed himself at Ro's bedside. He nodded to Beverly, and she administered a hypospray to the Bajoran's neck.

Slowly, wincing with fear and confusion, Ro Laren opened her eyes and struggled to sit up. When her vision focused on the concerned face of Captain Picard, she smiled weakly.

"Then it's true," she said in amazement, "this really is the *Enterprise*. Am I under arrest?"

"At the moment, you're under *my* care," said Beverly. "But I wouldn't worry too much about

Captain Picard—he went to considerable trouble to rescue you and your shipmates."

"Thank you." Ro sat up and looked around. "How are my passengers?"

"We saved all but five," answered Beverly. "Should I log you down as captain?"

"Yes," she answered hoarsely. "Can we talk somewhere?"

"Of course," said Captain Picard. "We have a lounge on this ship, much like the old Ten-Forward room. It's not the same as it used to be—with the war and all—but we could still go there." The captain looked at Crusher, who nodded her assent.

He tapped his comm badge. "Picard to Troi."

"Yes, Captain?" answered a lilting feminine voice.

"Counselor, meet me in the lounge right away."

"Yes, sir."

Ro swung her long legs over the side of the table and stood uneasily, holding the table for support. "Don't trust me, Captain? Have to make sure I'm telling the truth?"

"We are at war," said Picard gravely.

"Understood. Do you mind if I hold your arm? I'm a little wobbly."

"Of course." Like the gentleman he was, Picard offered a steady arm to his former foe.

It sure isn't like it used to be, thought Ro Laren as she surveyed the deserted lounge. Only a small corner of the cavernous room was lit, with only a handful of tables open for business. Even so, there was nobody in the lounge but herself, Captain Picard, and Deanna Troi, who looked as confident and beautiful as always.

Like Picard, Troi was dressed in a different Starfleet uniform than the ones she recalled. Evidently Starfleet's sartorial requirements had changed since Ro's departure.

Captain Picard returned to their table with a tray full of beverages, dispensed from a replicator. "It's self-service, I'm afraid," said the captain apologetically. "Table service is a luxury we don't have anymore. Nor do we have much time to sit and chat."

"I never thought I would say that it was good to see someone from Starfleet," said Ro, grabbing her glass of tomato juice. "But it's awfully good to see someone from Starfleet."

Deanna folded her hands and smiled pleasantly. "Suppose you tell us, in your own words, what happened to you?"

Ro set her jaw and nodded. "To keep from incriminating myself, I won't tell you what I was doing while we were still fighting the Federation. But life became peaceful for us after the Klingons went to war with the Cardassians, and Starfleet was fighting the Borg and others. Everyone forgot about us—we were even able to return to some of our old settlements."

She took a sip of tomato juice and smiled wistfully. "I used to grow my own tomatoes—they were much better than this." Ro paused and took a deep breath before continuing. "You can guess what happened to us. When the Dominion came, they rearmed the Cardassians and turned them loose on their old enemies. We tried to be neutral, like the Bajorans, because we were all tired of fighting. It didn't work. They destroyed our settlements and massacred us by the thousands."

"I'm sorry," said Deanna with heartfelt sympathy.

Ro shrugged. "It's happening everywhere, isn't it? The Maquis are nothing special anymore—just a bunch of pathetic refugees. Fortunately, I'm experienced at being a refugee—I know there's a time to run and a time to fight. We set out to run to Bajor, but we decided to fight instead. When we came upon that starship in trouble, we joined in."

"That was either very brave, or very foolish," said Picard.

"That's the story of my life," answered Ro, leaning back in her chair. "So . . . am I under arrest?"

"No," answered Picard resolutely. "We haven't got the luxury of holding grudges. I don't need to tell you that the war is going badly."

Ro scowled. "I'm afraid I have some more bad news for you, Captain. The Dominion is building an artificial wormhole deep in Cardassian space."

"What?" asked Picard, a stricken look in his face. "Are you certain about this?"

"I'm certain." She looked at Deanna Troi. "Tell him I'm certain."

Deanna sighed. "She's certain."

"They may be using Federation prisoners to build it," added Ro. "Slave labor."

Picard rose to his feet, his cup of tea untouched. "Could you repeat this for my staff? They may have questions."

The Bajoran nodded solemnly. "I will, but I want clemency for all my passengers."

"That's not mine to grant," answered the captain. "But we have your transport in tow, and Data says it can be repaired. Excuse me."

He strode from the lounge, his back stiff with

resolve. Ro watched him leave, then shook her head in amazement. "Still the same Captain Picard."

"Yes," agreed Deanna. "Still the best there is."

Ro Laren finished her report and dropped her hands to her sides, gazing expectantly at the officers gathered in the observation lounge. In her face was that odd mixture of intensity and indifference which Picard had come to expect from her. She hadn't given them any more than a secondhand account, hadn't furnished any proof, yet her statement was chilling, especially the account of ships full of Federation prisoners. They all knew that to be a tragic fact.

Still the captain could see doubt in the eyes of some of his staff, especially Will Riker's. Or perhaps Will's troubled expression was due to the disastrous implications of Ro's story. If the Dominion possessed an artificial wormhole in Cardassian space, then the mines in front of the Bajoran wormhole would be worthless. In fact, the Bajoran wormhole itself would be worthless, and ripe for destruction. The Dominion could stop protecting Deep Space Nine and move on to other objectives, such as Earth.

"Any questions?" concluded Ro.

"Why would they build this thing so close to the Badlands?" asked Riker suspiciously.

"I would guess that they assumed the Badlands would obscure it from your long-range sensors."

"That would do it," agreed Geordi La Forge.

"Could you locate this artificial wormhole on a chart?" asked Riker.

"Approximately," answered Ro. "I've never seen it, but I know Sector 283 fairly well."

Riker scowled. "You're sure of the reliability of the person who told you this?"

Ro's jaw stiffened, and her eyes became flint-cold. "I'm sure of everything that man told me. He never lied, had no reason to. He was certain that the Federation was going to lose this war, which is why he wanted to make friends with the Dominion."

After an uncomfortable silence, Picard managed a smile. "Thank you, Captain Ro. Ensign Craycroft will escort you back to sickbay. I believe that most of your passengers have recovered."

The lean Bajoran glanced at the gleaming models encased on the wall of the observation lounge—all ships named *Enterprise*—and she smiled wistfully. "Many times I thought about how I was such a fool to throw all of this away. And what happens? I find you—the *Enterprise*—in the same condition as me; we're all fighting for our lives. It's funny how time reduces everything to the essentials."

"I don't see anything funny about it," muttered Riker. His scowl softened slightly. "But I'm very glad that we were able to rescue you, and thank you for coming to the aid of the *Aurora.*"

"We can't choose where to die, only *how* to die." Ro Laren glanced at the security officer at her side. "I'm ready to go."

Ensign Craycroft touched a panel. The door opened, and she escorted the Bajoran out.

As soon as the door snapped shut again, Riker declared, "She's still a traitor. On top of that, we have absolutely no proof of her story. It could be a trap."

"Counselor Troi detected no prevarication." Troi nodded in confirmation. Captain Picard paced the length of the gleaming conference table. "We knew they were taking prisoners, but we didn't know *why*. Ro is the first person we've interviewed who has actually been living behind enemy lines."

"Judging by her general health," said Beverly Crusher, "she hasn't been living in luxury."

"I believe she is telling the truth," added Deanna Troi. "At least as far as she knows it."

"That's the catch," said Picard. "Is this fact or rumor? Either way, we can't ignore it. Data, is an artificial wormhole even possible?"

"In theory, yes," answered the android. "Three years ago, a team of Trill scientists, led by Doctor Lenara Kahn, set out to answer that very question. Using the Bajoran wormhole as a model, they determined that constructing an artificial wormhole would be possible, although there are many problems to be overcome. Without any working prototypes, one would have to construct a verteron collider of at least eight kilometers in length. I could give you a more exact estimate, if you wish."

"Perhaps later," said Picard. Geordi was leaning forward, anxious to say something. "Mr. La Forge?"

"In my opinion," said the chief engineer, "the biggest problem is not the size of the thing but the exotic construction material you would need to establish a permanent site. At the mouth of an artificial wormhole, the outward radial pressure would be tremendous—like the tension at the center of the most massive neutron star. We haven't got a building material that would stand up to that kind of pressure."

"Geordi, are you forgetting Corzanium?" asked the android.

The engineer grinned, his pale artificial retinas

glowing with mirth. "Come on, Data, there isn't more than a teaspoonful of Corzanium in the whole Federation. It has to be quantum-stepped out of a black hole with a tractor beam run through a metaphasic shield enhancer. But if you had enough Corzanium, I suppose, it would do the trick."

"The Dominion has considerable resources," muttered Picard. "I'm afraid they also have the personnel, some of it ours. So this artificial wormhole could be a reality?"

"Yes, sir," answered Data. "I believe we should take Captain Ro's report seriously."

That simple declaration dropped a pall over the meeting in the observation lounge. No one had to reiterate what a disaster it would be if the Dominion could bring through more Jem'Hadar warships, more unctuous Vorta, and more shapeshifting Changelings.

"We've got to go there and see for ourselves," declared Picard. "If it exists, we have to destroy it."

"Captain," said Riker, stroking his beard thoughtfully, "I feel I should point out that what you're proposing is . . . a suicide mission."

The captain sighed. "And if we fail to go, and she's right? That would be suicide for the entire Federation. I'm sending a message to Starfleet, asking them for permission to investigate Ro's report. Thank you for your opinions—you are dismissed."

Ro Laren sat in a small therapy room with Shon Navo, helping the young Bajoran exercise the repaired tendons in his right elbow and right knee. Of the injuries her crew had received, his were fairly mild, but the youth felt ostracized on this ship full of humans flying under the despised Starfleet insignia. Shon had known nothing but hatred for Starfleet for most of his life, and now he was being forced to depend upon their protection.

He bent and straightened his elbow as Ro monitored his progress on a medical tricorder. "Very good," she said. "Ten more times, and we'll work on your knee."

Shon let his arm flop onto the table. "What's the point? We're all going to be killed, anyway—or put in prison."

"We don't know that. In our case, there's a good chance we could be repatriated to Bajor."

"If we could ever get close to it," muttered Shon.

Ro frowned, unable to refute the fact that they were a long way from home, if indeed they could call anyplace "home." Being homeless had taken its toll, and Shon was much like her—cynical, disillusioned, with no respect for authority. Now there would be more refugees, more prisoners, more damaged and neglected lives.

She took a sip from her glass of tomato juice and replied slowly, "The humans and their allies are not bad people. In fact, they trust too much, always looking for the best, even in Cardassians. If they survive this war, perhaps they won't take so much for granted. The important thing is to realize that we're all on the same side now."

Shon's bravado slipped for a moment, and he looked like the frightened youth he was. "But won't they send us to a camp or a prison . . . just to wait until the Dominion finally gets us? Everybody says they're losing the war!"

"Then look out for yourself. Fight if you have to,

save people if you can, but survive. For once, it's a good time to be Bajoran." She rubbed his shoulder in a friendly gesture.

The door slid open, and Ro turned to see Captain Picard standing in the corridor, a concerned look on his face. Out of habit, Ro stiffened, tempted to bolt to her feet and stand at attention. Then she relaxed as she realized that they were now both captains of their own ships, a respect he had shown her in front of his crew. If she could only be sure that the rest of Starfleet would be as forgiving as Captain Picard, she would feel more comfortable about this new alliance.

He smiled at the boy as he entered. "I'm sorry to intrude, but it's rather urgent that I speak to Captain Ro. I'm sure one of the orderlies would be happy to help you with your therapy."

Ro gazed at the young Bajoran and nodded. With barely concealed hatred, the boy glared at Picard as he left, but the stalwart captain was too absorbed by more pressing concerns to notice.

"What's going to become of my passengers and crew?" asked Ro.

"They'll be protected, but if we lose the war—" Picard's glower finished his sentence. "All I know is, if you're correct about the Dominion building an artificial wormhole, then all is lost. Unless we destroy it. I've asked Starfleet for permission to investigate your report, and their response was . . . not entirely to my liking."

He sighed. "They refuse to allow us to risk the *Enterprise* on such a mission. That leaves us the option of using another ship, preferably one which isn't Starfleet and won't arouse suspicion."

Ro cocked her head and smiled. "Such as the *Orb of Peace?*"

"Precisely. Mr. La Forge says it can be repaired in thirty hours; that includes adding several improvements. A small, handpicked crew could slip into Cardassian space and deal with this threat, being careful not to endanger Federation prisoners."

Ro's smile grew larger. "Now you're talking about a dangerous spy mission, followed by a major act of sabotage. If we're captured, do you know how long the Cardassians will torture us? We'll be begging for death."

"I'm well versed in Cardassian torture," answered Picard grimly. "If you're worried about your crew and passengers, I'll make sure they're treated fairly; they'll be compensated for the *Orb of Peace*. I'm only asking for the ship, not your participation—although I would welcome it."

"I go with the ship. Besides, none of you know the Badlands like I do." Hesitantly, Ro asked, "What will be our chain of command?"

"You'll be captain of the ship, as you are," answered Picard. "I'll be in charge of the mission. I often find myself in *your* position with somebody else in charge of the mission, so this will be a nice change of pace for me."

"Do you have any Bajorans on board?"

"No, but Dr. Crusher has gotten remarkably good at disguises over the years. She can alter humans to pass for Bajorans, even on scans. We'll have a crew of fifteen, which is all I can spare. You know this mission has to succeed, don't you?"

The smile faded from Ro's gaunt face, and she looked like a soldier once again. "Yes. But you're asking for too much if you think we can sneak into Cardassian space, find this thing, blow it up, *and* save all the prisoners. We have to be realistic—the prisoners are lost."

"The mission comes first," agreed Picard somberly. "All we can do for the prisoners is to scout the situation. Only by defeating the Dominion can we avenge the suffering of our comrades."

Ro lifted her glass of tomato juice and gazed into the disheartened but determined eyes of Captain Picard. "Here's to vengeance."

Chapter Three

SAM LAVELLE FLOATED WEIGHTLESSLY through the void, his tethered space suit feeling like a gown of the finest silk against his chapped, grimy skin. The umbilical cord brought him air, security, and close scrutiny. Only when he tried to lift his arms too far above his head did he feel the restrictions of the cumbersome suit. Then he would relax and let himself float until he had found a better position in which to work on the exposed metal joint. He avoided using the jets on his suit, because they often caused him to overshoot his mark, losing precious seconds.

The large spanner in his hand had no weight—it felt like a feather—but it would make a formidable weapon, if he could only plant his feet. For the hundredth time that day, Sam fantasized about bringing the wrench crashing upon the head of his Jem'Hadar overseer.

"Number zero-five-nine-six," said a gruff voice in his ear. "You are falling behind the prescribed time-table. You have fourteen minutes to tighten that seal, or you will lose your privileges."

Sam held up his hand and waved, wondering if they could see that his middle finger was extended above the others. Probably not, with the thick, segmented gloves covering his hands. "Privileges" was a euphemism for food, water, oxygen, and a bunk—the bare minimum that was needed to stay alive. Those who lost their privileges only did so once or twice before they were expelled into space with the garbage.

His mind still wandering, Sam Lavelle stared down the length of the massive verteron collider, a skeletal tube over ten kilometers long and two kilometers wide. It was hard to envision the entire structure when all one could see of it were a few meters of spindly supports, surrounded by the daunting blackness of space.

The sight of thousands of space-suited workers, clinging to the structure like an army of inept spiders, gave him some perspective on its incredible length. The spectre of sleek Cardassian shuttlecrafts patrolling the center of the tube gave him some idea of its immense width. The fact that he hadn't moved since the Jem'Hadar had ordered him to do so made Sam think that he was prepared to die.

But he couldn't die, not now, when so many of his mates depended upon him. Through default and the force of his own personality, Sam had become the spokesperson for five hundred prisoners in Pod 18. He harbored few illusions that he was any more noble than his fellow captives, or any more likely to survive his imprisonment, but he was willing to speak up for them. For some reason, his jailers hadn't been troubled enough to kill him . . . yet.

He latched on to the bolt with his spanner, read the digital printout on the handle, and tightened until the seal reached the prescribed tension. Two meters away, a cylindrical verteron accelerator looked down at him like a bizarre cannon, reminding him of the war. As far as he knew, the war could be over and the entire Federation enslaved. On the other hand, the frenetic pace of the work and the Dominion's single-minded adherence to its schedules made it clear that the Federation was still a threat. The Dominion needed this wormhole.

And a remarkable achievement it was—a bridge to another quadrant, tens of thousands of light-years away. The artificial wormhole was a true mixture of Dominion and Federation technology, built by Federation and Dominion hands. It should have been a symbol of peace and cooperation; instead it sounded the death knell of the Federation.

Like thousands of other men and woman drifting inside the verteron collider or slaving in the laboratories or factories of the complex, Sam wondered how he could sabotage his own labor. Unfortunately, their work was tightly supervised, then inspected by Vorta engineers. Only when they started actual tests would they know if anyone had been successful in sabotaging the artificial wormhole. Sam waited for his moment to play the hero, but each passing day only brought the Dominion closer to its goals.

Like a robot trained to labor without thinking about the consequences, Sam finished checking the seal and logging it as completed. This was the last task to be completed on this segment, and he pushed himself away and drifted in space. There was no sensation in his body except lethargy and a gnawing hunger that could have been either his stomach or his soul.

Sam straightened his umbilical tether, watching it stretched back to the maintenance pod in the junction of six supports. "Ready to come in," he reported.

"There will be a delay in retrieval," answered the gruff voice of his overseer.

Sam breathed a loud sigh, which echoed in the hollow recesses of his helmet. He had just been threatened that if he didn't finish on time he'd be punished, and now he had been told to continue drifting in space. Wondering what the delay could be, Sam twisted around to look in the opposite direction.

That's when he saw it—a Cardassian tanker moving into position at the mouth of the verteron collider. Sam was no physicist, just a decent helmsman and navigator, but he knew that the gravitational and temporal forces would be greatest at the exit point of the wormhole. Only a few prisoners, kept in isolation, had seen the plans to construct that section of the collider. He assumed that it had to be a weak point in the machine, where sabotage could be very effective. Now he was about to watch an important development—from a distance of half a kilometer. He turned his dark brown eyes upon the figures in the distance.

Using the miniature jets on their suits, a squadron of workers maneuvered themselves into tight formation around the freight hatch at the aft of the tanker. There had to be fifteen white-garbed prisoners and an equal number of Jem'Hadar guards in gray space suits. Something big was coming off that tanker. With thousands of workers spread across ten kilometers, it was impossible to say that one spot was the center of attention, but Sam could feel the work halt as every eye and every viewscreen focused on the activity at the tanker.

The hatch opened, and what looked like a gleaming beam of sunlight emerged from the recesses of the tanker. Sam wished he could see more, but he also had a feeling that he didn't want to be much closer than he was. When it cleared the hatch, the stack of pure energy looked to be about ten meters long and a meter wide. Like the pallbearers at a funeral, the workers took positions around the blazing object and guided it away from the tanker.

Sam guessed that the mysterious material was encased in a stasis field, or perhaps a forcefield. He didn't think even the Dominion could use antimatter as a building material, but they treated this substance with the same respect.

The Cardassian tanker suddenly fired thrusters and tried to pull away. It got only a few meters when the space between the tanker and the glowing cargo rippled like a Texas highway in the summer heat. Sam caught his breath, knowing this chain reaction couldn't be planned. Sure enough, the glowing material increased in brightness until it seared his eyes.

Squinting, Sam could see the white-suited workers firing their jets and fleeing in panic. Ignoring the danger, the gray-suited Jem'Hadar began firing on the fleeing workers. Phaser beams crisscrossed the blackness of space, and several of his colleagues exploded in their suits like helium balloons set afire. He gasped and held out his arms, unable to do anything but watch the tragedy unfold.

Those who escaped the massacre did not escape the deadly chain reaction that followed. The stasis field flickered out, and the glowing material within it expanded like a solar flare, engulfing the workers, the Jem'Hadar, the Cardassian tanker, and the collider. The tanker exploded in a vivid burst of silver confetti and golden gas clouds, and the mouth of the collider was consumed by a monstrous fireball.

Sam braced himself as the wake of the explosion struck him and flipped him over and over like a leaf caught in the wind. He could feel a momentary warming in his suit, which worried him until he crashed hard into a metal pylon. He caromed off the structure and spun to the end of his tether, which jerked him like a puppet on a string. He watched the tether stretch to a dangerous length, and he jammed on his jets in time to compensate.

Now Sam was hurtling in the opposite direction as debris from the explosion shot past him. Miraculously, none of it ripped his suit, and he was able to pilot himself back into a controlled drift behind a thick pylon. He finally had time to glance behind him, where it was complete chaos along the entire length of the collider.

Quickly Cardassian and Jem'Hadar ships converged on the scene of the disaster, but there was no one and nothing to be saved. People who had been his shipmates and fellow prisoners now floated in the void, little more than scraps of charred flesh and cloth. The Cardassian tanker was a quickly expanding sphere of dust.

"Stay where you are!" bellowed an angry voice in his ear. "Do not move!"

Sam barked a macabre, frustrated laugh. Scores of lives had been snuffed out in an instant of Cardassian carelessness, and all his captors could think about was preventing the escape of their slaves, most of whom were floating helplessly in space. Where could they go? How far could they run in a space suit containing a few minutes' worth of breathable air, minus the cord?

If it weren't so tragic, it would be funny, thought Sam Lavelle. Maybe this accident was a harbinger of good luck, and the artificial wormhole would never operate as planned. That might be good news for the Federation, but thousands of Federation prisoners would then become expendable, even more so than they were already. If it failed, no doubt the Dominion would take out their anger and frustration on the prisoners.

We're all dead anyway, Sam decided as he floated aimlessly, watching a misshapen dust cloud in the distance. That massive cloud was called the Badlands, and it had once been a refuge of the Maquis. Now it was a tempting mirage, promising them escape and freedom, when there was little point in thinking about such goals.

His life had ended with the capture of the *Aizawa,* the cruiser on which he and his best friend, Taurik, had been serving as bridge officers. Sam couldn't help but wonder if their previous ship, the *Enterprise,* had survived the war so far. He hadn't met any prisoners from the *Enterprise* or heard of its fate, but that didn't mean much. By now, the *Enterprise* could be a cloud of space junk, like the Cardassian tanker which sparkled all around him.

He thought back to those days aboard the *Enterprise*, where his closest friends included Taurik, Sito Jaxa, and Alyssa Ogawa. With all their neurotic fretting over crew evaluations and promotions, those days couldn't be called carefree, but that group had real camaraderie. They were gung-ho. Jaxa's death on a covert mission had been their first taste of reality, and of the sacrifices they would be called upon to make.

Something twinkled in the corner of his eye, and Sam was glad to turn his attention elsewhere. He twisted around to see a squat, bronze shuttlecraft hovering over his head. "Uncouple," commanded a voice. "Prepare to be retrieved."

Sam sighed and closed off the intake valve of his umbilical cord. He attached the spanner to its holder, unscrewed the valve, and watched the cord retract slowly into the maintenance pod. Sam floated free in space for a few seconds, thinking this was as close to freedom as he would ever come. A familiar tingle along his body alerted him that the transporter beam was scrambling his molecules.

He materialized inside the transporter room of the shuttlecraft, with three Jem'Hadar guards training their weapons at him. "Move!" ordered one of them, brandishing his phaser in a threatening manner.

Sam staggered off the transporter platform, suddenly clumsy and leaden in his space suit. His captors looked particularly edgy today, and usually he was met by only one or two of them, not three. Under the cold gaze of their pinched, spiny faces, Sam quickly stripped down to nothing. He dropped his suit into a chute in the deck and stood there, shivering in his nakedness.

Modesty and decency had long been abandoned in this weightless and silent hell, and Sam was ushered into a holding cell where three male and four female prisoners huddled, all naked. They looked wild-eyed and spooked from their recent brush with disaster.

At one time, seeing young women nude would have excited the handsome lieutenant, but now they were nothing but victims, stripped of their humanity and will. They were his sisters in this dark tragedy, not objects of desire. All of them needed a bath, and there was no pretext of trying to maintain proper appearance. Like most of the males, Sam sported a dark, ragged beard. Even Taurik, who was normally as fastidious as any other Vulcan, looked unkempt as he sat stoically with his naked back resting against a cold bulkhead.

Sam nodded wearily to his fellow prisoners as he slumped down beside Taurik. Just outside the force-field entrance of the cell, an armed Jem'Hadar stood watching them. Sam wondered if he would allow the prisoners to talk. Some Jem'Hadar guards didn't care, while others strictly forbade talking among the prisoners until they were locked safely in their pods. Cardassian guards, who loved to be overbearing, would often beat prisoners for talking.

Deciding to test the guard, Sam turned to Taurik and asked softly, "What did you think of that explosion?"

The Vulcan cocked his head thoughtfully, as if he had been asked a normal question under normal circumstances. "It appeared to result from the mishandling of a very volatile material. Possibly a stasis field was disturbed. I could only speculate on the material they are using to build the mouth of the wormhole."

A loud shuffling grabbed their attention, and the prisoners looked up to see two Jem'Hadar guards dragging an injured human with burns over most of his naked body. They carried the injured man like a bag of garbage and flung his body into an open cell. If he was still alive, it couldn't possibly be for long—unless he got treatment soon.

One of the male prisoners began to weep. They all knew the man would never get treatment, or even a funeral. He would die, alone and forgotten, in a cage.

Sam turned to the man and said, "It's all right. Stay alive, so we can remember this."

"I don't want to stay alive," rasped the man in despair. "And I certainly never want to *remember* any of this!"

"He's a collaborator," hissed a woman, glaring at Sam.

"That is inaccurate," replied Taurik. "Lieutenant Lavelle has volunteered to be Liaison Officer of Pod Eighteen, which does afford him more access to our captors than a typical prisoner has. But in no sense is he aiding and abetting the enemy as a true collaborator would do. He argues on our behalf."

"Never mind, Taurik," muttered Sam. "Let them think what they want."

"This one is all right," grumbled the oldest of the four women, a lean Klingon with scars over most of her body. "You want a collaborator, you take that turncoat Trill—Enrak Grof! Give me a knife, and I will slice the worm right out of him!"

"I believe Professor Grof is an unjoined Trill," said

Taurik. "But I agree with you—he is a collaborator in the accepted sense of the word."

Sam looked at his friend, wondering if he had detected a trace of bitterness in the Vulcan's tone. He couldn't blame Taurik if he was bitter, because Enrak Grof was close to solving one of science's most elusive puzzles, unraveling the mysteries of wormholes and actually re-creating a tunnel through space and time. In exchange for this privilege, Grof was collaborating with the enemy. His name was all over schematics and memos, and he seemed to rank in importance with the Vorta engineers. He was particularly useful in telling the Dominion what kind of work best suited their prisoners.

Come to think of it, maybe Grof did deserve to be gutted with a dull Klingon knife.

Taurik shook his head. "It is highly unlikely that any of us will get an opportunity to harm Professor Grof. To my knowledge, few prisoners have seen him since his capture on Deep Space Nine."

"How was he captured?" asked the youngest woman. Swapping capture stories was a favorite pastime among the prisoners.

"He refused to abandon his experiments on the Bajoran wormhole," answered Taurik, "and was captured when the Dominion took over. This would indicate that his work is more important to him than anything else."

"Even his *honor*," hissed the Klingon woman. "He may not have a worm inside of him, but he *is* a worm."

"They pulled me out of an escape pod," said the youngest woman with a haunted look in her pale eyes. Her freckles went all the way down her back.

A clank and a slight shudder informed Sam that they had docked at the pod complex. Although he had never seen it from the outside, he imagined that it looked like a giant model of a complex molecule, with long, narrow shafts connecting large, windowless spheres in which both they and their jailers lived. The place felt decentralized, with easily defended modules instead of a central hub. At any rate, it was unheard of for anyone to escape from the pod complex. Where would they go, surrounded by freezing space?

Sam often thought about stealing a ship, but their captors never left the shuttlecraft docked for more than a few seconds. Both the Jem'Hadar and Cardassians were skilled and experienced jailers, and they considered every possibility.

"Lucky devils," muttered one of the men. "The ones who died, I mean."

No one disputed the man's morbid assessment. Some days, it did seem as if death was a preferable option to numbing, soulless labor that would only benefit the enemy. The war and imprisonment had made death a constant fixture of their lives, like the darkness of space.

Armed Jem'Hadar gathered around the cell, and one of them turned off the forcefield. Waving their weapons, they ushered the prisoners out of the cell and into the gangway. Most of the prisoners made a point of not looking at the dying man in the adjoining cell, but Sam pointed at him.

"Can't you do something to help him?" demanded Sam.

"He is damaged," replied a Jem'Hadar. "Move along."

Sam thought about arguing, but the Jem'Hadar treated their own with the same disregard. The strong survived, and the weak were best weeded out. Besides, to die in the service of the Founders was the greatest reward of all for a Jem'Hadar, and why should prisoners be any different? Did they grieve the loss of their comrades in the accident? No. Their only reaction was to increase security and cut short the work shift.

He followed the others down the gangway, through the hatch, and into the freight pod. Situated near the outer bulkhead, the hold was freezing, and the prisoners hurried to grab frayed white jumpsuits from a rack of used clothing. They gratefully covered their shivering bodies.

The woman who had accused Sam of being a collaborator gave him an embarrassed glance. He nodded, knowing the glance was as close as he would ever come to receiving an apology. In this place, distrust was easier to come by than hope. The guards motioned the females into the turbolift marked with vertical red stripes, and the men shuffled silently toward the turbolift with the horizontal blue stripes. There was a good chance they would never see each other again.

Sam had once demanded that the women and the men be housed together, but a Jem'Hadar had informed him that pregnant women would have to be killed. That was as far as the request went.

Taurik, Sam, and the other man entered the lift and waited for the door to close. The Jem'Hadar guards were smart—they never rode the turbolifts with the prisoners, preferring to avoid tight places where their charges could jump them and take their weapons.

Come to think of it, Sam had never known the Jem'Hadar to be careless or make mistakes. They would fight to the death if ordered to do so, but it would be a controlled, measured suicide.

As the men rode in the cramped turbolift, Sam wondered for the hundredth time if there was any escape from the seamless chamber. A prisoner named Neko had once told him that he could escape from the turbolift, but Sam had never seen Neko again after that boast.

The door opened, and a gruff voice said, "Prisoner three-six-one-nine, this is Pod Fifteen. Exit now." The man who envied the dead shuffled off the lift and vanished down a narrow corridor.

When the door shut, Sam and Taurik continued their diagonal journey. The long turbolift rides were the main reason why Sam envisioned the complex as being individual pods separated by long shafts. Not that it made much difference, but it was something to think about when a person was trying to avoid thinking.

"It has been a difficult day," said Taurik in the Vulcan equivalent of small talk.

"Yes, it has been," agreed Sam. "And the most difficult days are ahead of us."

Somehow, before their work was done, they would have to revolt and try to destroy the artificial wormhole. Certainly it would be the day they all died in utter futility, but the effort had to be made—or they couldn't live with themselves. But each day, if they could be called days, slithered by with lethargy and hopelessness as the prisoners' constant companions.

The door slid open, and a gruff voice said, "Prisoners zero-five-nine-six and zero-five-nine-seven, this is Pod Eighteen. Exit now."

Sam and Taurik filed off the turbolift into the dimly lit corridor which led to their barracks. After a walk through a featureless hallway, they came upon a narrow metal hatch, which snapped open at their approach. Sam entered a high-ceiling room which always reminded him of the gymnasium in the basement of his church in Brooklyn. It had the same sort of Spartan, no-nonsense utility.

Five hundred bedrolls lay on the floor, and most of them were occupied with bored male prisoners representing a score of Federation species, from blue-skinned Andorians to beaked Saurians. They sat staring at the observation lenses along the ceiling, from where, it was assumed, the guards stared down at them.

Half a dozen prisoners rushed Sam and Taurik as they entered. "Did you see it? We heard there was an accident! What exactly happened out there?" they demanded in a babble of voices.

Sam motioned them to be calm, then he told them what he had witnessed, not mentioining how many prisoners had been caught in the explosion.

"Were there many casualties?" asked a young ensign.

Sam shrugged. "Only a few of ours, but they lost a tanker full of Cardassians and a bunch of Jem'Hadar guards."

"All right!" crowed a prisoner, thrusting his fist into the air. An excited discussion ensued.

Taurik shot Sam a look that said that he recognized the lie but wouldn't correct it. Like all of them, the Vulcan had learned to deal differently with the world since becoming a slave laborer. Taurik was willing to overlook the truth if it gave some comfort to his dispirited comrades.

A twinge of pain reminded Sam that he had crashed hard into the metal supports, and he rubbed his shoulder. "What time is it?" he muttered. "Time for chow?"

"More than an hour to go, we think," answered a prisoner. They were driven by chronometers while outside working, but timepieces were not allowed inside the prison pods. There was no day or night to measure the passage of time, and the jailers never changed the lighting. Still the prisoners kept a running estimate, as best they could, based on changes of shifts and meal delivery.

A klaxon blared, causing Sam to jump nervously. He stared up at the observation lenses in the ceiling, as did hundreds of his fellow prisoners. The excited conversation dissolved into an apprehensive whisper.

"Prisoner zero-five-nine-six, prepare to exit," said a voice.

Sam licked his lips nervously and stepped toward the door. With a jovial smile, he told the others, "I'll see you later at chow." They stared at him with a disconcerting mixture of fear, distrust, and envy.

The door flew open, and Sam stepped into the dimly lit corridor. When the door slid shut behind him, leaving him alone, he felt ostracized from his fellow prisoners. It was getting harder and harder to cap his temper and remain cordial to everyone— when all of them expected so much of him. More than anything, Sam just wanted to keep the lines of communication open between captors and captives. They weren't animals, as long as they could communicate their needs and wants.

He heard footsteps, and he turned to see an armed Jem'Hadar marching his way. The guard was flanked by a short Vorta named Joulesh, whom Sam had met only twice before when making official requests. He was not in the habit of meeting with the Vorta; usually a Cardassian glinn was as high as he got.

"This is quite an honor," said Sam, keeping his sarcasm in check.

"You have no idea of the honor," replied Joulesh with an enthusiastic smile. "It is only the beginning."

The little humanoid turned on his heel and strode briskly down the corridor. Under the stern gaze of the guard, Sam followed him. To his surprise, the Vorta stepped into the turbolift and motioned him aboard. Sam entered, expecting the Jem'Hadar guard to follow, but he remained behind in the corridor, glowering at them. The door shut, and they began to move.

Joulesh wrinkled his nose at Sam. "I wish we'd had an opportunity to clean you up somewhat, but this is an emergency. We'll make do. I advise you to behave."

"That depends on what you plan to do to me," said Sam.

The Vorta's silvery eyes twinkled. "What happens to you depends entirely on your interview. You aren't the only candidate for this post. However, I have been keeping an eye on you, and I believe you are the one."

"May I remind you that I'm a prisoner of war," said Sam, "not an employee of the Dominion, Incorporated."

The Vorta brushed some lint off his elegant, silver-brocaded jacket. "You are an asset of the Dominion. Whether you fulfill your potential or end up as waste is your decision. Thus far, you have proven yourself an able worker, and you have tried to improve relationships between our people. These traits could take you far in the Dominion."

Sam forced himself to keep still and not argue with the popinjay. The fact that the Dominion operated under the guise of business and mutual cooperation didn't make them any less a dictatorship. He wondered how long it would take the Cardassians to realize that they were the lackeys in this operation—temporary help until more fleets of Jem'Hadar warships arrived.

"I wish the Federation could understand that we only want to bring them under our protection and influence," said Joulesh, sounding like a used shuttle-craft salesman. "Your people don't do us any good if you are dead or imprisoned."

"Then let us go," suggested Sam.

As the door slid open, the Vorta gave him an amused smirk. "We might do so, one at a time. Follow me."

They walked down a well-lit corridor that actually had doorways and multiple exits . . . and no Jem'Hadar guards. Sam followed Joulesh into a second turbolift, which had diagonal yellow markings on it. This lift was the deluxe version, Sam decided, as he inspected the plush carpeting and tasteful instrument panel. The lifts he rode were controlled from outside, and this one was controlled by Joulesh's deft fingers. After a trip so smooth that Sam couldn't tell they were moving, the door opened.

"Remember," warned the Vorta, "you are about to meet a god."

The words didn't register until Sam stepped off the turbolift and found himself in a large observation lounge, with a spread of food and drink in one corner and a lovely window in the other. A few people were scattered about, but the scent of food commanded Sam's attention. Halfway across the room, he saw a remarkable creature—a slim figure dressed in a sparkling beige robe—standing like an angel at the head of the table. His features were hairless and oddly unformed, as if this incarnation were so simple that it didn't require much detail.

A Founder! thought Sam with alarm. It was the first Changeling he had ever seen, and he wasn't certain how to react. Joulesh was practically scraping the floor, so Sam gave his host a respectful bow. He couldn't offer his hand as he could scarcely imagine touching such an ephemeral creature. Despite his halfhearted attempt at a humanoid appearance, the Changeling looked more like an illusion than a real being.

Sam reminded himself that a handful of Changelings had nearly destroyed the Klingon Empire from within. It was disconcerting to know that the creature in front of him could morph into any object or person in the room.

There were other persons in the lounge, and Sam looked at them, wondering if they were really what they seemed. Two Jem'Hadar guards were stationed near a golden basin, and a second Vorta conferred in whispers with Joulesh. Standing by the observation window was a hulking man in a white laboratory coat; he had an uncouth brown beard and brown spots running down his forehead, temples, and neck into his collar.

Enrak Grof. It has to be him, thought Sam. This was quite a meeting. If his cellmates knew he was in this company, he would never be trusted again.

Sam edged toward the food. "Excuse me," he asked the Changeling, "may I eat?"

"Not until the Founder has blessed the food," cautioned Joulesh, sounding aghast at his impertinence.

"It is allowed," said the Founder in a silky voice, nodding at his minion. Bowing low, the Vorta backed away.

Sam attacked a plate of what looked like ham. He didn't care what it was, as long as it was solid food that wouldn't kill him. Assuming he would probably say no to whatever proposal they offered him, Sam figured he should eat as much as he could before they kicked him out.

"Lieutenant junior grade Samuel Lavelle, or has he been promoted?" said the Founder, relishing the unfamiliar syllables of his name. "Captured aboard the *Aizawa,* formerly stationed on the *Enterprise,* now technician and Liaison Officer for Pod Eighteen."

Sam mumbled through a mouthful of wonderful food. He was afraid to say much, lest he slobber all over the plates, but he was impressed that the Founder had used his name instead of a number. He glanced toward Professor Grof, wondering if he would get a chance to speak privately with the most notorious collaborator in the complex. The Trill edged forward, looking as if he wanted to say something; but he also held his tongue. Sam guessed that a smart collaborator didn't interrupt a Founder.

He grabbed some more food. Whatever happened, he was going to try not to get kicked out of this shindig too quickly. With his determined chewing, Sam nearly choked on the next words he heard from the Founder's smooth lips:

"Lieutenant Lavelle, we would like to give you a ship to command."

Chapter Four

Sam Lavelle lowered his plate and stared at the Changeling. What a poker face—there was no way to tell if he was the butt of a cruel joke, or they were actually trying to recruit him for some nefarious purpose. Changelings were rare in the Alpha Quadrant, and he didn't think one had summoned him only to have a laugh at his expense. Wherever this was going, it had to be dangerous and probably treasonous.

"You'll give me a ship to command?" he repeated slowly. "There's got to be a catch. Why don't I continue to eat, and you can explain to me what you want. Exactly."

"First," said the Changeling, "do you know anything about the act of sabotage which occurred today?"

Sam looked around the tasteful observation lounge,

and he could tell from their earnest faces that they were serious. "Sabotage? Do you mean the *accident?* I was out there at the time, and that accident was caused entirely by the boneheaded Cardassians."

From force of habit, he looked nervously around the room, but there were no Cardassians present. Every other race of importance was represented at this meeting, but not the lackeys. So Sam decided he could speak freely.

"I don't know what you were moving out there, but they put on their thrusters too early and disturbed the stasis field."

"Bumbling fools!" muttered Grof, unable to contain himself any longer. "I've warned them often enough."

"You said it wasn't entirely their fault," whined Joulesh. He looked accusingly at Grof.

The Trill folded his thick arms. "I warned you that the compound was too unstable, and that *they* were the wrong ones to handle it. I believe I was proven right on both counts."

"But all of our models—"

Sam was beginning to enjoy this bickering when the Changeling glided gracefully between the Vorta and the Trill. "Enough. Explain it to him so that he can understand it."

Dumb it down for the stupid human, thought Sam, bristling at the tone of the Changeling's words. But he was willing to listen until the food ran out.

Grof pointed accusingly at the Vorta. "*They* chose the wrong material to reinforce the mouth of the wormhole. I'm sure you know enough physics, Lieutenant, to realize that we can't use a common building material for the opening. Unless we use the right substance, the collider will get torn apart by the extreme pressures."

The scientist paced the length of the table, looking with disgust at the Vorta. "They listened to the Cardassians, who assured them they could use a material made of sub-quark particles, despite the volatility. After the stasis field was destroyed, the sub-quark particles recombined.

"There is a far more elegant approach. The Federation isolated the perfect substance only a few years ago—it's stable after it's extracted and recombined. *We* are the only ones who have succeeded in extracting it."

"Corzanium," answered Sam.

"Ah," said Grof with satisfaction, "I see you are versed on the latest research."

"Not really," admitted the human. "My friend, Taurik, was telling me about it. He admires your work, but he doesn't think much of you personally."

"A common sentiment," muttered the Trill, "but misguided. We are on the verge of great discoveries, great leaps forward—after our cultures merge. In the short term, Federation personnel are the best equipped to find and extract the Corzanium. We certainly can't rely on the Cardassians."

"Lieutenant Lavelle, will you command the craft?" asked the Founder bluntly. Joulesh's oversized ears twitched expectantly as the Vorta awaited his answer.

"Into a black hole?" scoffed Sam. "Isn't that where this stuff comes from? I can see why you don't want Cardassians—they're probably too *smart* to undertake such a crazy mission."

Despite the bravado, Sam was stalling for time as he tried to reason it out. Even though he might go down as the greatest traitor in Starfleet history, the chance to escape from the prison with a ship under his command was too tempting to pass up. Survival instincts that he thought were long dormant suddenly surged to the surface, and Sam envisioned himself making a break for freedom.

Besides, he knew that if he refused, he would be dead. They had told him too much to let him return to Pod 18 and the general prison population.

"Will you give us an answer," said Joulesh, "or simply continue to eat and make snide comments?"

"What do I get out of it?" asked Sam.

"You will receive your freedom," answered the Founder somberly, as if this were the greatest gift he could bestow.

"I get to pick my crew," said Sam.

"Boy, don't make this difficult!" snarled Grof. "Just say yes to the Founder, and let's get on with it."

Sam cautioned himself to remain as stone-faced as the Changeling and his retinue. He truly was not in a position to bargain, but maybe he was in a position to make a difference. It would appear that his patience, gift of gab, and good work habits were about to get him promoted in the prison hierarchy—into his real job. Sam wished he didn't have the spectre of Enrak Grof staring at him as he decided his fate. Either way, he doubted whether he would live to reflect on this decision.

"I'll do it," he said. "I won't be going back to Pod Eighteen, will I?"

"No," answered Joulesh. "Would you be afraid for your safety?"

Sam smiled. "Around here, I'm always afraid for my safety."

"Eat," said the Founder, sounding like a friendly relative. He wasn't exactly androgynous, but his masculine traits were underplayed. Sam imagined that he could just as easily present a pseudo-female façade. The creature was fascinating to study, up close, and it was all Sam could do not to ask him to morph into a chair. He tried to imagine what it was like on their home planet, where they merged into a sea of their kind called the Great Link.

Sam fought the temptation to ask this advanced being why it was so important to conquer the Alpha Quadrant. He supposed it was the same arrogance that had driven Europeans to conquer the Americas or Cardassians to conquer Bajor—a certainty of their moral and intellectual superiority.

With the slightest nod from the Founder, the Jem'Hadar guards suddenly picked up the basin and carried it out of the room. The Founder walked after them, and the two Vorta brought up the rear of the entourage. This left Sam alone with Professor Grof, plus enough food for a barracks.

"They're not much for good-byes," remarked the human.

"I think the Founder was tired," said Grof. "He probably has to revert to his liquid form soon. Dominion upper management is spread very thinly through the Alpha Quadrant. Besides, they got what they came for."

"Me?" Sam asked incredulously.

"Yes, but you could have shown them more respect. This is quite an honor."

"So everyone tells me." Sam glanced around the room. "Can I speak freely in here? Are we being watched?"

"Don't bother bawling me out," said the Trill. "You were going to tell me that I'm a traitor, a collaborator, and so on and so forth. You're going to say that we ought to escape, or sabotage the artificial wormhole. Well, let me tell you—what we're building here will last longer than either the Dominion or the Federation. The war will be a footnote to this invention. I'm on the side of science, and what we're building is going to revolutionize the galaxy."

"At what cost?" asked Sam. "You would destroy a federation of hundreds of planets for a *machine?* Whose side are you on? Are you a prisoner here, or are you one of the jailers?"

Grof scowled and lowered his voice. "I'm both. I want to see my work to fruition, and I'm not going to let politics stand in the way. I would like to take my findings to the Federation. In fact, I hope that this work brings both sides together, and ends this stupid war. Meanwhile, I'm still a prisoner. Would I welcome a chance to escape? Perhaps at a later date, but only if it's foolproof."

Sam picked up a slice of yellow melon and took a bite. The delicious juice ran down his beard. "You're obviously doing something right to have all of this handed to you."

"I'm just doing my job," snapped Grof.

At that moment, Sam decided not to trust Enrak Grof, who seemed entirely too wrapped up in his own self-interests. Sam would plan his escape without the Trill, unless his participation was absolutely necessary . . . and foolproof.

"What's the ship like?" asked Sam.

"It's a Cardassian antimatter tanker, specially equipped. You start training on it right away. You will need additional crew of six, and Joulesh and I have prepared a preliminary list of names. We have everyone we need right here."

"I'm sure of that," muttered Sam.

Grof ignored his sarcasm and went on, "We need two specialists in material handling, a tractor-beam specialist, and a senior transporter operator."

"And Taurik. I want the Vulcan."

"That leaves one more," said Grof. "Me."

Sam blinked at him. "You're going along on this mining expedition?"

"Everything depends upon it," answered the Trill. "Now that their engineers have been proven wrong, it's up to us to finish the job. And show them how valuable we are."

"How dangerous is this going to be?"

The Trill smiled. "Only as dangerous as we make it."

"It's too dangerous," insisted Will Riker. "Captain, please, I beg you to reconsider."

Captain Picard, who was lying on an operating table in sickbay, closed his eyes and tried to block out the concerned voice of his first officer. He concentrated instead on the sound of Dr. Crusher and Nurse Ogawa preparing their instruments. It sounded like fine silverware in use at a banquet.

"Captain, we have many other people who could do this mission," insisted Riker.

"Nonsense," said Picard. "We're so shorthanded that every able-bodied crew member is indispensable. The fact is, *you* can captain the ship, making *me* more dispensable than the majority of the crew. I also have the most expertise working with Ro Laren, and she can be a bit prickly."

"She's one of the reasons this is so dangerous," growled Riker with frustration.

"I'm sure Mr. La Forge and I can handle whatever she throws at us." *Literally and figuratively,* Picard thought, recalling her formidable fighting spirit. "And Data will keep us on long-range scans."

"What if he loses you in the Badlands?" Riker persisted.

"Nothing is without risk, Number One. If we need rescuing, we'll release our subspace beacon with a coded distress signal."

"Still, Captain—"

The captain finally opened his eyes and gazed sympathetically at his first officer. "You won't be able to talk me out of it, Will. The truth is, I need a break from this hit-and-run fighting, and you're better at it than I am. If I can investigate Ro's story, I'll feel I'm making a difference."

"I hope this isn't a wild-goose chase."

"I hope it is," said Picard gravely. "A false rumor—even a trap intended to catch us—would be preferable to finding an artificial wormhole in Dominion control. If we find that it actually exists, then the fate of the Federation rests upon our actions, right here."

Riker scratched his beard. "I suppose it's pointless to tell you to be careful in the middle of a war, but *be careful.*"

"You, too."

Beverly Crusher strode over to the table and shook her head. "Captain Riker, your persistence will be duly noted in my log, but you failed yet again to talk some sense into him. That makes two of us. Now we need to get on with the procedure, because I have a full schedule of appointments today."

Riker glanced quickly at the tiny implants resting on a tray held by Nurse Ogawa. Picard tried not to look too closely at them either. When he awoke, his face would be altered to look Bajoran, and he would be given an earring.

"I'll check on the repairs to the *Orb of Peace,*" promised Riker as he backed out of the operating room.

Brandishing a hypospray, Beverly gave the captain a professional smile. "Relax, Jean-Luc. I have to give you an anesthetic, but you'll only be out for a short time."

Picard nodded, thinking that he wouldn't mind a few minutes of blissful ignorance. As he felt the pressure of the hypo on his neck, he allowed his tense shoulders to relax. The urge to *do* something would soon be over. Like Don Quixote, he would be chasing either windmills or the biggest dragon in the kingdom.

Sam Lavelle stood on the somber, gray bridge of the *Tag Garwal,* studying schematics of the antimatter tanker under his command. Sam had studied Cardassian vessels for years, and never more intently than in the weeks leading up to the war. This design was well known, on a par with Starfleet tankers of similar vintage. The *Tag Garwal* was no speed demon or luxury liner, but it was built to be sturdy, dependable, and uncomplicated. Sam didn't think he and his handpicked crew would have any trouble mastering the craft.

Professor Grof sat at an auxiliary console, running diagnostics on the tractor beam and the transporters a deck below them. He occasionally glanced at Sam to see what he was doing. The uncomfortable silence between them was beginning to make Sam nervous, and he tried to think of a subject safe enough for small talk.

"Thank you for translating the manuals," said Sam.

"You're welcome," replied Grof brusquely. "But that was really Joulesh's idea. Are you satisfied with the ship?"

"I won't know for sure until I take her for a little spin."

"About those little spins," said Grof. "You'll be closely watched. An attempt to make a break for it would be suicide."

"You don't have to lay the company line on me," said Sam angrily. "I know how things work around here. We're more expendable than the Jem'Hadar, or even the Cardassians . . ."

"*You* may be expendable, but I'm not!" protested Grof. "I'm irreplaceable, no matter who wins this thing."

"Don't you even *care!*" Sam scowled. "Why should you? You're already on their side."

"There's more to being a prisoner than your feeble mind can envision!" hissed the Trill. "The Federation is the power in the Alpha Quadrant, and that's why the Dominion is testing us. Although you can't see it, everything we do in this secret complex is being judged and tested. For example, you had no idea they were paying such close attention to *you*, but your ability to voice dissatisfaction while being calm and reasonable was very impressive to them."

Grof sighed with frustration. "As you know, the Dominion has no real faith in the Cardassians—they're just convenient locals. Someday this war will be over, and we'll have to live with the Dominion. If you and I are a success on this mission, the worth of the entire Federation will go up in the eyes of the Founders."

"Oh, wonderful. Do you think they'll give me a promotion?" Sam winced, knowing that he was losing the battle to avoid controversial subjects. He had to end this topic, before he said something he regretted to this traitor.

"Listen, Grof, I'll do the mission, and I'll work with them—but don't expect me to like it. I'm in this for survival, not science, or to score brownie points."

The Trill looked deeply disappointed, but he managed to say, "As long as your attitude remains pragmatic, we should succeed."

"Fine," snapped Sam. Although he knew he should keep his mouth shut, he didn't like Enrak Grof. There had to be some way to needle him without talking local politics.

"So, what's it like to be an unjoined Trill?" asked Sam.

Grof snorted. "You mean, what's it like to be a second-class citizen? Imagine your planetary society has a small segment of people who are automatically considered superior to everyone else, and they automatically get the best careers. Imagine that these people have several lifetimes of experience to draw upon, and you're just starting the only lifetime you will ever get. How would you like to compete against them?"

"I take it you didn't pass the program?"

"No, I failed," admitted Grof. "My field docent didn't like my attitude, or some such. Of course, when eighteen initiates apply for every available symbiont, they can afford to be choosy."

"So you found a field in which to excel, to spite them."

Grof's dour, hirsute face broke into a slight smile. "I suppose I can thank them for some of my ambition and drive. But I firmly believe that I would have been doing this same work even if I had joined with a symbiont."

"Maybe that's why they didn't take you," said Sam, "too headstrong."

Grof frowned. "At any rate, it has taken me twice as long to have my work and my theories recognized. I should have led teams on which I was only a member, because we had to have a joined Trill in charge."

"But the Dominion accepted you right from the start," said Sam, putting it all together.

"Yes," snapped the Trill. "Being unjoined has never been a detriment here. They recognized me as a man of science. In many respects, the Dominion represents a clean slate for the Alpha Quadrant."

"That seems to be what they're going for—a clean slate with us wiped out. And you're helping them." Sam inwardly cursed his one-track mind. This was the very same conversation he had just tried to derail.

Grof stroked his beard and looked around. Then he lowered his voice to say, "Don't you see, this technology cuts both ways—it allows *us* to attack *them* through wormholes of *our* making. It democratizes the galaxy."

He shook his spotted head. "To depend on a natural wormhole inhabited by semi-mythological beings— only seen by one person—is absurd. What we're creating here is the transportation of the future, as important as warp drive or artificial gravity! Ships won't need to carry dangerous fuel like antimatter, because artificial wormholes will take you to the next solar system or the next quadrant in seconds."

"And with slave labor, you'll have plenty of people to keep building them," muttered Sam. "But suppose I'm hardly any better than you. My friends think I'm a brave soul who disappeared fighting the good fight, and here I am with decent food and my own ship. That reminds me, where do I sleep?"

"Right here." Grof motioned around the cramped, utilitarian bridge. "The captain's quarters are quite nice, I understand. There is even a sleeping alcove directly behind us, off the bridge."

Sam looked behind him and saw a small, curtained lounge where there would be a ready room on a Starfleet vessel. "Yes, this crate was built for long-range hauls. Well, if this is going to be home for a while, let's see what kind of entertainment we have."

He tapped the console, and the main viewscreen flickered on. A row of closed airlocks greeted Sam's eyes for a few seconds; then the angle cut to a view of empty cargo holds, followed by vistas of the verteron collider and the prison complex. To Sam's delight, the spheres and shafts of the complex *did* look like a giant molecule floating in space.

"Hey, we're patched into the security feed," said Sam. "There's nothing like being part of the gang."

They were treated to several tantalizing glimpses of various spacecraft docked around an outer sphere. Sam plied the console and found a way to cycle more quickly through the images until he found their own oblong tanker. Its hull was gray with yellow stripes, and it was mostly featureless except for the dents and pits.

"That's us, huh? We won't win any beauty contests."

Sam continued paging through the images until they had inspected a number of interesting locations, including laboratories, factories, and guard posts. He could see Grof getting nervous about scanning the security channel, and he was about to stop when they were suddenly thrust into a women's prison pod. Sam looked away with embarrassment, hoping the scene would switch soon.

A blur of action caught his eye, and Sam looked back at the screen to see a squad of twenty or so Cardassians rush into the pod. The Cardassians were wielding clubs and were wearing vests, helmets, and riot gear; they quickly surrounded the unarmed prisoners. The free-cycling program chose that moment to cut to another pod, which was full of bedrolls but otherwise empty. Sam frantically worked the controls, trying to page back to the first pod.

"Don't," said Grof softly.

Sam ignored him and finally cut back to the occupied pod. Two Cardassian guards were holding a woman by her arms and shaking her violently, while a glinn grilled her. There was no sound, and Sam couldn't tear his eyes away from the viewscreen to find it on the console. The other guards herded the prisoners away from the action, but the women pushed closer, anxious to see what was happening to their comrade. It looked like a disaster in the making, and Sam gripped the handrail in front of him.

Sure enough, when the glinn struck the woman across her face, her fellow prisoners revolted. This resulted in a ruthless crackdown, as the club-wielding Cardassians waded into the women, forcing them against the walls. As Sam watched in horror, he was glad there was no sound.

Grof finally reached over and pounded the console, turning off the viewscreen. By the stricken look on his face, it seemed as if the Trill was about to have a heart attack, or maybe an attack of conscience.

"See, they have a good use for the Cardassians," hissed Sam. "I'm not sure Federation personnel could replace them."

Grof sputtered, looking as if he wanted to say something but had no words. He hurried off the bridge of the *Tag Garwal*, and Sam heard his footsteps clomping down a ladder to the lower deck.

Despite a rush of murderous impulses, Sam tried to stay calm. He thought about turning the viewscreen back on, but what was the point? His hatreds were already etched into his soul, and watching more atrocities wouldn't change anything. He had to maintain his cool, jaded façade until there came a chance to strike hard against the Dominion—or die trying.

Eventually Sam put on the viewscreen, but he tuned it to an innocuous view of the starscape, dominated by the swirling gases and dust of the

Badlands. In all of this vast universe was there no one to help them? Where was the might of Starfleet, and the vaunted resources of the Federation?

For all he knew, the war could be over, and no one was out there to give a damn. In which case, maybe he should be looking out for number one, as he pretended.

Sam reclined in the alcove off the bridge and tried to sleep, but his mind kept dwelling on images of space-suited prisoners, exploding like balloons in the cold darkness of space.

Ro Laren stood on the bridge of the *Orb of Peace,* marveling at the appearance of her crew. Dressed in rust-colored uniforms with dangling earrings and pronounced nose ridges, they could have been the cream of Bajoran youth. Of course, there was the older Bajoran sitting at the conn station. He was mostly bald except for two tufts of unruly gray hair hanging over his ears, which made him look vaguely absurd and absentminded, like an old librarian. His earring was also slightly askew, and Ro couldn't help but to smile at her former captain.

"She's your ship," said the pilot. "Take her out."

"I'm going to need a code name to call you by," said Ro. "Your real name is a bit too well known. Do you know who you remind me of? Boothby, the old gardener at the Academy."

Picard grinned. "That's quite a compliment, as I had Boothby in mind when we devised this disguise. Not very Bajoran, of course, but it will pass for a nickname—and a code name."

"Okay, Boothby, set our course for the Badlands."

Ro tapped her comm badge, a distinctive Bajoran design of a sphere and a fin, surrounded by concentric ovals. "Ro to La Forge. Is everything ready?"

"Yes, sir," came the cheerful voice of Starfleet's best engineer. "We'll coax every parsec we can out of our warp drives, but this isn't a long-range craft. We can't cruise hours on end at maximum warp."

"I know we're not going to outrun or outfight anybody," agreed Ro. "Stealth and guile—that's what I learned from the Maquis."

"That's well and good," said La Forge, "but I'm also worried about those plasma storms in the Bad-lands."

"There are bubbles of calm in the storms," explained Ro. "That's why you have me along. Did you run the scans?"

"Yes. We'll register as a Bajoran ship on anything but the most detailed inspection. Biological scans came up all Bajoran, too."

"Thank you, La Forge. Bridge out." Ro tapped her comm badge again and said, *"Orb of Peace* to *Enterprise:* we are ready to launch."

Captain Riker's somber face appeared on the viewscreen. He was still exhibiting his displeasure over this mission. "Launch sequence completed. We are opening shuttlebay doors. Good hunting."

"Thank you," answered Ro. The viewscreen shifted to an impressive view of the thick doors and smooth silver walls that enclosed them. The sight only served to remind her how large the *Enterprise* was—her transport had been swallowed whole inside one shut-tlebay. Slowly the huge doors slid open, revealing the star-studded depths of space beyond the womb of the *Enterprise.*

Ro nodded to the conn. "Take us out, one-quarter impulse to a thousand kilometers."

"Yes, sir," snapped the dark-skinned woman.

Picard smiled at his captain. "By the book. You still remember procedures."

"Old habits," said Ro with a shrug. "They seem to work."

With thrusters firing, the boxy transport lifted off the deck of the shuttlebay and floated out the open door. Picking up speed while it rushed past the twin nacelles of the *Enterprise,* the *Orb of Peace* soared into space.

Chapter Five

SAM HEARD FOOTSTEPS on the ladder, and he turned away from the ops console to see a thin, cadaverous-looking Cardassian emerge onto the bridge of the *Tag Garwal*. His first reaction was to grab a weapon to protect himself, but then he realized that it had to be official business. He was part of the gang now, Sam reminded himself; and this was *his* ship.

Nevertheless, the Cardassian gave him a suspicious glare as he stepped aside and let the elegant Vorta, Joulesh, rise from the hatch and join them on the bridge. Footsteps continued clattering on the ladder, and a moment later Taurik's head popped out of the hatch. The graceful Vulcan lifted his lanky body from the hole and stood before Sam, looking nonplussed by this sudden change in fortune.

"Taurik!" exclaimed Sam with delight. He started to rush forward to embrace his friend when he

80

remembered where he was, and with whom. "It's good to see you."

"And you," said Taurik with a slight nod. "There are more of us."

He stepped aside to allow four more dazed Starfleet officers to join them on the bridge. Unlike the Vulcan, their faces ran the gamut from confusion to curiosity, and they glanced with apprehension at the Cardassian and the Vorta.

"Here is your crew," said Joulesh with pride, "except for Professor Grof, who will join us shortly. I believe you know Lieutenant Taurik."

"Yes."

The Vorta motioned to the remaining two men and two women, who were unfamiliar to Sam. All looked to be older, career officers. "Chief Leni Shonsui, transporter operator; Commander Tamla Horik, tractor-beam operator; Chief Enrique Masserelli, stasis engineer; and Lieutenant Jozarnay Woil, material handler. All were department heads on their own ships."

The Vorta smiled, quite pleased with himself. "Two men and two women. Two are human, one is Deltan, and the other is Antosian. When you include the Vulcan and the Trill who are part of our team, I believe we have put together a representative cross section of the Federation. All humanoids, I'm afraid. I would have liked to have a Horta or one of your more exotic species, but this ship is built for humanoids."

Sam pointed to the Cardassian on the suddenly crowded bridge. "What's *he* doing here?"

"Trainer," answered Joulesh. "I know you pride yourself on knowing everything, but you are bound to have questions which can only be answered by an experienced officer. In particular, I'm concerned with tractor-beam operations."

The Vorta clapped his hands together. "I almost forgot—I should introduce *you*. Ladies and gentlemen, this is the ship's captain, Lieutenant Sam Lavelle."

The newly summoned crew looked suspiciously at Sam, as if he were one of the unfamiliar consoles that surrounded them. He couldn't expect to have this crew's loyalty or respect, so he would have to make do with their fear and curiosity. Plus Sam knew he would have their instincts for survival on his side.

"How much have any of you been told?" he asked.

"Very little," answered Taurik. "I was told that I was needed for a special task. Until I saw you here, I considered it likely you were dead."

"Likely, but not quite." Sam scratched his bare chin, which he had shaved for the first time in weeks. He was also wearing a nondescript but new blue jumpsuit, while his shipmates were still dressed in rags, with unkept hair and unshaven faces.

"It's very simple," he began. "We're going on a mining expedition to extract Corzanium from a black hole. Sounds like fun, doesn't it?"

Woil, the Antosian material handler, gaped at him. "Corzanium? But we've only been able to extract that in minute quantities. What are they going to do with it?"

"Reinforce the mouth of the collider," answered Sam bluntly. "But that's not our concern. We have a ship and a job to do—if we're successful, they've promised us our freedom."

His new crew stared at him with expressions ranging from incredulity to belligerence. Taurik merely looked thoughtful. *Can't they read between the lines?* thought Sam with frustration. In the company of a Vorta and a Cardassian, they weren't going to be able to talk frankly. It was time for this group to realize that they were being given a rare opportunity.

Sam thought back on how frustrated Grof had been when he hadn't jumped immediately at the chance to join up. He frowned. "I know none of you volunteered for this duty, but you were specially chosen. Each of you impressed our captors in some way or another. If you don't want to join this detail and go back into space, just let me know. You can go back to your pods and your normal duties."

With a half smile on his face, Joulesh looked curiously at Sam. Both of them knew that these people were never going back to their regular pods and work routines, no matter what happened. When no one called Sam's bluff, the Vorta allowed himself a full smile.

"Very well," said Joulesh. "Shall we begin?"

After securing clean uniforms for everyone and taking a tour of the tanker, they began the long process of familiarization. There was special emphasis on operations of the bridge stations, tractor beam, transporter room, stasis fields, and the antimatter containers that had been converted to store Corzanium. By the end of the day, the reluctant crew members had embraced the challenges of their task and were offering suggestions on how to proceed. Sam could tell that Joulesh was quite pleased by their progress, while the Cardassian trainer barely hid his contempt.

Sam and Taurik found themselves observers during

a session on how to manipulate the robotic arm mounted to a mining probe.

"I've got a side job for you," Sam whispered to the Vulcan.

"Yes?" answered Taurik, keeping his voice low.

"I want you to inspect the ship and see if there are any monitoring devices aboard."

The Vulcan glanced at him. "You wish to know if we can speak freely?"

"Right."

Taurik nodded in response, and they went back to listening to the lecture.

By the end of a long shift, they were joined by a taciturn Enrak Grof, who barely grunted as he was introduced to the rest of his shipmates. The Trill briefly explained that he had been occupied with finishing his regular work and calculating how much more Corzanium they would need to complete the project. He assured them he would not have to return to the laboratory, and he was joining them for the duration.

As they continued their training, Sam watched his new crew. They were as experienced and competent as any captain could possibly hope for, but they were hardened by their weeks of captivity. Except for Grof, they were probably loyal to the Federation, but were they loyal enough to give up their lives? Was he kidding himself in thinking that they could accomplish anything but saving their own skins for a few extra days? The chances were good that they would all die in this foolhardy undertaking.

"Very good!" exclaimed Joulesh, clapping his hands with delight and snapping Sam from his reverie. "I believe we have made wonderful progress, ahead of schedule. In fact, let us move up the test flight to the next shift. The Founder will be so pleased!"

The Vorta nodded to the Cardassian, who had been surly but helpful for most of the training. "You are dismissed."

With a parting snarl, the Cardassian climbed down the ladder and disappeared, and Joulesh considered his cadre of prized pupils. "We are entrusting you with an enormous responsibility, I hope you realize that. Yes, you have an opportunity to act foolishly and register your discontent, but you also have an opportunity to further science and improve relations between our peoples."

Sam looked around at his crew. Almost all of them were stone-faced over this twisted reasoning, even Grof, who had avoided Sam since his late arrival. Was he still thinking about the beatings they had witnessed? Or was he still angry over the senseless loss of life caused by the Cardassians?

The burly Trill had barely hidden his contempt for their Cardassian trainer, and Sam was beginning to consider him neutral but still unpredictable. If any of them had any sense, they would avoid being drawn into a conversation over motives and politics with this slimy Vorta.

Joulesh continued to smile gamely at his impassive audience. "I know it's been a difficult shift, and you must be tired. This ship has lodging for a crew of twelve, so you have ample room to spread out. The replicators in the mess hall have been reprogrammed for Federation tastes, and everything on this craft is fully functional, except for the weapons systems, of course. They were never much to speak of, anyway."

The Vorta started for the ladder, then he waved

back to them. "Use your intelligence, and don't act rashly. I will see you at your test flight. Yes, the Founder will be so pleased!"

As soon as the Vorta left the ship, Taurik moved to the ops console and began to run diagnostics and scans of the ship. Sam hovered over his shoulder, as Grof and the four new crew members looked uneasily at one another.

"What's the catch to this?" asked Enrique. "They're not going to give us a ship and let us fly off into space, are they?"

"Yes, they are," answered Grof. "As I've been telling our captain, the bond between the Dominion and the Cardassians is weak, because the Cardassians are incompetent. We have a chance to make a favorable impression."

"Belay that," growled the bald-headed Deltan, Tamla Horik. "Despite the pretty words, I say we're aiding and abetting the enemy."

"Keep it down," warned Sam. "We don't know that we're not being observed."

"Actually, Sam, I detect no monitoring devices or listening coils," said Taurik. "I believe the ship is, as Joulesh said, unaltered except for improvements to the containment lockers and the absence of weapons. There is no reason why we should not speak freely. In fact, our odds of success depend upon the ability to communicate."

"Finally somebody is making sense," muttered Grof. "Listen to the Vulcan. This isn't a joke or a test—this is a vital mission for the success of the greatest invention in our history. I've already explained all of this to Lieutenant Lavelle, but the artificial wormhole will outlive all of us, including the Dominion and the Federation. This invention turns the entire galaxy into one neighborhood."

"Giving the Dominion the chance to take over the whole Milky Way," snapped Leni Shonsui.

"Don't bother arguing with him," muttered Sam. "I've already said everything you're going to say, and he won't listen."

"And what's the deal with you?" asked Leni. "What did *you* do to make captain in the Dominion?"

"I could ask you the same thing about your assignment to this ship. All of us have been blessed, or cursed, by the same fate. We're here, we have a ship, and we have a job to do. Let's get on with it, and we'll worry about everything else later."

Enrique edged toward the ladder. "Does that replicator really have any food we want?"

"I think so," answered Sam. "Go ahead and enjoy yourselves, because I figure we probably won't survive, even if we don't do anything stupid."

"The odds of completing this mission without being destroyed are approximately ten to one—against," added Taurik.

Sam chuckled, letting the tension drain out of his handsome face. "Thank you, Taurik. Do you see? There's no sense fighting with each other. The chances are good that we're going to die in each other's company, aboard this strange ship, no matter what we do. But at least we'll die in space, not chained in a cell."

Grof scowled and strode toward the ladder, pushing Enrique out of the way. "We're not going to die—we're going to *succeed!*" He clomped down the ladder, his footsteps ringing all over the small ship.

Sam watched the Trill disappear into the hatch, then he whispered, "With or without *him,* we're going to make an escape. But not until I say so."

"Approaching ships," warned Data.

Will Riker bolted upright in the command chair of the *Enterprise.* "How many? From where?"

"Three ships, Jem'Hadar battle cruisers, traversing sector nine-four-six-two on an interception course at warp eight," answered the android.

The acting captain of the *Enterprise* jumped to his feet and strode toward Data's station. "Who are they after? Us, or the *Orb of Peace?*"

"It would seem to be us, sir. It has now been nine minutes and thirty-two seconds since the *Orb of Peace* entered Cardassian space, and they appear to be undetected." The android looked earnestly at Riker. "Estimated arrival time of the Jem'Hadar: twenty-one minutes and thirty seconds."

"Are there any Starfleet vessels that can help us?"

"None that can reach us in time."

Riker scowled. "We can't stand up to three cruisers. We have time to run, but we'll have to stop tracking the away team."

"Not necessarily, sir." Data cocked his head. "The *Enterprise* must retreat, but I could take a small shuttlecraft and land on the sixth planet of the Kreel solar system. With the shuttlecraft's sensors, I could monitor the transport until the danger has passed. If I maintain my relative position, I could monitor them indefinitely."

"That's a class-Q planet," said Riker with distaste, imagining its cold temperatures and deadly methane atmosphere. Then he realized that class Q or class M was all the same to Data.

"Its inhospitality will prevent the Dominion from following me. I can land in the polar region where the methane is frozen."

"We can beam you down," said Riker.

"I would prefer to have a shuttlecraft, so I can be mobile."

Making an instant decision, Riker motioned toward the turbolift. "Go."

In a blur, the android leaped from his seat and rushed off the bridge. A replacement officer, who looked young enough to be Riker's daughter, settled into his vacated seat.

"Bridge to shuttlebay one," said Riker, "prepare a shuttlecraft for Commander Data. He's on his way."

"Yes, sir," came the response.

The acting captain tugged on his beard as he paced the circular bridge of the *Enterprise.* This was his worst nightmare—taking over the ship in the midst of a crisis without Captain Picard, Geordi, or Data. Not only was he worried about his friends, but he was worried about the effectiveness of the crew without her senior staff. He was surrounded by newly minted ensigns fresh from the Academy; half their names he didn't know. Riker wondered whether Beverly Crusher would like to take over for him now.

"Estimated arrival time of enemy ships: nineteen minutes," reported the young ops officer with a slight tremolo to her voice.

The captain stopped behind the conn. "If they want to chase us, let's lure them to the rendezvous point and get some help. Set course two-five-eight-mark-six-four."

"Yes, sir." The blue-skinned Bolian plied his console. "Course set."

Riker strode toward Ensign Craycroft. "Tactical, send a message to Starfleet and tell them we're on our way, and that we're bringing company—three Jem'Hadar battle cruisers."

"Yes, sir." Ensign Craycroft turned on her communications panel and began to enter the message.

Riker looked back at ops. "Commander Data?"

"He is entering the shuttlecraft *Cook.* Launch sequence in progress . . . opening shuttlebay doors."

"On screen." Riker stepped back to see the hurried launch on the viewscreen. For the second time that day, he watched a small ship soar from the belly of the *Enterprise,* looking like a bat escaping from a cave into the dead of night.

"Five hundred kilometers, six hundred kilometers, seven hundred kilometers—" droned the ops officer.

"Good luck, Data," muttered Riker. "Conn, prepare to go to maximum warp. Engage."

In a halo of golden light, the sleek starship elongated into the sparkling starscape and vanished. Thousands of kilometers away, a tiny shuttlecraft veered toward a medium-large planet engulfed in noxious ivory gases.

Ro Laren paced across the tastefully illuminated but cramped bridge of the *Orb of Peace,* thinking their return to Cardassian space had been too easy, too uneventful. Unless a big operation was afoot and most of the Dominion ships were occupied, they should have been hailed or intercepted by now. After all, they were making a straight shot across a war zone toward one of the Dominion's most sensitive areas.

"No sign of any ships?" she asked Picard, who was still seated at the conn. In their agreed-upon chain of command, she was captain of the ship, and he was in command of the mission. For a veteran officer, the captain had been remarkably calm about taking a subordinate role to her own. Perhaps a real captain didn't need to have a special chair, extra pips on his collar, and everyone saluting him. Captain Picard's bearing and dignity were enough to warrant the respect of anyone in his presence.

He shook his head. "There is traffic in several solar systems along our route, but no one seems overly interested in us."

"It's too easy," said Ro with concern. "We're being watched, evaluated—I can feel it. By the time they come after us, it will be too late; they will have made up their minds."

Picard tugged on his earring, a tic he was beginning to develop.

"Then let's alter our course," Picard suggested. "Pick a typical solar system that is inhabited, go there and look like we're doing some trading."

"That will throw us off our timetable," said the ops officer.

"Getting killed will throw us off even more," replied Ro, glowering at the man.

Picard nodded to his officer. "Find us a likely planet. Quickly."

"We have goods to trade, don't we?" asked Ro.

"Yes," answered the captain. "We replicated a supply of zajerberry wine, Bajoran silk, and tetra-lubisol. Plus, we have a box of Bajoran religious tracts."

"If we survive this, maybe I'll read them," muttered Ro.

"Won't it look odd for us to be trading with a Cardassian colony?" asked the ops officer.

"I wouldn't be terribly concerned about that," answered Picard. "According to Starfleet Intelligence, the Cardassians developed quite a taste for Bajoran goods during the occupation, and Bajor is still trying to rebuild its economy. Under the circumstances it will just look like a wise business decision."

Behind her, the ops officer sighed loudly, not happy with his options. "There's a Cardassian farming colony on the sixth planet of System H-949."

"All right then. Set course for it and make our way slowly, at warp one," ordered Ro. "I want them to see that we've changed course."

Since Picard was stationed at the conn, it was his decision whether to obey the order, and everyone on the bridge was watching him. Without hesitation, he punched in the new coordinates. "New course entered. We'd better come out of warp to change course."

There was a slight tremor in the primitive craft as it slowed and made an awkward course correction. Then the warp engines revved once more, and the transport shot into space, headed toward an obscure Cardassian colony.

Ro sighed, not certain whether her relief was over the course change or the fact that the fake Bajorans had obeyed her order. Her authority over this crew extended solely from Captain Picard, and no one else. Without his faith in her, she was nothing but a grubby refugee to this crew of young upstarts. They were brave and eager to face the enemy, while she was jumpy and cautious. In Cardassian space, surrounded by the enemy, she much preferred her collection of well-earned fears to their naïveté.

"They're here," said Picard grimly as he studied his screen. "Two warships are now in pursuit of us. One Jem'Hadar and one Cardassian."

"I *knew* they were watching. Maintain course and speed." Ro turned to face the crew. "We have to confront them and prove who we are—to get them off our tracks. Had we waited too long, heading directly for the Badlands, they would've decided on their own that we were spies. How much time do we have?"

"Eleven minutes until interception," said the ops officer, a trace of fear in his formerly condescending voice.

"When they hail us," said Ro, "be friendly and do whatever they ask. Remember, the Cardassians treat their riding hounds better than they treat Bajorans. We're awfully lucky that we got a Jem'Hadar ship in the mix."

"We usually don't feel that way," said Picard with a wan smile.

Ro tapped her Bajoran comm badge and spoke in a loud voice. "Captain Ro to the ship's complement: all off-duty personnel are to go immediately to the cargo bay and unpack the zajerberry wine. Put out samples of all the cargo. Arrange it nicely, as if it's always on display. Bridge out."

"Shall we go on yellow alert?" asked the ops officer uncertainly.

"No, don't do anything that looks even remotely aggressive. We'll either talk our way out of this or die here and now."

The lanky Bajoran gazed at Picard. "I notice that

one of the 'improvements' you made to my ship was to add a self-destruct sequence. Feel free to ready it. I, for one, don't want to be tortured. How about you?"

The captain cleared his throat and returned her gaze. "I'll bring it up on my console, keeping it in the background. I won't move from this station. If capture looks imminent, I'll arm it with a ten-second delay."

Ro nodded. "We always did think alike."

"We're being hailed," said tactical.

"On screen." Ro turned to look at the viewscreen framed with platitudes, and fear clamped her spine. Instead of the spiny Jem'Hadar face she had hoped to see, a bony, scaly Cardassian face stared at her. He smiled with the delight of a sadistic schoolmaster having caught a tardy student.

"And what have we here?" he said snidely. "Bajorans in the Cardassian Union? Roaming freely?"

"Good day to you, noble captain," replied Ro in as obsequious a tone as she could manage. "We are no longer enemies—we are practically allies, thanks to the benevolence of the Dominion."

That wiped the smirk off the Cardassian's face. "Come to a full stop and prepare to be boarded."

"We would welcome that," said Ro brightly, "as we are looking for the opportunity to trade with your people."

"What do *you* have that *we* could possibly want?" asked the Cardassian doubtfully.

"Zajerberry wine," answered Ro slyly. She knew that Picard's comments had been on the mark. The Cardassians *had* developed a taste for the stuff while they occupied Bajor. She had once smuggled some out of Quark's place on Deep Space Nine to buy the release of Maquis prisoners.

"Prepare to be boarded." The Cardassian scowled, and the screen went blank.

With movements that were so fast they could not be fully appreciated by a human eye, Data scurried around his type-9 personnel shuttlecraft, the *Cook*. He quickly filled two shielded cases with tricorders, weapons, tools, a distress beacon, and emergency supplies, leaving food and water behind. The android took a final glance at his console and confirmed that one of the Jem'Hadar battle cruisers had indeed broken off from the others and gone into orbit around Kreel VI, the uninhabited planet on which he had taken refuge.

If Data didn't want his shuttlecraft to be detected and destroyed, he had to shut down all systems. Plus, he knew it would be prudent to run some distance from the shuttlecraft in case the Jem'Hadar sent down a probe and discovered it. Fortunately, a scan of the planet for life signs would not reveal his existence. Unfortunately, after he turned off all systems, he would be unable to track the *Orb of Peace*. After the danger passed, he would have to depend upon the transport's last known position and scan from there. It would be highly imprecise.

Experiencing a sense of urgency, Data powered down the shuttlecraft. After a brief pause, the interior of the small vessel was plunged into total darkness. Data could sense his surroundings perfectly well as he opened the hatch manually, something which would have required two humans to accomplish in the heavy gravity of Kreel VI.

Monstrous winds and sleeting methane snow pelted Data as he darted outside, carrying a large case in each hand. His feet crunched on the frozen tundra, and he didn't even want to think about how cold it was. Data set down the cases long enough to shut the door; then he surveyed his surroundings.

Visibility was almost zero in the blizzard, and Data relied upon his built-in sensors to locate an outcropping of rocks about three kilometers away. As the only landmark in the area, it would have to serve as his destination.

At a fast jog, leaping over fissures, he crossed the uneven ground, conscious of the opaque ice beneath his feet. The very fact that the Jem'Hadar had stopped to look for him on this inhospitable planet proved that their technology was quite advanced. They were thorough and determined—a dangerous adversary. Although the Jem'Hadar were biological beings, Data felt some kinship with them. Like himself, they had been engineered to serve without question in a multitude of situations, and they did so without complaint or selfish motives.

He heard a wrenching explosion somewhere behind him, and a sheet of methane blasted his back. A human would have been pitched off his feet by the impact of the shock wave, but Data just kept loping across the uneven terrain, hardly able to see his own legs in the driving snow. He suddenly detected high readings of radiation, enough to kill most creatures.

With his emotion chip turned off, the android felt no fear, but he spent a microsecond deciding that he was in serious trouble. His shuttlecraft probably destroyed, his shipmates scattered in different directions, he was all alone, except for an enemy cruiser with a complement of several hundred Jem'Hadar. If the *Enterprise* was destroyed, nobody in the universe would know where he was, even if he did manage to survive this incident.

Data's most unsettling conclusion, however, was that his mission had already failed. If the shuttlecraft was destroyed, he could not track the *Orb of Peace,* nor could he catch their distress beacon when they released it. They were also on their own.

His legs began to pump uphill through ice and rubble, and Data realized that he had reached his destination. The rocky tor offered scant shelter, but it stood forty meters tall and might disguise his mass and metallic components from their sensors.

As there was nothing to see, Data didn't bother to look for a vantage point. He set his cases down at the first level ground he came to, then crouched between them, ready to use them for shields. The tor seemed to consist of bedrock, which was some consolation to the android, because it might withstand an attack. Data waited, watching for the Jem'Hadar to emerge from the dense clouds and snow that swirled all around him.

A dabo-girl smile plastered to her face, Ro Laren stood by in the cargo bay, which had been hastily converted into a showroom. She watched half a dozen Cardassians paw her merchandise and shove her crew around, while another half a dozen trained their weapons on the helpless Bajorans. A gray-haired gul named Ditok had beamed down with the inspection team, and he rifled through the silks, then moved on to the red-clay bottles of wine.

"An excellent vintage," chirped Ro. "Would you like to try some?"

He glared at her. "You have the impertinence to think that I would drink while on duty. Or that I would even like this Bajoran urine?"

His men chuckled politely, while Gul Ditok grabbed a bottle and hefted it. "Probably replicated, if it isn't totally fake."

"I can verify its authenticity," promised Ro, "although the truth is in the tasting." She hoped the Starfleet replicators had been up to the task—some Cardassians were experts on zajerberry wine.

"Doesn't matter," snarled the gul, "you have a bigger problem, *no documents.*"

Ro offered him a smile of regret. "As I have told you, we have just entered this sector, and we were about to make our first stop, where we could apply for permission. We welcome your visit."

The gul scowled, as if he much preferred Bajorans who made trouble. "Is this what your proud people are reduced to, slinking around with trinkets, like a tribe of Ferengi?"

Ro lowered her voice. "To be frank, we are curious to get to know the Dominion better. We are neutral in this war, you know, and it's fairly clear how it's going to end."

The gul laughed. "Ah. So now you're cowards, but at least *smart* cowards."

A young glinn hovering nearby whispered something in the ear of the gul, and he glowered at them. "I'm reminded that your flight pattern shows you came from Federation space, or what's left of it. How do you explain that?"

"We did come from Federation space," answered

Ro. "We were trading there first. In fact, that's where we obtained the tetralubisol. It's the finest space-rated lubricant you can buy."

"I know what it is," muttered the Cardassian.

One of the young pseudo-Bajorans approached the gul with a pamphlet in her hand. "Would you like something to read? It's very inspiring."

He slapped the padd out of her hand. "Get away from me! You're all sheep, the lot of you. Bajorans!" He spat on the deck.

Despite the burning bile surging up her throat, Ro stuck to her plan. "We honestly come in peace. With the Dominion rolling over two quadrants, we haven't got anything to gain by remaining loyal to the Federation. The Federation did nothing but interfere, anyway."

"There's a grain of truth," said the Cardassian. "Have you got any more truth in you?"

"Only that you once fought against the Dominion, and now you regard them as allies. Can't you do the same with us?"

For a moment, it looked as if the old warrior would accept her entreaty of peace; then he burst out laughing. "Bajorans, my dear, are hardly the Dominion."

His sunken eyes ran down her lean body. "You personally are quite attractive, Captain, and perhaps you *do* offer something of worth. We must have a private conference later to discuss it."

Ro gritted her teeth and tried not to vomit. "Then I could offer you some wine."

"I'm afraid not," he said with a sympathetic smile. "We have to confiscate all of the wine. Contraband, you know."

"What? *What!*" sputtered Ro, although she had

expected this turn of events. "You can't take our whole cargo . . . I mean, we need to make a profit!"

"Experience is always a great profit." Gul Ditok snapped his fingers, and his soldiers roughly herded the Bajoran crew away from the cases of wine. Within seconds, they had transported every bottle from the cargo bay to their warship.

Ro tried to feign a mixture of indignation and horror at this outrage, while she was secretly relieved that they had accepted the bribe. Could she possibly hope they would leave it at that?

"Now are you satisfied? Can you let us go?" she demanded.

"Not yet. I want to see your bridge and your weaponry. Our scan suggests that you have photon torpedoes."

"Only six," said Ro. "You never know when you'll confront an asteroid belt, pirates, or some other obstacle that requires intervention."

"We don't have pirates in the Cardassian Union," said the gul testily.

"Ah, but we were just in Federation space, where they have no respect for law and order."

Once again, the gul looked disappointed that his prey was so amenable. "Take us to your bridge."

Gritting her teeth, Ro led the way to the bridge, which was only up one level via a spiral staircase. When she entered the control room, she was glad to see that the lights were dimmed to a soothing level. Captain Picard and two other duty officers were the only ones present.

The Cardassian gul and his entourage muscled their way into the cramped room and began peering at everything and everyone. Captain Picard stood immediately and smiled at the visitors.

The gul looked at his conn screen. "What is your maximum speed?"

"Warp three," answered Picard.

The Cardassian laughed. "Aren't you embarrassed to be flying this thing?"

"It's preferable to fighting in the war," said Picard with a shrug. "We have a message of peace to bring to the Dominion."

"We shall see about that." The gul gave a sidelong glance at his retinue, and they grinned knowingly.

"Gul Ditok!" snapped a voice. "Look what I have found."

They all turned to see a female glinn standing beside an open cabinet, holding a Starfleet hand phaser. It was a shock to Ro and everyone else in the crew, as they had been careful not to bring any obvious Starfleet equipment on board. All of their phasers were Bajoran or Ferengi.

"Aha!" declared the Cardassian. He was so melodramatic about it that Ro instantly knew what had happened—the phaser had been planted!

"You are enemies of the Dominion, in league with the Federation," proclaimed the gul. "We are seizing this vessel and taking you prisoner."

Picard shot her a glance, then immediately turned to his console. His fingers pressed several membrane panels before the gul slapped him in the head and knocked him out of his chair. The captain tumbled to the floor, but he gazed up with a satisfied look on his face.

"What have you done?" bellowed the gul.

"We have eight seconds to live."

Chapter Six

RO HAD NEVER SEEN a Cardassian's eyes widen, because of the thick bones which encircled their eye sockets. But Gul Ditok's eyes grew very wide when Picard told him that he had seconds to live. Every person on the bridge of the *Orb of Peace* looked terrified, and Ro's eyes went instinctively to the platitudes framing the viewscreen. "Place yourself in the hands of the Prophets," suggested one phrase, which was a proper sentiment under the circumstances.

Gul Ditok barked into his communicator, "Beam us up! Immediately!"

As their sparkling shapes vanished from the bridge, Picard leaped into his chair and punched his instrument panel. Ro flinched, certain that the next instant would be their last.

When they weren't blasted to bits, she opened her

eyes and looked around. "I counted more than ten seconds."

"I changed my mind and set it for thirty," admitted Picard. "I put the shields up, so they can't transport us off. You'd better start talking to them."

Ro motioned to Tactical. "Open a channel to the Jem'Hadar ship. Put me on screen, whether they acknowledge or not."

She strode in front of the viewscreen and pouted angrily. "This is Captain Ro Laren of the *Orb of Peace*. Is this how the Dominion treats its neutral trading partners? We come here in peace, and you *steal* our shipment of zajerberry wine, you threaten my crew, and you plant a weapon on our ship so that you can illegally seize us!"

She closed her eyes again, expecting quantum torpedoes to slam into them. When that didn't happen, Ro went on. "We know there's a war, but our work goes on. We are a religious people, and we just want a chance to trade goods and ideas. In this modest vessel, we couldn't do you any harm."

Ro tried not to think what a huge lie she had just delivered, but she was doing the best she could in this one-way conversation. Ro glanced down at Picard and saw that he had only paused the self-destruct sequence. There were fifteen seconds left, and his fingers were poised to resume the fatal countdown.

The viewscreen was filled with two imposing warships—the mustard-colored Galor-class warship and the Jem'Hadar battle cruiser, its hull pulsing with a vibrant blue light. Ro looked at tactical. "End transmission."

"Yes, sir."

"Are they arming weapons?"

"No," said the officer on tactical. "They're sending coded messages back and forth to each other."

Ro looked at Picard, and he gave her an encouraging smile. "You're doing fine."

She nodded and swallowed. It felt good to yell at them, even if every word was a lie.

The tactical officer gasped with surprise. "They are . . . they are sending us documents! One set allows us passage in this sector, and the other is an order to appear on Cardassia Prime in seventy-two hours to discuss a fine for our offenses."

"They gave us a *ticket,*" commented Picard with a touch of amusement in his voice.

Ro looked puzzledly at the human. "A ticket?"

"It's an old Terran phrase," said Picard. "It means that we received a summons to appear later, so trial and punishment is put off. Acknowledge it and thank them."

"Yes, sir."

Ro didn't breathe calmly until the two great warships glided into graceful turns and disappeared into space. For several seconds, the bridge crew stared at the glittering starscape, scarcely believing that the threat was gone.

"Keep them on sensors," ordered Ro, "for as long as you can."

"Yes, sir," answered the ops officer.

"Resume course for the farming colony until we're sure they're gone," said Ro, her mouth feeling parched.

"Aye, sir," replied Picard as he carried out the order. "We'll have to make a run for the Badlands sooner or later."

"I know," answered Ro grimly. "Let's calculate exactly how much time we'll need to make it. When we get a window, we'll go."

"Let's hope for a large window," added the captain.

While buffeted by swirling winds and heavy methane snow, Data set up a portable scanner on the rugged outcropping and tried to take readings. Although the electromagnetic interference and radiation levels were high, they weren't disruptive enough to hide his shuttlecraft, which was still sitting out there, an alien artifact on an icy plain. At least it hadn't been totally destroyed.

He couldn't detect any other machines, vessels, probes, or life signs near the shuttlecraft, but that didn't mean the area was safe. The range of his portable instruments didn't allow him to tell if the Jem'Hadar ship was still in orbit around Kreel VI.

Data was neither impatient nor imprudent, and he could have sat there for weeks, waiting until it was absolutely safe to venture forth. But every moment he delayed reduced the likelihood of finding the *Orb of Peace* with the shuttlecraft's sensors. His own safety was not an issue, except that if he was captured or destroyed, his mission couldn't possibly succeed.

Overriding these concerns was the necessity of finding out if the shuttlecraft itself was still intact. In the pelting blizzard, he repacked his cases and began his descent from the tor. Not only was the storm worse than ever, but the daylight was beginning to fade. By the time Data covered the three kilometers to his shuttlecraft, the visibility was terrible, and he was forced to plug directly into his tricorder to scan the area.

Thirty meters from the shuttlecraft, he discovered a

dark crater brimming with radiation, and he set down his cases and crouched between them. He assumed the crater was the remains of the blast he had felt earlier, which meant that the Jem'Hadar had missed his shuttlecraft. Or perhaps it had been a warning shot, intended to flush him out of hiding. Data grabbed a phaser, a tricorder, and a bandolier loaded with photon grenades, which he slung over his shoulder.

Despite all indications that the Jem'Hadar had left the planet without finding him or his ship, Data hesitated and continued to take readings, both with his tricorder and his internal sensors. His friend, Geordi, had an expression: "If it looks too good to be true, it probably is." In this case, it looked too good to be true.

As he searched for esoteric pulses and energy readings, Data detected the low-resonance hum of a light source which shouldn't be there in the foggy darkness. It wasn't a strong light source, more like a photo cell or a photoreceptor.

A motion detector. On a planet with no life, it was a simple but effective warning device.

He concentrated his search on the few meters in front of the shuttlecraft and pinpointed the location of the motion detector—directly in front of the hatch. Was the alarm intended to alert the Jem'Hadar that he had returned? Or was it even more basic—a bomb intended to turn both him and the shuttlecraft into scrap? If he took another step closer, he would probably find out.

The trick was to get closer without getting closer. The android did a careful calculation and determined that he was seventeen meters away from the device, and it was at ground level. He stepped backward several paces, ran forward, and leaped twenty meters into the air.

In a high arc, Data soared through the methane atmosphere and landed with a thud on the roof of the shuttlecraft. He paused, waiting to see if he had activated the alarm, but the device continued to emit a low-resonance hum. Because it was on the ground, its range apparently didn't extend to the roof, and the shuttlecraft itself hid his movements.

Because a bomb was a more immediate concern than an alarm, he had to deactivate it. But getting too close would have just the opposite effect. Despite all of his precautions, Data realized that direct and swift action was required.

He looked around the roof of the shuttlecraft and spotted a deflector dish, which had to weigh at least two hundred kilograms. He grabbed the dish with both hands and yanked it from its mounts, snapping the metal as if it were plywood. Calculating the exact location of the motion detector on the ground below him, Data leaned over the edge of the roof and dropped the dish on top of it.

With a satisfying crunch, the humming stopped.

Data noted that both he and the shuttlecraft were still intact, but he crouched down and drew his phaser, making sure it was set on heavy stun.

They came quickly. Four figures in gray space suits materialized on the ground below him, and Data didn't wait for them to react. He fired two bursts from his phaser, felling two of them; then he leaped off the shuttlecraft as they returned fire.

Data dropped into a crouch and fired twice more. The space-suited figures twisted from the impact of his phaser beams and slumped to the ground. Figuring the casualties would be retrieved quickly, the android grabbed a plasma grenade, armed it, ripped off the adhesive, and stuck it to the chest of the closest Jem'Hadar in less than a second. With movements so swift that no one could have followed them, Data planted a live grenade on each enemy body and leaped back. It was a particularly brutal way to dispatch with a foe, Data knew. But he also knew that brutality was unavoidable in war.

In the dark, swirling fog, the fallen Jem'Hadar soldiers sparkled brightly as their molecules were swept off the planet. Data calculated the horrible chaos that would erupt on the Jem'Hadar ship when the four plasma grenades exploded in their transporter room—in point-five seconds. With any luck, the rupture would be bad enough to cause a breach in the hull, occupying his pursuers until he could get away.

Data fetched his equipment and opened the hatch of the shuttlecraft, dragging his reflector shield and supplies after him. His movements a blur, the android powered up the small craft, fired thrusters, and zoomed away from the surface of the planet. The fact that he was still alive a few moments later assured him that his diversion had been a success.

Reaching full-impulse speed in seconds, Data piloted the craft in an elliptical arc which put him on the other side of the planet, away from their sensors. He ran a brief scan before he vanished over the dark horizon and noted with satisfaction that the Jem'Hadar battle cruiser was in low orbit and descending quickly. He doubted whether the massive ship was capable of atmospheric reentry, which meant they were in serious trouble.

There was no time to appreciate his unexpected victory over the much larger ship, because Data had a Bajoran transport to find. He zoomed out of orbit and entered warp drive, missing the spectacular explosion that sundered the ivory clouds of Kreel VI.

Will Riker gripped the arms of the command chair and held on as the *Enterprise* was jolted by a Jem'Hadar torpedo. An ominous rumbling sound surged along the length of the vessel.

"Shields down to thirty percent!" shouted Ensign Craycroft on tactical.

Riker checked his readouts. "If we can hold on just a little bit longer . . . Where the devil is the fleet?"

It was a rhetorical question, because he didn't expect an answer. Apparently, the Dominion had launched a massive offensive all along the Cardassian border, and the ships chasing the *Enterprise* were just two of many. The fact that there were only two was also troubling, because it meant that one of them had broken off to pursue either Data or the *Orb of Peace*.

He couldn't worry about them now. The *Enterprise* shuddered again from the impact of another torpedo against her weakening shields. Riker glanced at Craycroft, and the ashen expression on her face told him everything he needed to know.

"All residual power to shields," ordered Riker through clenched teeth. It was tempting to come about and make a stand against the enemy, but Riker knew it would be the last stand. He wasn't prepared to lose the *Enterprise* until he could run no farther. The fleet had to be out there . . . somewhere.

"Sir!" gasped Ensign Craycroft. "The *Carla Romney* and the *Sharansky* have responded to our hails! They'll intercept in two minutes."

Riker allowed himself a grateful sigh. "All right, hail the Jem'Hadar and tell them we want to surrender. Conn, come out of warp to full impulse."

"Verifying that order to surrender," said Craycroft.

"Yes, because we know they like to take prisoners. Don't lower shields, but ready phasers. Conn, be ready to go to warp on a moment's notice." Riker settled back in his chair and straightened his rumpled uniform. He had lost about ten kilos since the war began, and the tunic hung on him. Too bad there was no time for anyone to appreciate his thinner physique.

Craycroft listened intently to her earpiece, then reported, "They say to lower shields."

"On screen," ordered Riker, sitting upright in the command chair.

When a glowering Jem'Hadar appeared on his viewscreen, with a stream of white surging into the veins on his neck, Riker gave him his most charming smile.

"I am Commander William Riker of the *Starship Enterprise.* We are prepared to surrender. However, our shield strength dropped to a point where an emergency backup system took over, and our computer currently has command of the ship. We apologize. We hope to rectify this problem in—" He glanced at his panel. "One minute."

"They're arming phasers!" warned Craycroft.

"Fire phasers!" barked Riker.

They got off the first salvo, which rocked the

Jem'Hadar battle cruisers at point-blank range and delayed their barrage for a few seconds.

"Maximum warp!" shouted Riker, leaping to his feet.

The young Bolian on the conn responded instantly, and the *Enterprise* shot off into space as the Jem'Hadar cruisers pounded the region they had vacated.

Riker had no illusions that he had crippled the battle cruisers in any way, and he was running for his life even as the *Carla Romney* and the *Sharansky* zoomed past them on the viewscreen, two blurs of light in the infinite blackness.

"Reverse course and go to one-third impulse," he ordered. "Let's hang back and see what's happening. Ready photon torpedoes."

There came a chorus of "Yes, sir"s as his young crew executed his commands. A moment later, the birdlike form of the *Enterprise* glided into a graceful holding pattern, framed by the serene starscape.

On the viewscreen, it was anything but serene, as the Jem'Hadar cruisers were caught flat-footed by two Akira-class starships, which unleashed a phaser barrage as they swooped past. Space rippled around the Jem'Hadar warships as they absorbed a devastating bombardment of pure directed energy.

"Target four torpedoes on closest foe," ordered Riker.

"Targeted," reported Ensign Craycroft.

"Fire!"

While her allies came about for another attack, the *Enterprise* launched a stream of shooting stars at the closest of the stunned Jem'Hadar ships. The cruiser's sleek hull glowed with brilliant phosphors as she powered up to go into warp, but the torpedoes slammed into her before she could get away. Explosions rippled along the hull of the battle cruiser as her sister ship successfully escaped into warp.

Riker watched with grim satisfaction as the *Carla Romney* and the *Sharansky* swooped back into view, hurling a dozen more quantum torpedoes at the crippled ship. The barrage obliterated the cruiser's shields, then the cruiser itself; it exploded like a sun going nova, hurling flame and debris into the cosmos. There had been no opportunity to take prisoners, not that the Jem'Hadar were ever known to surrender.

Without taking time to gloat over their kill, the *Sharansky* and the *Carla Romney* shot off into space in pursuit of the second cruiser. Riker sighed and slumped back into this chair. "Any other ships in the area?"

"No, sir, all clear," answered Craycroft, the tension draining from her voice.

The captain rubbed his eyes. "Inform Commander Troi that she's on bridge duty, and set course for Starbase 209. Before we go back into action, we need to unload those Maquis passengers."

"Yes, sir."

Riker rose stiffly from the command chair, feeling as though he had been caught in a barroom brawl. He wanted to go chasing after Data's shuttlecraft, the Bajoran transport, and the escaping Jem'Hadar cruiser, but there was only so much they could do in a day. Despite all the business left unfinished, it was time to rest and lick their wounds.

Against the odds, they had survived this day, earning the chance to do it all again tomorrow. He could only hope his friends had also survived one more day.

Captain Picard stood on a dusty patch of ground, surveying a speckled field of waist-high, black-tasseled grain. He couldn't believe how odd it felt to be standing on terra firma, gazing at a leafy horizon and a cloudless blue sky. A warm breeze stroked his face, bringing greasy smells of Cardassian food bubbling in communal pits.

It had been a long time since he'd had any liberty—so long he couldn't remember the last time. Although the visitors were surrounded by sullen Cardassians, inspecting their wares, the war seemed far removed from this peaceful farming community. What had begun as a forced stop to bolster their cover story had turned into an unexpectedly pleasant respite.

Picard turned to see Ro talking to the leader of the village, a gangly Cardassian dressed in simple brown clothes. At first they had appeared standoffish and suspicious, but now they were relaxed and cordial. These farmers were not typical of the Cardassians with whom he had dealt. For one thing, they didn't even possess spacecraft or transporters, which necessitated the trip down to the planet. The tetralubisol was of only minor interest to them, but they wanted to buy the whole load of Bajoran silk. They postured very little, as if the typical Cardassian arrogance had been beaten out of them.

Ro was supposed to be haggling over a price for the silk, although the farmers didn't seem to have much to offer except for food and hospitality. Picard had the feeling that these lonely people welcomed contact with anyone from outside their limited sphere, even Bajorans, and they were in no hurry to conclude the deal.

He knew he should be mingling with the customers, but he wanted to look around. They had to find out whether Ro's story about the artificial wormhole was true, and every minute they delayed could be vital. Picard stepped away from the outdoor bazaar, which consisted of gray tarpaulins strung between window-less geodesic domes. The domes were an all-purpose design that would have suited humans as well, except for the lack of modern facilities. It almost seemed as if this place were purposely kept primitive.

The captain strolled nonchalantly along a path that ran beside the field of grain. When he was sure he was out of earshot of the noonday shoppers in the bazaar, he tapped his communicator badge.

"Boothby to *Orb of Peace*," said Picard.

"Bridge here," answered the cheerful voice of Geordi La Forge. "How goes it down there?"

"Fine. We've moved most of the Bajoran silk, but I'm not sure how much our captain is going to get for it. The crops are very impressive down here."

"If you're inquiring about our friends," said La Forge, "they're still hanging around. It must be a slow day for them."

Picard tried to hide his disappointment. It was hard to imagine that a Galor-class warship and a Jem'Hadar battle cruiser had nothing better to do than observe one tiny merchant ship, but that seemed to be the case. "Keep me posted if the situation changes. Out."

He turned away from his self-absorbed conversation and bumped into a Cardassian woman who was strolling down the path. She sprang back, cradling her basket of fruit to her chest, and stared at him as if he were a bandit.

"Pardon me," said Picard with concern. "I'm so sorry. Did I injure you?"

He instantly regretted his feeble words, because this was a fit woman in excellent health who was much more offended than injured. He couldn't be too certain of her age, because their leathery skin didn't show much wear, but she was a handsome Cardassian.

"Who are you?" she asked accusingly.

He pointed lamely to the sky. "We're merchants—we came to trade. Our ship is in orbit."

"Bajorans?" she asked doubtfully.

"Yes," answered Picard. "Have you met our people before?"

"Yes, in prison." The woman scowled, as if she had said too much. She brushed past him and hurried down the path.

But Picard now was intrigued, and he charged after the woman. "Madam, can I give you something for your inconvenience?"

"Give me something?" the woman asked, peering strangely at him as if she had never gotten a break in her life. *Just as well*, Picard thought sadly. There wasn't enough latinum in the Alpha quadrant to compensate this woman for the unhappiness evident in her vivid green eyes.

"Have *they* sent you?"

"Who?"

"Don't be coy. Are you telling me that you don't know what this place is?"

"I don't know much about this place," admitted

Picard. "It was just a name on a chart to us until a while ago."

She snorted a laugh. "Well, somebody in your party must have a sense of humor. This colony, this communal farm, is an indoctrination center. Despite the lack of guards and fences, it's a glorified work camp."

Picard nodded gravely, thinking that explained the absence of off-world transportation and modern technology. "What crimes have you committed."

"Things like this," answered the woman snidely. "Talking to the wrong people, saying the wrong things. I can't help myself."

"You're dissidents," said Picard, realizing that they had indeed picked the wrong colony to call upon. Instead of throwing off suspicions, coming here might have aroused them more.

"Ah, but we're toothless, powerless dissidents," whispered the woman. "We've been spared, but we can't leave here. We've been genetically altered—if we try to eat anything but the food we grow on this planet, we'll die."

She offered him a shiny yellow fruit. "Want some?"

Picard shook his head, feeling terribly sorry for the woman and her fellow political prisoners. He wanted to tell her that Dr. Crusher could reverse the genetic engineering, but Beverly wasn't with him. He reminded himself of his conversation with Ro; they couldn't save the prisoners, only the Federation, if they were lucky. No doubt this was one of the colonies that the Cardassians had insisted they had the right to build in the Demilitarized Zone, and the Federation had let them. What appeared to be idyllic farmland was just another prison camp for the most forgotten of Cardassia's victims, her own people.

"How long have you been here?" he asked.

She gave him a sidelong glance. "Are you sure you're not a spy?"

"No," lied Picard, wondering which side she thought he was on. "How do I know *you're* not a spy?"

"You don't. However, it was *you* who ran into me, and you are the stranger here. Plus, you are the only one of us who is allowed to leave."

"I wish that were so," muttered Picard, "but we're under observation by two warships."

The woman smiled. "We are always under observation. As they tell us when we complain, if you're innocent, why should it matter that we're watching you?"

"I'm called Boothby," said Picard, appreciating her sarcastic wit. Her eyes narrowed, perhaps in response to the odd nickname, Picard thought.

"Letharna," she said, apparently deciding not to comment as she sauntered down the path in the direction of the bazaar. "If you were to get away from these warships, where would you go?"

The captain knew he should be careful. But this was a fact-finding mission, and he couldn't overlook any possible source of information, especially a dissident Cardassian. Still, Picard had made a career of judging character, and he decided that Letharna was on his side.

But he was guarded as he replied, "We may never be in Cardassian space again, so we would want to see the biggest, most important sight there is."

"Hmmm. There is a dust cloud called the Badlands which is very unusual."

"Yes, we need to go there." Picard gazed at her, hoping that his trust wasn't misplaced.

"But those ships won't let you go there. That is, unless they were called away to other duty."

"Yes," said Picard, gazing benignly at the fields. "That would be ideal, if they were called away."

As some of her neighbors strolled past, Letharna held out a plump piece of fruit to Picard, and this time he took it. "This planet doesn't have just farms," she whispered. "There is also a subspace relay station on the southern continent. From there, it might be possible to fake a general alert that would bring them back to their base. It might only distract them for a short time, but that could be enough to get a jump."

Deep in thought, Picard stared at the fruit in his hand, and she finally smiled at him. "You can eat it. It's safe."

He nodded, thinking that he had already decided to trust Letharna. With a grateful smile, he bit into the fruit. "Are you sure you can't leave here?"

"Yes. We lack the enzymes required to digest food grown anywhere but the soil of this planet. It's a rather ingenious punishment, isn't it? We require little security, and we're tucked safely out of the way. Yet we're available to be displayed when visitors want to see a nonmilitary colony. And if we don't work hard, we starve."

Picard wanted to say that Cardassians were masters of torture and imprisonment, in all their myriad forms, but his hostess already knew that.

"Your help will not be forgotten," he assured her.

"I have only begun to help you," said Letharna.

Ro Laren stared at him, aghast. "You want to take one of these people aboard our ship, show them what we're doing, and use them to take out a subspace relay station?"

"Not take it out," said Picard. "We just want to send a fake message, a general alert. Those ships are close enough to get their relays from this station, and it might throw them off long enough for us to get away."

Ro shook her head vigorously but kept her voice low. "I believe you—that these people could be dissidents—but that doesn't mean we can *trust* them. Some of these farmers are sure to be government plants, and the others could be crazy. What if she's just looking for a way to escape, or to hijack our vessel?"

"She can't leave the planet," said Picard. "Those two warships are sitting at the edge of the solar system, watching us. If you know a better way to get rid of them, I'm listening."

Ro scowled, and he knew that she didn't have a better solution. Picard pressed his point: "In three days, we're expected to go to Cardassia Prime, a trip which could land us in a Cardassian prison. Maybe they're hoping we'll just head back to Bajor, and that will be the end of it. But we can't do that. We can't shoot our way out, and we can't talk our way out. As you say—we need to use stealth and guile."

Ro nodded politely to a clutch of Cardassians as they walked by; then she strolled farther away from the bazaar. "What kind of garrison are we looking at?" she asked.

"According to Letharna, maybe ten. I believe she's thought this out fairly well."

"I wish we had a backup plan," muttered Ro. "When do we go?"

"To allay suspicion, I would like to leave you and the others here. You seem to have quite a few crates of vegetables to inventory, and Letharna thinks that with our transporters, we can be there and back in less than an hour. We won't even have to change our orbit."

Picard motioned toward the sky, which was turning a salmon color with traces of vibrant orange. "It's already dark on the southern continent."

Before Ro could reply, the head man of the village strode up to them, a concerned look on his face. "You look unhappy. Is everything all right?" asked the gangly Cardassian.

"Yes," answered Ro, mustering a smile. "My shipmate here doesn't like the price we got for the silk, but I overruled him."

"It's simply vegetables I don't like," said Picard with a friendly smile. "I'll return to the ship and make room for them in the hold."

"A gift for you then," said the Cardassian, "for accepting an uneven trade."

He handed Picard a small scroll, which the captain politely took. It wasn't until his hand closed around the object that Picard realized it was solid, not paper—the scroll was wrapped around another cylindrical object. The intense look on the Cardassian's face told Picard that he had better accept the gift with no questions asked, and no examination until later.

"Thank you," said the captain solemnly. He tapped his comm badge. "One to beam up."

A few moments later, Picard materialized in the stylish but small transporter room of the *Orb of Peace*. La Forge was at the controls, looking quite dashing with his dangling earring, nose ridges, and pilot's goggles, which hid his ocular implants.

"Captain," said Geordi. "Anyone else?"

"One more person," said Picard, jumping off the transporter platform. "But first, help me unwrap this gift."

He carefully removed the scroll to find a copper-colored cylinder with magentic strips along its length and a blue label at the top.

"Hmm," said the engineer with appreciation, "an isolinear rod, Cardassian design. What does it control?"

"I think we'll find out soon." Picard leaned over the transporter console and entered prearranged coordinates into the computer. "Beam up one, from that location."

"Yes, sir." La Forge completed the procedure, and another figure began to materialize in a column of sparkling light. Even wearing goggles, it was evident that the engineer's eyes widened considerably when he got a good look at the newest arrival.

Letharna stepped down from the transporter platform and glanced around at her ornate surroundings. "I can't believe I'm in space again . . . on a Bajoran vessel."

"Unfortunately, there's no time to show you around," said Picard. "Are you ready?"

She pointed to the object in his hand. "Good, you have the isolinear rod. That will help."

Picard was having second thoughts, realizing that he had jeopardized their entire mission on a hunch. If he was wrong about Letharna—if she was well meaning but unstable—they could very well doom themselves to capture and torture. For his own satisfaction, he had to ask, "Why are you doing this?"

Letharna glared at him. "I'm no traitor if that's what you're getting at. The Dominion is exactly what we have always feared. While our military leaders strut and preen, they let an outside force take over our civilization. Wasn't it a terran who said, 'Absolute power corrupts absolutely'? The absolute power of the military made us weak and corrupt, unable to resist the lure of the Dominion. This is why I help you, whoever you are."

Picard glanced at La Forge, and the two old comrades exchanged a shrug. It wasn't the first time they had gambled.

"Stay here, Geordi," said the captain. "We're going to need an experienced hand on the transporter."

Chapter Seven

ON BOARD THE *TAG GARWAL,* Sam Lavelle took personal control of the conn, deciding to pilot the antimatter tanker himself on their first test flight. Taurik sat nearby on ops, monitoring ship's systems. The towering Deltan, Tamla Horik, was on tactical, manning the tractor beam in lieu of weapons. Grof, the two material handlers, and the transporter chief were also available, but Sam knew that he and Taurik were basically the bridge crew. In fact, the others weren't even on the bridge but below, fussing over the transporter, mining probe, and recombination storage chamber.

He was glad this wasn't a Jem'Hadar ship, because he didn't think he'd have time to get used to an eyepiece for visual input instead of the more traditional viewscreen. Cardassian technology was roughly equivalent to Federation technology, and they had all studied Miles O'Brien's compendium of Cardassian technology.

It helped that today's mission wasn't very difficult. They were to disengage from the docking sphere and take a short spin five thousand kilometers into space, where they would grab a dummy cargo bin with the tractor beam and bring it back. Sam presumed all of this would take place under the watchful eye of the military vessels docked around them.

He tapped the comm panel on the arm of his chair. "Lavelle to crew. We've run through our checklist, and the bridge systems are ready for launch. Does anyone need a delay?"

"No, get moving," grumbled the voice of Enrak Grof. "We're ready."

"Affirmative," said Sam, pressing another button. "This is tanker *Tag Garwal* to station control, seeking permission to launch on test flight zero-zero-one."

On his screen came the familiar face of Joulesh, the Vorta, looking delighted with his charges. *"Tag Garwal,* you are clear to launch. We've rerouted incoming traffic for you. Good luck."

Sam didn't know whether to thank Joulesh for his precautions or not. All of them had flown more difficult flights than this as second-year cadets, and he anticipated no problems. He supposed that Grof was right about one thing: they were constantly forced to prove themselves to their captors.

"Retracting airlock and disengaging," said Sam. He wiped Joulesh's grinning face off the viewscreen and put up the view from the nose of the tanker. Sam felt as if he should be nervous, but it was such a relief to be back at the conn of a ship, doing what he had been trained to do. Without hesitation, he fired thrusters and slowly piloted the bulky tanker away from the spacedock.

Once they were cruising at full impulse power through space, Sam couldn't help but to look at Taurik and smile. The Vulcan, of course, gave him only a blank stare, and he was forced to look at the Deltan to convey his pleasure. The bald female beamed back at him, sharing his joy at this momentary taste of freedom.

Sam set his course and put the ship on automatic pilot to insure it was working properly. Once they got to the black hole, they would be depending a great deal on the automatic settings, and there would be no room for error, human or machine. He carefully monitored their progress, and they covered the five thousand kilometers in what seemed like seconds.

Looking like a trash bin floating in space, a large rectangular object loomed ahead of them, and Sam slowed to one-third impulse.

"Ready tractor beam," he ordered.

"This is too easy," grumbled the Deltan. "Graviton levels steady, tractor beam ready."

Sam brought the ship to a full stop and used his thrusters to reverse her heading. "All right, latch on."

The Deltan plied her controls as Sam watched the invisible bonds twist their cargo around and draw it closer to the tail of their ship. "Tractor beam holding," reported the Deltan. "Levels steady."

"I would love to take it to warp," said Sam, "but I think that would surprise our trainers too much. I'm setting course back to the dock."

Reluctantly, Sam piloted the craft and its dummy cargo back to the sphere they had left about ten minutes earlier. The successful but rapid conclusion of their test flight left him feeling oddly disappointed, and he didn't want the mission to end.

In some respects, this was the cruelest punishment of all, he decided, waving a tantalizing glimpse of freedom and normality under their noses before forcing them back into their cage. He began to understand how Enrak Grof had evolved into a collaborator. It would be hard to give up feeling useful and responsible—to go back to being a prisoner awaiting death.

"We're docked," he announced to no one in particular. "Mission complete."

He heard footsteps clomping up the ladder, and he turned to see the rotund, beaming face of Enrak Grof. "Excellent!" bellowed the Trill. "Very efficient piloting, Lieutenant, and excellent work with the tractor beam, Commander."

The Deltan scowled. "My baby sister could have retrieved that cargo bin."

"Baby steps are what we must take," said Grof, "until we are allowed to take the big step."

The Trill flashed Sam a look, and then he climbed back down the ladder. There was something in his choice of words and his expression which made Sam wonder how hard he would resist an escape attempt. When the moment came, it would be hard to predict how any of them would react. It would either be escape or death, so they would have to choose the moment carefully. If Grof resisted, they would be forced to deal with him themselves.

There were more footsteps, and Joulesh poked his web-eared head over the top of the hatch. "I wish to convey the Founder's extreme pleasure with your progress," said the Vorta. "Two more test flights, and we believe you will be free to make history."

Whose history? wondered Sam. *Who will end up writing it?*

Jean-Luc Picard materialized inside a narrow, low-ceilinged tunnel that linked the subspace relay station to the barracks of the permanent garrison. He was glad that Letharna had warned him to duck, or his head would have materialized inside a concrete ceiling. More black-garbed guerrilla fighters were standing by in the transporter room of the *Orb of Peace,* in case they were needed, but the initial assault team consisted of himself, Letharna, and two young humans who looked Bajoran.

He and his crew members were armed with phasers set to heavy stun, although they hoped to slip in, broadcast the alert, and escape without being detected. Letharna was armed only with the isolinear rod. In a crouch, she motioned them to follow her as she scuttled down the dank tunnel toward a shadowy doorway.

Feeling unexpectedly nervous, Picard nodded to his subordinates to follow her, while he brought up the rear. The tunnel was intended for use during bad weather, to move from one building to another, but it had apparently fallen into disuse. According to Letharna, it wouldn't have sensors capable of detecting a small force beaming down, but the tunnel was giving Picard an uncomfortable feeling of claustrophobia. He didn't have enough knowledge of the station to take over the point from Letharna, so he had to trust her. Trusting Cardassians, even dissidents, did not come easily.

He thought of another Cardassian he had trusted, Joret Dal, a Federation operative who had infiltrated the Cardassian military. Dal disappeared in a shuttle-craft with Ensign Sito Jaxa, attempting the same thing his team was trying to do—sneak into Cardassian space. Was Dal found out, or was he a double agent? They would never know. What a tragedy it had been to lose Ensign Sito, recalled Picard. Putting people in danger was his least favorite aspect of command, especially when he lost the gamble, as he had with Sito Jaxa.

A moment later, the captain arrived at the solid metal door where Letharna and his two officers were gathered. Confronted by a card entry system, Letharna drew a handful of Cardassian security cards from her belt, and she intently fed them into the slot, looking for one that would work.

"They don't change the codes that often," she whispered. "After all, their nearest neighbors are on another continent, with no way to get here."

While she worked on the door, Picard checked his chronometer. He was worried that if the operation took too long, their ship would move so far in its orbit that it would be out of transporter range. Then the ship would have to backtrack, possibly raising suspicions.

He was about to tell Letharna to hurry up, when the lights on the door turned white and the lock clicked. Letharna pushed the door open, and it squeaked on rusty hinges. Stealthily they climbed a flight of metal stairs.

On the move again, Picard felt more confident. When they got to the open door at the top of the stairs, Letharna dropped into a crouch, and Picard moved into position behind her, his Bajoran hand phaser leveled for action. They crept into a large bunker filled with electronic equipment, computer stations, and the chirping sounds of a constant stream of subspace radio traffic. The only window was a narrow slit in the wall which afforded a partial view of a giant parabolic antenna on the outer grounds. Although it was night, the floodlights outside were as bright as day.

No one seemed to be present in the bunker, and Picard felt a mixture of relief and dread. Just as before, it was going too smoothly. He motioned to one of his officers to remain by the door, and she did so, crouching down on the upper landing. The other officer followed Picard and Letharna as they crept through rows of shelves, boxes, and electronic equipment.

Suddenly they heard voices mixed in with the subspace chatter, and all three of them dropped to their bellies and remained prone as two Cardassian guards entered from an outside door. Laughing, the guards seemed to share a joke as they checked the readouts on a console by the door.

Picard saw Letharna draw a long, curved knife from her bosom and clutch it in a trembling hand. He quickly tapped her leg. After getting her attention, he shook his head vigorously, then he held up his phaser, hoping she would get the idea. Letharna had a look of bloodlust in her dark eyes which he had seen before in Cardassians. Looking somewhat disappointed, she nodded at him.

A moment later, Picard felt a tap on his leg, and he looked back at his young officer to see him urgently pointing. The captain turned to see one of the Cardassians strolling nonchalantly across the room, checking various readouts as he went. He was coming closer.

For the moment, they were hidden by stacks of equipment, but there was no way of telling when the Cardassian would walk down their aisle. There was also no way of knowing how long these workers would remain on duty in this bunker, and time was running out.

With both of his comrades staring at him, awaiting a decision, Picard made one. He held up his phaser, motioned to his officer, and pointed to the guard making the rounds. Then he pointed to himself and motioned to the guard farther away on the main console. A sense of urgency gripped the captain when he saw his target insert an isolinear rod into the receptacle on the instrument panel.

He jumped to his feet, seeing his comrades do the same. Picard took quick but sure aim and unleashed a red beam, which streaked across the room and struck his target in the back. The Cardassian gasped and slumped over his console, unconscious.

Picard heard shuffling and crashing sounds, and he turned to see that his officer had missed his target. The second Cardassian scrambled down the aisle, making a dash for the exit, and there was another flash of movement to Picard's right.

With a total disregard for her safety, Letharna leaped over a computer console and pounced upon the escaping guard. Picard watched in horror as she neatly slit his throat with her curved blade. His body slumped uselessly onto the floor, yet she continued to shake him, looking annoyed that the life had so quickly seeped out of him.

"That's enough!" hissed Picard, grabbing her arm.

"He was going for the alarm," she said defensively.

"That could be," muttered Picard. As disappointed

as he was in her rash actions, he still needed Letharna, so he swallowed the rest of his words.

"I'm sorry, sir," said the officer who had missed his target. The young man looked quite mortified.

"Dispose of his body," said Picard. He took the young man's phaser and set it to vaporize. The officer nodded and went about his grim task.

Letharna was already at the main console. She grabbed the unconsious guard and tossed his body to the floor; then she sat down at his place. Picard looked nervously over her shoulder and studied the unfamiliar readouts.

"Can you do it?" he asked.

"Oh, yes, that was never in doubt." Letharna gave him a sardonic grin, and for the first time Picard saw a look of madness in her sunken eyes.

"I have control of the whole station from here, the whole security grid—the whole planet!" With confident fingers, Letharna worked the instruments. "Do you know how long we've waited to get in here?"

Picard tried to curb his anger and impatience. "The message to the warships," he reminded her.

She removed the rod from the console and replaced it with the one given to them by the village leader. "This should give us access to the interrupt codes. Yes, there it is. You want them to receive a general alert that will cause them to return to base?"

"Yes," breathed Picard, worried that Letharna was beginning to look upon this as an opportunity to right as many wrongs as possible.

As she entered commands, an urgent beeping caused all of them to jump, and Picard looked accusingly at the blinking communications panel. Letharna kept working, a delighted grin on her face, and Picard finally slapped the panel to silence it. A moment later, a stream of spoken Cardassian erupted from the panel, and he tapped it again to squelch that.

"Hurry," he breathed.

"Your part is done," she said. "Now I have to collect as many new codes as I can, while we have this chance. I'm going to fill up this rod."

The man on the floor groaned, and Picard adjusted his phaser to a heavier stun and drilled him at point-blank range. A second later, they heard footsteps running outside the bunker, and Picard knew it was time to go.

He looked around, took stock of the situation, and tapped his comm badge. *"Orb of Peace*—five second delay, then *six* to beam up."

"Yes, sir."

Picard motioned to his officer stationed by the tunnel, and she hustled over. He heard more footsteps and voices outside, plus the comm panel began to beep again. "It's time to go," he told Letharna.

"One more minute," she growled, her fingers working furiously.

Picard grabbed her precious isolinear rod and yanked it from its slot. The screen went blank. Enraged, Letharna screamed and jumped up with her knife over her head, but Picard shot her in the stomach. Stunned, she slumped to the floor, and Picard caught her falling body just as their molecules turned into a swarm of swirling fireflies. When the Cardassians burst in a moment later, they found no one.

Captain Picard, two humans disguised as Bajorans, and two unconsious Cardassians materialized in a heap on the transporter pad of the *Orb of Peace*. Picard staggered off, setting Letharna gently on the floor and tucking her knife and her isolinear rod into her belt. The blacked-garbed officers quickly surrounded the fallen Cardassians. The wounded one appeared to be dead.

"Mr. La Forge," said Picard urgently, "what about the warships?"

The engineer grinned. "They lit out right on cue, twenty seconds ago."

"Accelerated orbit," ordered Picard. "I want Ro and the rest of the team back here as soon as possible."

La Forge carried out the command on his transporter console, while the captain gazed down at Letharna. "A remarkable woman—I wish I had time to thank her properly. I'm glad she was willing to help us. Beam her back down to the planet."

"Like that, unconscious?"

"Yes, we don't have time for good-byes." He looked with distaste at the living Cardassian. "I hadn't intended to take a prisoner, but now we have one. Starfleet may want to interrogate him."

"But, Captain," said La Forge, "we don't have a brig. And no internal forcefields either."

Picard turned to the security detail. "Put the prisoner in the captain's quarters. We haven't been using it. Strip the furnishings, except for a mattress, and put restraints on his legs. I want him to feel as if he's being well treated—but watch him closely."

"Yes, sir," they replied in unison.

"Captain," said Geordi, "we're coming up on transporter range."

"Notify the away team and tell them to keep their

good-byes short," ordered Picard, striding toward the door. "We're getting out of here."

It was a peaceful evening aboard the *Tag Garwal*. At least, it felt like evening, with both their test flights over and almost everyone asleep. The bridge was quiet, with only Sam Lavelle on duty. There was no particlar reason why he had to be on duty, because they were docked and safely cocooned within the might of the Dominion. Their comrades were suffering only a short distance away, but no harm could befall the chosen ones.

That is, no harm could befall them until tomorrow, when they set off on their mission. Perhaps that was why Sam couldn't sleep, why he had to haunt the bridge long after his shift was over. He wasn't worried about their official mission, only the unofficial one. He had promised his crew that they would try to escape; it was their duty as prisoners of war. But how could he pull it off? Did he have the right to jeopardize all their lives in what could well be a futile gesture? Especially when they had a chance to survive this hell.

Survival versus honor—it was a tough choice.

Sam was startled by heavy footsteps on the ladder, and he knew before he turned around that it was Grof. The big Trill lumbered up the steps, veered toward him, and slumped into the tactical station.

"Can't sleep?" asked Sam.

Grof scowled. "No, of course I can't sleep with the voices coming from the quarters next door. That Deltan is up all night, entertaining her friend, Enrique."

"Oh, let them be," replied Sam, putting his hands

behind his back. "Sex is a kind of religious experience to Deltans. Besides, weren't you ever young . . . and about to die?"

"We aren't going to die," muttered Grof through clenched teeth. "The Dominion should have continued to keep us segregated by sex even here."

"I guess they don't think of everything," said Sam with a sly smile. "And if we manage to live through this, it will be a miracle."

"I wish you would stop saying that. Although it's dangerous, there's no reason why we can't successfully complete this mission."

Yes, there is, thought Sam, but he wasn't going to tell Grof why. Besides, it was time to change the subject. "Tell me about our destination, the Eye of Talek."

Grof shrugged. "It's the smallest black hole in Cardassian space. Probably the oldest, too."

"It's not an imploded star?"

"No," answered Grof, "the Eye of Talek dates from the formation of the universe. At least that's the legend according to the Cardassians, and the cosmology tends to bear it out. Had we tried to go with an imploded star, the gravity would have been too great for our operation. You know, a typical black hole keeps the same mass it had when it was a star. As for the small ones, like the Eye of Talek, and the huge ones, like that monster at the center of our galaxy— we can only guess where they came from."

"Some people think it was a supreme being who created the universe," said Sam. "What we call God. Some people wouldn't like the idea of you creating an artificial wormhole either. Don't you sometimes feel like you're playing God?"

"Yes," answered Grof proudly, "but it's necessary to play God. Once we discovered that space and time were curved, it was essential that we try to exploit the intersections where they curve back upon themselves. Where God failed was that he made wormholes unstable. The Bajorans consider the Prophets to be gods, simply because they stabilized a wormhole. Imagine what kind of god I'll be after I stabilize *hundreds* of wormholes, connecting every corner of the galaxy?"

Sam shook his head in amazement. "You have a big enough ego for the job."

"I'll take that as a compliment," said Grof smugly.

The lieutenant yawned and pointed to the sleeping alcove off the rear of the bridge. "You're welcome to bunk back there if you don't want to go below."

Grof glowered at the injustice of it all, but he finally acceded. "Thank you."

The bear of a Trill rose to his feet and shuffled off; then he looked back. "You know, Lavelle, this mission depends entirely upon you. You're our leader. If you crack—or you pull something stupid—we'll all go down with you."

"Not that you would put any pressure on me," muttered Sam.

"I just want you to know how much is riding on this. Our equality—"

"Equality?" Sam burst out laughing. "We're *slaves*, Grof. Maybe someday a few of us could aspire to attain the status of a Jem'Hadar or a Vorta. Well, thanks but no thanks. There's only one race who matters—the Founders. The rest of us are just the help. If you try to be a god, they'll squash you like a bug. The Founders are the gods around here."

Grof opened his mouth and started to respond, but Sam let him off the hook by jumping up and brushing past him. Stomping as loudly as the burly Trill, he headed down the ladder.

In the corridor outside the captain's quarters, Ro Laren compressed her lips in annoyance as she listened to the sounds of their prisoner kicking the bulkhead. Even though he had restraints on his arms and legs, he was still thrashing around like a fish in the bottom of a boat. She couldn't understand why Captain Picard had put the Cardassian in their best cabin; whatever impression he wished to make, it was obviously lost on the brute.

The captain stood beside her, his jaw clenched. He motioned to four armed officers behind him and said, "Phasers set to heavy stun."

"We can't keep him stunned all the time," said Ro.

"I know. And I am open to other suggestions."

"We could throw him out an airlock."

The captain scowled. "That's not an option. If we could only interrogate him, he might be useful."

"Chances are good he doesn't know anything about the artificial wormhole," said Ro, "stationed in the middle of nowhere like he was. The Cardassians are good at keeping secrets, even from each other. We could jeopardize the mission if we take him with us into the Badlands, and we'll be there soon."

"Nonetheless, Captain," said Picard with determination. "It is always worthwhile to try talking." He tapped his comm badge. "This is Boothby to the captain's quarters. Please quiet down and listen to me. You are our guest, and we would like to send you home."

But the ferocious thrashing went on, and it was now centered on the door itself. He could wreak some serious damage if left alone like this, thought Ro.

Picard glanced at the crew assembled to help them, and he picked the two stoutest officers. "You two, hand your weapons to the others, and let's subdue him by hand. Stand on either side of me. The rest of you, be prepared to use your phasers."

Ro hefted her Bajoran phaser rifle as Picard stepped closer to the door. After the two unarmed officers took up their places on either side of him, the captain reached a long arm across the bulkhead to touch the wall panel and open the cabin door.

As soon as the door slid open, the Cardassian head-butted Picard sending him reeling into the bulkhead. Then came a howl of indignation as the Cardassian hopped out, his legs bound together and his hands tied behind him. Lowering his shoulders, he bulled into the two unarmed guards and knocked them back on their heels. He hadn't looked so big lying on the deck, but now he looked huge, with his thick neck muscles bulging like the hood of a cobra.

"Surrender!" ordered Picard staggering to his feet.

"Die!" shrieked the Cardassian. He lowered his head and charged toward the captain.

Ro lifted her rifle, ready to protect the captain, but he stepped gracefully away from the charge as he brought his knee upward in a swift kick. He caught the Cardassian in the nose, and he howled as his head bounced. Then Picard grabbed him by the seat of his pants and tossed him headfirst to the deck. That should have subdued him, but the bloodied Cardassian rolled onto his knees and tried to stand once more.

"Cease resistance!" warned Picard.

"No!" Eyes bulging from their bony sockets, the Cardassian flopped onto his back and tried to kick Picard. Amidst his enraged grunts and groans, the captain's comm badge sounded.

"That's enough," he told Ro. "Stun him."

She shot her weapon, and the red beam finally put the wild prisoner back into blessed unconsciousness. Only then did Picard answer his comm badge. "Boothby here."

"Sir, you'd better get to the bridge," said a nervous voice. "We've picked up enemy ships on our tail, closing fast!"

Chapter Eight

Ro followed Captain Picard onto the bridge of the *Orb of Peace*. The relief personnel had an edgy look about their eyes, and they didn't seem Bajoran anymore, despite the nose ridges and earrings. Maybe it was the human scent of their sweat.

The man on the conn jumped to his feet when he saw Picard.

"Status?" barked Picard as Ro headed toward the conn.

"Three Jem'Hadar attack ships are on an intercept course with us," reported the officer, stepping aside to let the Bajoran take his seat. "They're going twice our speed, and they'll be in weapons range in approximately thirty-six minutes."

"And how much time to the Badlands?"

"Approximately forty minutes," answered Ro.

Picard scowled, and she could feel his frustration.

They were so close to reaching a hiding place, only minutes away, but the hounds were running them aground. Ro knew this feeling of dread—to run for her life with time counting against her.

"Evasive maneuvers?" she asked.

"Not yet," replied the captain, tapping his finger to his chin. "Steady as she goes."

Ro knew that Picard was reviewing his options, but they weren't many. They were no match for one Jem'Hadar ship, let alone three, and they couldn't explain making a mad dash to the Badlands. This time, they probably wouldn't even get a chance to talk to the enemy before the attack began.

"They must have us on scanners," said Ro. "I'm sure they're watching every move we make. Evasive maneuvers might work against bigger ships, but not against these. The Jem'Hadar attack ships are the most maneuverable vessels we've ever seen."

"The *Orb of Peace* has two operational escape pods. Let's put our Cardassian friend into one of those pods and launch him toward a planet. If they're watching us, they'll have to stop to investigate, especially after they scan and find a Cardassian on board," said Picard.

Ro tugged thoughtfully on her earring. "We'll have to come out of warp, which will cost us some time, but it will be worth it."

"Captain," said the officer on ops, "may I remind you that we need both of those escape pods to evacuate the ship's crew. If we're missing one, eight crew members cannot evacuate."

The captain gazed at Ro, and the Bajoran knew from his determined expression that they were still on the same frequency. This mission would either result in success or death, perhaps both, so there was no point in planning for survival in Cardassian space. When Picard armed the self-destruct sequence, they had both known it would be all or nothing.

Will Riker had been right—this *was* a suicide mission.

Picard leaned over her. "Attend to it, Ro. Ready escape pod one, and put the prisoner into it. Tie him down securely."

"Don't worry about that," she assured the captain.

A short while later, a snarling Cardassian strapped to a vertical seat tried to spit in Ro's face, but she jerked away just in time. He ended up drooling on his angular chin and staring hatefully at her. She didn't want to sink to his level, but she lifted a spool of metal-coated tape and waved it in his face. "I could shut you up."

"You . . . you are cowards!" sputtered the prisoner. "Terrorists!" He gasped when a muscular officer tugged sharply on the belt stretching across his chest.

Because the cramped sphere was designed to fly automatically toward an inhabited planet and make an atmospheric reentry, anyone aboard would have to be strapped in his seat. The Cardassian was simply strapped in more securely than usual, with his hands and legs bound together with metal tape and strips.

"We're letting you go," said Ro, "so I don't know why you're so angry with us."

"Bajorans!" he hissed. "We should have killed you all!"

"You tried," said Ro evenly. "In fact, if our roles were reversed, I'm sure you would just toss my body out an airlock. But we've treated you like a gul. We put you up in the captain's quarters, and now we're sacrificing this whole escape pod just to let you go free. You ought to be grateful."

The Cardassian growled and tried to twist out of his bonds, but they held tightly. Ro had made sure to get the same two officers who had tried to subdue him earlier; they had scores of their own to settle. She wanted to ask him about the artificial wormhole, and she would have, if they were going to slit his throat instead of let him go. But asking him about the wormhole would reveal their mission, and it probably wouldn't garner them any information.

In fact, maybe this was a good time to impart some false intelligence. "We're neutral, you know," explained Ro. "We're not interested in your stupid war with the Federation. We have some terrorists still hiding out in the Badlands, and we're only trying to rescue them. So if you leave us alone, we'll finish our mission and go home. You'll never know we were here."

"I'll know, because you've ruined my career!" wailed the Cardassian. "Why don't you just kill me? After failing to protect the station and being kidnapped, I'll be lucky not to be sent to a work camp!"

"These are dangerous times," replied Ro. She looked at her comrades, and they nodded, signaling they were through. "Sorry for the inconvenience. Have a nice flight."

Ro and the two officers ducked through the hatch, which she secured herself. Then she cleared the airlock and listened to the air escape with a hiss. Like most escape pods, this one was jettisoned into space by an array of tiny thrusters, and its flight was totally automated. All that was needed was to enter the coordinates of the destination planet, hit the launch button, and hope for the best.

She tapped her comm badge. "Ro to bridge. Our passenger is secure in escape pod one."

"Good," answered Picard crisply. "We're working on his itinerary. We've got several possibilities, but we need to find a planet which will allow us to jump out of warp and back quickly. We can enter the coordinates from here, so you can return to the bridge."

"Yes, sir."

A minute later, Ro stood on the bridge, explaining to the captain how she had told the prisoner they were on a simple rescue mission to the Badlands.

"Do you think he believed it?" asked Picard.

"That's hard to say," answered Ro. "He was mostly upset that we wrecked his career."

"Coming within range of H-574," announced the conn. "Optimal launch window in forty seconds."

Picard turned to tactical and asked, "How far are we from our pursuers?"

"At present speed and course, we will make contact in approximately twenty minutes."

"Come out of warp, half-impulse," ordered Picard, "and prepare to launch escape pod one."

"Yes, sir," answered three voices at once.

Stepping out of the way, Ro watched the viewscreen as the *Orb of Peace* slowed down just long enough to jettison the escape pod. The tiny sphere shot into space like an ancient musket ball and swerved toward a nearby planet covered with shimmering blue water and emerald islands, sparkling in the sun. The Cardassians had all these beautiful planets, thought Ro, and they begrudged the Maquis even one little rock.

"Escape pod on course," reported the officer on ops.

"Set course for the Badlands, maximum warp," ordered Picard. "Engage."

Once again, they were streaking through space at an incredible speed that was faster than light but wasn't faster than the three Jem'Hadar attack craft. There was silence on the bridge and little to discuss until they saw how their pursuers responded to the escape pod. Ro wondered whether they would take the bait, and if so, how many of them would be delayed.

When the tactical officer spoke, her voice betrayed the uncertain nature of the news: "Captain, one of the Jem'Hadar ships has broken off in pursuit of the escape pod. The other two remain on an intercept course with us. Contact in approximately twelve minutes."

Picard glanced at Ro. "That's about the best we could expect. Any more ideas on how to even the odds?"

"Well," answered the Bajoran, "there's an old trick we used to use on Starfleet. When you have a small craft traveling at warp speed, it's almost impossible to distinguish it on long-range scans from a photon torpedo at warp speed, especially if you set it for indefinite distance and no detonation."

Picard scratched his chin, and a smile of appreciation crept across his face. "You mean, use torpedoes as decoys?"

"Yes. We could launch two torpedoes, one of them on the course we're traveling now, and the second one on another likely course to the Badlands. We'll pick a third course and hope they go after the two decoys."

"We'll have to match speed exactly," said Picard, sounding excited—or concerned, it was hard to tell. He hovered over the tactical station. "Do you understand what Captain Ro is proposing?"

"Yes, sir," answered the officer, plying her console. "I'm configuring torpedoes now: one for our exact heading and one for ten degrees to port. They're set for no target, indefinite distance, no detonation, and warp speed matching ours."

"Right, stand by." Picard stepped across the cramped bridge to the conn. "Set course ten degrees to starboard. We'll enter the Badlands at a different place than we planned, but that can't be helped. We'll slow our warp speed by point-zero-five to launch torpedoes, then change course and resume maximum warp."

"Yes, sir," said the pilot. He glanced at Ro and gave her a grateful smile. Although she hadn't saved his life yet, the young man was hopeful that she would.

"I should point out that we will be reduced to four torpedoes," said the tactical officer.

"Acknowledged." If it pained the captain to use his torpedoes for subterfuge instead of a real attack, he didn't show it.

"Course changes laid in," reported the conn.

With a glance at Ro, Picard brought his hand down. "Reduce speed."

"Speed reduced," echoed the conn.

"Fire!"

"Torpedoes away," announced tactical.

"Changing course," said the conn. "Resuming speed."

Now it was time to wait again, to see if the Jem'Hadar fell for the parlor trick. A tense silence fell over the bridge, and it wasn't assuaged by the fact that they could see the Badlands on the viewscreen, shimmering in the distance. Although the forbidding cloud appeared relatively close, it was a long way in an underpowered Bajoran transport chased by swift fighters.

"This is a trick I hadn't heard of before," said Picard conversationally. "And we've been studying Maquis tactics very closely the last few months."

"You need a small ship," answered Ro. "I'm worried that this one may be too large."

"It's worth a try," said Picard. "If they change course at all to chase the decoys, we'll pick up valuable minutes."

With everyone staring intently at their readouts or the viewscreen, the gasp of the tactical officer made them jump. Ro whirled around to see her triumphant grin. "Both Jem'Hadar vessels are following the decoy on our old course."

She stared intently at her instruments, and everyone else stared intently at her. After a minute that seemed like a day, the implants over her nose wrinkled into a frown. "Now one attack ship has changed course and is in pursuit of us. They'll be in weapons range in eight minutes."

"How long to the Badlands?"

"Eleven minutes."

"All right, we're down to one," said Picard. "That is certainly much better odds than I expected. Maintain course and speed."

"Yes, sir."

Now it was Ro's turn to hover over the conn station. "Listen, the Badlands are a plasma dust cloud, and instruments are completely useless there.

So the sooner we reach it, the better. Like most dust clouds, it has fingers and tendrils which stretch into surrounding space. If we can find a tendril, maybe we can cut our time getting there."

Picard walked to the viewscreen and studied the octopus-like cloud that loomed in front of them. He pointed to a massive finger of dust shaped like a horse's head. "There—that looks promising."

"If I change course," said the conn, "we could reach it maybe two minutes sooner. But we wouldn't have time to scan the area before we entered."

"We don't have much choice." Picard turned back to Tactical. "What's the position of the second craft?"

"They've broken off pursuit of the decoy," answered the young woman, not hiding her disappointment. "They're on an intercept course, but they won't reach us in time. Only the first one is a threat."

"Change course, most direct route," ordered Picard.

"Yes, sir. Course laid in."

The captain tapped his comm badge. "Bridge to Engineering. Geordi, we need you to boost our warp speed—right now. Any increase would help."

"We're in the red zone now, Captain," replied the engineer, "but I can shut down the safety overrides and coax a bit more out of her."

"Make it so."

"Captain," interrupted the woman on tactical, "they're sending a message, demanding that we stop and surrender. The message is repeating on all frequencies."

"They don't want to talk," said Ro.

"Ignore it," replied Picard. "How many of our torpedoes are aft-mounted?"

"Only two."

Two or twenty, it didn't matter, thought Ro, because the *Orb of Peace* wasn't a warship. If they didn't make the Badlands in time to hide, the Jem'Hadar would pick them apart.

"Lead ship has launched a torpedo," cut in the tactical officer, surprise in her voice. "But they won't be in optimal range for several minutes."

"But their torpedo will reach us a few seconds before they do," said Picard. "We're both playing for seconds now. Conn, maintain course and speed, but be ready to go to evasive maneuvers."

"We can't use our standard patterns," replied the officer.

"Devise something simple but effective, based on the alpha pattern, but keep us headed toward that tendril."

They could see it clearly now on the viewscreen— the daunting cloud of dust and debris which rose over the darker body of the Badlands like a horse's head. The colors kept shifting from a murky brown to a golden orange to a vibrant magenta, as plasma storms glimmered behind the clouds like lightning in a far-off thunderstorm.

Ro couldn't help but to remember all the times she had made this mad dash to the Badlands, thinking each time would be her last. Unfortunately, she had never been in a vessel so ill equipped for fighting. Ro also remembered all the ships that had entered that forbidding region but had not come out. Brave comrades, deserving Cardassians, bumbling Starfleet— the plasma storms and anomalies played no favorites. Decrepit shuttlecraft or great starships, when the Badlands claimed them they were gone.

The Cardassians and Starfleet had developed a healthy fear of the massive cloud, but Ro had no idea how seriously the Jem'Hadar took the legends. With their vaunted superiority, they might think they were immune to the sinister lure of the Badlands. Perhaps they would pursue them into the heart of it, although that wouldn't be easy once their instruments deserted them.

That's it! thought Ro as a shiver gripped her spine. *We have to fool their instruments* now!

"Contact with torpedo in one minute," reported the officer on tactical.

"Ready aft torpedoes," said the captain grimly. "Target our first one on their torpedo and the second one on the lead ship."

"Yes, sir."

In the confines of the small bridge, Ro was already at Picard's back. "Sir, if we detonate both of our torpedoes directly behind us, we can blow up the torpedo and disrupt their sensors."

"That will only last a few seconds," said Picard thoughtfully, "but we can go to evasive maneuvers right after."

"Captain," insisted tactical, "contact in thirty seconds."

He strode toward the young woman. "Target both torpedoes on the lead craft, but detonate two seconds after launch. Conn, go to evasive maneuvers on my mark."

"Yes, sir," came the tense replies.

"Launch when ready."

"Torpedoes away!" barked the tactical officer.

Silently, Ro counted to herself, *one thousand one, one thousand two.*

"Mark," said Picard, pointing at the conn.

While the pilot worked his console, Ro tried to imagine the brilliant light, like a miniature nova, as the two photon torpedoes exploded inside a warp corridor. That would make a very large blip on their pursuers' scanners, not to mention sending their torpedo haywire. For several seconds, the *Orb of Peace* would be invisible. When they found her again, they would have to change course, but which course? If the pilot were good, he could send them the wrong way again, buying the transport a few more seconds. She fought the temptation to hover behind him and watch what he was doing.

"They're firing more torpedoes," said tactical. "Phasers, too. But we're out of phaser range."

"They're desperate," said Picard. "We're losing them."

The viewscreen filled with an ominous cloud of debris and dust—the scene of some cosmic cataclysm and the resting place of countless ships. The twinkling of plasma storms in the swirls looked like some exotic lighting in a smoke-filled nightclub.

"I'm losing instrumentation," said the conn.

Picard motioned for Ro to take over for the young man, who bolted to his feet. "Good flying," said Ro as she took his seat.

"Thank you." Beaming, the young man shuffled behind Captain Picard.

"Keep the viewscreen on as long as possible," ordered Ro. "And keep adjusting to correct for static."

"Aye, sir," answered the officer on ops.

"They're closing on us," warned Tactical.

"That's all right. By now, they're losing sensors and

instrumentation, too. I'm coming out of warp—to full impulse. Shields up!"

"Shields are up," echoed the woman on tactical, "but I've lost the Jem'Hadar! They're nowhere to be seen."

"Keep looking," said Ro, knowing it was useless; but it would keep her busy. Flying through the Badlands was not for the faint of heart, especially with the enemy hot on your tail and no reconnaissance ahead of you. If they hit a major plasma storm, nothing in the universe could save them.

The scene on the viewscreen changed very little as the boxy transport plowed into the thick of the plasma-charged cloud. She couldn't see the sleek attack ship with its pulsing blue lights, but she knew it had followed her in.

Without slowing speed, Ro piloted them through the thickets of smoke and mist, which flowed past on the viewscreen like some psychotropically induced dream. She tried to navigate the pockets of calm, avoiding the plasma streaks, which lit up the cloud like electrical impulses shooting across a nerve ending. Ro didn't mention to her comrades that at any moment they could get struck by plasma and evaporate—or whatever ships did when they disappeared in here. Ideally, she would pick her way through this morass at one-quarter impulse, but there wasn't anything ideal about this mission.

The viewscreen crackled with streaks of static, and she slowed to half impulse. She had to find their pursuer while there was still a chance.

"Ops, give me a view from aft," she ordered.

"Want a split screen?" asked the man.

"No, give me what I ask for," demanded Ro.

"Flying like this through the Badlands requires more luck than sight."

Stiffening his back, the ops officer changed the view to the aft lens. It was hardly any different than the view from the front, except that their wake was like a tunnel in the colorful dust. She saw a small beam of light in the distance, and at first she thought it was another bolt of plasma—until the *Orb of Peace* shuddered from a sudden impact.

"Torpedo," said Tactical. "I'm not sure it hit us—no damage."

"It was discharged by the plasma," said Ro. "They'll quickly figure out they'll have to use phasers, or whatever kind of beamed weapons they have. Front view."

The ops officer obeyed her order instantly, showing Ro the thickening, stringy fog of the Badlands, shot through with brilliant streaks of plasma. For the first time, Ro set course for the brightest storm in the area and increased speed to full impulse.

"You are aware, I take it, that we are heading into the storm?" asked Picard, controlled concern audible in his voice. *Just how far does he trust me?* Ro wondered.

"I'm coming about now, before we reach it." Ro eased the transport into a steep turn, finding that the craft was surprisingly easy to handle. At least her people built simplicity and elegance into all their creations.

"You're hoping to draw their fire," said Picard, comprehension dawning on his face.

She squinted into the filmy swirls of dust and debris, searching for their nemesis. When she finally spotted the Jem'Hadar ship, they were almost nose to nose, streaking toward each other at speeds too fast for the limited visibility. Ro ignored the gasps behind her as she dropped the transport into a steep dive. In the same instant, the warship fired a deadly beam that streaked through the dust, barely missing the transport.

Instead the phaser beam struck a bolt of plasma in the storm that Ro had lured them into. The plasma rippled along its new path and hit the Jem'Hadar attack ship like an avenging bolt of lightning. Ro turned her ship around just in time to see the sleek vessel light up like a fluorescent bulb and then burst into a billion shards of shimmering crystal.

When the gasps quieted, Picard said hoarsely, "Well done."

Ro sighed and brought the craft to a complete halt. She was finally able to rub her eyes and brush the hair off her clammy forehead.

"For once," she said, "it was good to fight a Jem'Hadar ship. I couldn't have pulled that trick on a Cardassian."

"I can truthfully say, we would not have made it without you," answered Picard. The faces of the young crew beamed at her with relief and respect, and they began to look Bajoran again. Maybe they would hop to when obeying her orders next time.

"So we're here," she declared. "What now?"

"First of all, we have to see if the artificial wormhole exists," answered Picard. "We have to know if it's there. Data said they need a verteron collider of large size, so we should be able to find it."

He wrinkled his artificial nose ridges. "Of course, that means we have to cross the entire Badlands, without knowing where it is on the other side. I wish we could get some intelligence first. I understand that the Badlands are inhabited by people who like their privacy, for one reason or another, and they're willing to risk the plasma storms."

"There is a place——" mused Ro, turning back to her console. "I wonder if it's still there? I'll get an approximate fix from our last known position, and we'll use dead reckoning from there. Settle back, and let me take you on a tour of the Badlands."

On the shuttlecraft *Cook*, Data put in another day of work without relief, staring at instruments as he drifted through an asteroid belt for cover. He would not have thought to complain; in fact, Data believed his time had been remarkably well spent. He had located the *Orb of Peace* on long-range scanners and had followed her all the way until her disappearance in the Badlands, which was to be expected. He had also seen the transport somehow manage to shake four enemy ships, with a fifth one still in pursuit.

Had his emotion chip been turned on, the android would have been extremely apprehensive about the mad chase he had witnessed from afar. Now it was simply a successful incursion into Cardassian space, unless the fifth ship had destroyed them. But from what he knew of the Badlands, Data considered it far more likely that the plasma storms would destroy them.

His vigilance was far from over, as now he planned to vacate the asteroid belt and sneak even closer to Cardassian space. From peripheral scans, Data had concluded that the fighting had moved on from this sector, leaving him some room to maneuver. For as many days and weeks as it took, he would scan the

Badlands, looking for a craft which could be the *Orb of Peace*. At the same time, he would be looking for the *Enterprise* to rendezvous with him. Since they were currently overdue, there was a very good chance *they* had been destroyed as well.

No, concluded Data, he had no intentions of turning on his emotion chip.

Chapter Nine

AT LONG LAST, THE *TAG GARWAL* was cruising through space under the command of Federation prisoners, with orders to stay out until her mission was accomplished, or they were all killed. Despite the dire circumstances, Sam Lavelle felt almost giddy as he stood on the bridge and watched the endless expanse of stars stream past. He could easily forget the war, the Dominion, the artificial wormhole, and everything else in the mistaken belief that he was free to explore this dark infinity. Space was oblivious of their petty quarrels; it always looked the same—endless, vast, imponderable.

For a taste of realism, Sam put the aft view on the screen. Now he could see the Jem'Hadar attack ship keeping a respectful but watchful distance behind them. The craft was smaller than theirs, but Sam knew it superior in every other way. The tanker had decent shields but no weapons, whereas the Jem'Hadar craft was a flying arsenal with no other purpose but to destroy enemy vessels. Their shadow was friendly at the moment, but Sam had no doubts that the Jem'Hadar would destroy them with all aboard at the slightest provocation.

"Their relative distance has not changed in twelve hours," observed Taurik, seated at the conn.

"I know," replied Sam. "I didn't expect them to be gone."

"Staring at them will not change the situation."

"I know!" groaned Sam. *Vulcans!* Sometimes their literal nature drove him crazy. Of course, it made no sense to stand here and watch the Jem'Hadar ship, hoping it would go away, but that was precisely the sort of thing humans did.

How could he make it go away? That was the question. Without their shadow, they were in a good position to make an escape and get back to Federation space. The *Tag Garwal* was a common type of supply ship found everywhere in Cardassian space, and she would typically be traveling alone. Nobody would pay any attention to them.

He looked around the bridge. As usual, only he and Taurik were on duty, with Grof and the rest of the crew below, fretting over their tractor beams, transporters, mining probes, and recombination chambers.

Sam tapped the ops console and put the starscape back on view, then he lowered his voice to ask Taurik, "How can we get away from that Jem'Hadar ship?"

The Vulcan raised an eyebrow. "I hope you are asking in the theoretical sense, because eluding them would be virutally impossible."

"Impossible?" repeated Sam, not liking the taste of

the word in his mouth. "Then we just carry out this operation and put them closer to victory? We don't even try to escape?"

"I did not say that," answered Taurik, "only that escape from that Jem'Hadar attack ship is virtually impossible. We have no weapons, and they are well armed and three times faster than us."

Sam bent down and whispered into the Vulcan's pointed ear, "Could we beam over to their ship? We have a larger crew—we could take them in hand-to-hand combat." Taurik raised an eyebrow. Sam knew the Vulcan was calculating the abysmal odds of such a fight.

"We could if only they lowered their shields and came within transporter range, neither of which they appear inclined to do."

"Then we'll have to make them do it," said Sam determinedly. He heard footsteps on the ladder, and he asked loudly, "How much longer to the Eye of Talek?"

"Twelve more hours. We are approximately halfway there."

"Excellent!" barked the voice of Enrak Grof as he lumbered out of the hatch and strode toward them. He was followed up the ladder by Enrique, the lucky material handler.

"Is the ship handling well?" asked Grof expansively, as if this were his private yacht.

"Fine," answered Sam with false cheer. "It feels good to be out in space again."

"I would imagine," Grof replied. "I would hate to be separated from my work for a lengthy period."

Sam bit his tongue and didn't say any of the several nasty things that occurred to him. Despite everything he had seen and heard, Grof was steadfastly determined to get the Corzanium and return to the Dominion. The war, the slave-labor camps, the subjugation of the Federation—these were all annoying side issues to the important matters of Grof's wormhole and his place in history.

Sam once again decided not to trust the Trill with any knowledge of their escape plan, when they had one. Grof's only purpose was to provide cover until they were ready to make their move. Sam had to make sure they got a realistic opportunity to sabotage the mission and escape. He hated to think about killing Grof with his own hands, but he would if he had to.

The professor motioned toward the glimmering starscape ahead of them. "Even without this wormhole business, we are making history on our little mission. No other operation has ever succeeded in extracting more than a few cubic centimeters of Corzanium from a black hole, and we're going to mine fifty cubic meters of the stuff."

"If we live long enough," added Taurik. "There are logical reasons why no one has been successful. Shall I list them?"

"No, thank you," muttered Grof. "Nobody has ever had as good a reason as ours, or else they would have done it before. All the models say it's possible with standard equipment. Right, Enrique?"

But the material handler was staring off into space with a moonstruck expression on his face.

"Right, Enrique?" asked Grof testily.

"Whatever you say, boss," replied the avuncular human. "I'd better get below and recheck those calibrations." Whistling cheerfully, the lithe man dropped into the hatch and was gone.

Grof scowled and opened his mouth undoubtedly to offer another tiresome prudish opinion, Sam thought. He cut the Trill off before the tirade even began.

"Oh, let him be," said Sam. "We've got twelve more hours before we have to get serious. The important thing is not to get overconfident or careless. No one's ever been sucked into a black hole and lived."

"Or ever been found again, except for some minute trace particles," added Taurik.

"The Eye of Talek is perfect for this operation," insisted Grof. "We've got nothing like it in the Federation. But I agree with you, Sam—we have to be careful. You just keep reminding me of that, because I *do* have a tendency to be overconfident."

Sam blinked at this outburst of humility. "I'll remember that, Grof."

The Trill nodded and looked uncomfortable for a moment, as if he wanted to be accepted into their circle but knew he never would be. "See you at chow!" called Grof, heading for the hatch.

"Yeah, at chow." Sam waved lazily and turned his attention to the viewscreen. Once the footsteps had stopped clomping down the ladder, Sam switched the view back to the sleek Jem'Hadar ship on their tail. Taurik would never agree, but maybe staring at it would give him an idea on how to lure it close enough to board it and capture it.

At times during their tense but sluggish cruise through the Badlands, Picard wanted to ask Ro if she really knew where they were going. He admired her ability to navigate by dead reckoning, only getting her bearings on rare occasions when they found a bubble, as she called them, where the dust and interference were thin enough to take sensor readings. He could tell that Ro was tempted to remain awhile in the relative safety of the bubbles, but she knew they had to push on.

Once, it seemed, they came very close to another ship, but they passed so quickly in the surreal fog that it was impossible to tell for sure what it was. Maybe it was only a plasma storm, thought Picard. Perhaps they were hallucinating. The Badlands struck him as the kind of place where a person's imagination and fear might get the better of him.

So dense was the dust and debris in some stretches that Picard felt as if he were on a submarine floating through a sea of mud. The shields took a beating, but the transport held together and somehow avoided the ubiquitous bursts of plasma.

Through all of this, Ro piloted the craft in a businesslike calm, talking very little and only relinquishing the conn for a few moments. Picard had little to do but watch the bizarre light show.

After hours and hours, Ro began to peer intently at the viewscreen, and Picard began to watch more closely, too. He saw it at the same moment she did— something black and ominous that sat like a gigantic spider in the middle of a vast neon web.

"There!" she said excitedly, pointing toward the viewscreen. The relief in her voice surprised Picard.

"What is it?" he asked.

"I think it started life as a space station," answered Ro. "Don't ask me whose, because it's ancient. I don't know how anyone thought they could build a station that would survive in this mess, although maybe it was here before the cloud. The Maquis call it the 'OK Corral.'"

Picard smiled. "It seems fitting that the Badlands should have a famous corral."

"And that's what it's used for," added Ro, cautiously steering them closer. "It's been hit so many times over the years by the plasma blasts that it's developed a repulsion effect—now the plasma actually stays away. The hull is nothing but a black hulk—you can't even tell what it's made out of."

"It sounds fascinating." Picard stared with interest at the spidery structure hanging in the magenta-brown haze. When it was illuminated by a far-off streak of plasma, he could see that the "legs" of the spider were broken spokes coming from a central hub. In its prime, this station must have been bigger than Deep Space Nine, and it was built in a similar gyroscopic design. Despite its familiar traits, the OK Corral seemed otherworldly, perfectly suited to its bizarre surroundings.

Ro circled the blackened ruin from a respectful distance, as if she were afraid something was going to pop out. Close up, the structure looked more like a lopsided, pitted asteroid than a creation of civilized beings; but its shape and symmetry were too exact to be accidental. It reminded Picard of an ancient burial mound he had seen in North America—beaten into something natural by the elements yet unmistakably a work of intelligence and artistry.

Without warning, they were jarred by a sudden blast, and Picard had to grab Ro's chair to remain upright. "What was that? Plasma burst?"

Ro scowled. "More like a photon torpedo."

"She's right," agreed the tactical officer. "No damage."

"A warning shot," added Ro grimly. "But we're not going to be warned off. We've got as much right here as anybody else. Still, keep those shields up."

Picard was about to ask where the shot had come from when a burst of plasma reflected off something silvery lurking within the hulk of the old station. As they continued to circle the OK Corral, the captain spotted a gaping crater that was big enough for the *Enterprise* to fly through. It looked as if something had taken a huge bite out of the central hub, leaving a blackened, hollow wreck. Sure enough, docked inside this unlikely safe harbor were two Ferengi marauders; they looked like sleek, bronze horseshoe crabs.

"Ro," said Picard, pointing at the viewscreen.

"I see them," she answered with a smile. "The old neighborhood is still active. They're most likely pirates and smugglers, so let's keep on our guard. Tactical, all auxiliary power to shields."

"May I remind you," said the woman on Tactical, "we're down to two torpedoes."

"They won't do us much good, anyway," answered Ro. "When they see how small we are—and that we're Bajoran—maybe they'll let us in."

"If they don't?" asked Picard.

"Then we'll look for friendlier pirates and smugglers. A good friend of mine used to say that you don't meet any choirboys in the Badlands." When Ro mentioned her friend, her eyes got a faraway look, and Picard glimpsed the grief she had been hauling with her.

Acting as if the *Orb of Peace* were the equal of the two battle-scarred warships, Ro Laren swept through the crater and into their midst. Picard half-expected the Ferengi to rake them with withering phaser fire; then he realized that these ships were not going to risk destroying their refuge. He had seen enough of the Badlands to know that safe places to stop were few and far between.

Now that they were inside the hollowed-out ruins of the main hub, the captain marveled at the bizarre sights that surrounded them. In addition to the two garish warships, he could see a cross section of the devastated space station, complete with decks, chambers, and bays; it all looked like a massive burnt honeycomb. He made a pact with himself that if he were ever free to travel Cardassian space—with no war—he would come back to the OK Corral and investigate this wondrous artifact.

"Have we got anything to trade for information?" asked Ro.

"Perhaps some tetralubisol," Picard suggested.

Ro shrugged. "I guess that's worth a try. I'm going to hail them. Ops, let's dim the lights."

"Yes, sir."

"Remember," said the captain, "they're smugglers and pirates."

"And fellow neutrals." Ro stood up and nodded to Tactical.

"Hailing frequencies open," reported the young woman on duty.

"Greetings. This is Captain Ro Laren of the *Orb of Peace,* from Bajor. We were forced off course by some unusual circumstances, and we hope you don't mind if we stop—"

"Quiet!" growled a voice, and the viewscreen popped on, showing a flurry of moving figures, most of them naked. They were clearly in the master stateroom of the Ferengi captain, because his wives were scurrying to get out of the way. But it was a muscular, unclothed Orion male who stepped into their view. The green-skinned humanoid grabbed a shimmering blue robe and pulled it around his thick body; then he motioned to the unseen shadows.

"Shek, get out here!" bellowed the Orion. His rough voice seemed to have only one volume—loud.

Accompanied by giggles and women straightening his clothes, a scrawny Ferengi strolled toward them from the shadows. He looked a bit taller and more fit than the typical Ferengi, although he was still dwarfed by the big Orion.

With a snaggletoothed grin, the Ferengi asked them, "What is this? A Bajoran vessel sneaking around Cardassian space—in the middle of a *war?* Are you lost? Or crazy?"

The muscular Orion glared suspiciously at her. "Nobody knows about this place . . . nobody who's still alive."

Ro put her hands on her hips and sighed. "Okay, we're really trying to find some terrorists we left here. We think they're still fighting the war with Cardassia and don't know that we're neutral. This used to be a place we could find them."

The Orion and the Ferengi looked at one another, and Picard thought they would buy it—until the Orion turned and shook his fist at them. "I say we loot their ship! You have ten seconds to *surrender!*"

"Wait a minute, Rolf," said Shek, patting his large partner on the shoulder. "You never dispose of merchandise until you find out its worth. They have exhibited considerable skill and knowledge just getting here. Unless I am a worse judge of appearance than usual, they have nothing of value aboard their ship. Their ship isn't worth anything either. I *know*. I tried to sell one of those once—took a real loss. Had to sell it to the *Maquis!*"

The Orion scratched his chin and leered at her. "I know a place where they pay dearly for young Bajoran females. It's not far from here either."

"We're not young," scoffed Ro. "We're all old and haggard, like me." She reached out and pulled Picard into their view. "See, this is my first officer. He's typical of this crew. This is a humanitarian mission to rescue some of our warriors who no longer need to fight. Do you think somebody young and beautiful would take a job like this?"

Shek laughed. "I like her. Let's have dinner with her. Anyone who can find her way here has got to have some interesting stories."

The toothsome Ferengi wiggled his finger at her. "We'll beam you over in one hour—you and your first officer. Unarmed, please."

"Thank you," said Ro evenly. "We accept your invitation."

The screen went dark, and Ro's tense shoulder blades finally dropped into their regular position. She looked so worn, Picard thought as he placed a tentative, but he hoped comforting, hand on her shoulder.

"It's worth the risk," he said gently. Ro glanced back at him with a rare glint of insecurity in her dark eyes.

"Those are fast ships out there," Picard continued, pointing to the two bronze marauders filling the viewscreen. "They can outrun Jem'Hadar and Cardassian ships, so they've probably seen a lot of this sector. They may also have dealings with the Dominion. If the artificial wormhole is real, they ought to know."

Ro looked back at her young crew and whispered, "On the other hand, our relief should be prepared to run for it, if we don't return."

"We'll work out a signal," said Picard grimly.

Ro smiled. "Make sure your earring is on straight. Believe me, how you wear that earring is nine-tenths of being a Bajoran."

"Understood," answered Picard gravely.

Will Riker paced outside the office of Commander Shana Winslow on Starbase 209, fuming. Winslow was head of the repair pool, and she had refused to release the *Enterprise* for active duty. Sure, Will knew they were a little banged up, but *unfit for duty?* He didn't think so! Besides, he had friends and comrades out there who needed him, and Starfleet forces were spread too thin to worry about one little fact-finding mission. Picard, Data, La Forge, every member of the away team—they were counting on the *Enterprise*.

Commander Winslow's assistant was a bookish-looking Benzite, who sat behind his desk and watched Riker with thinly veiled contempt. Every so often, he clucked like a chicken, which was driving Riker crazy.

"Where is she?" grumbled Riker. "Doesn't she know there's a war going on?"

"Oh, she's quite aware there's a war going on," answered the Benzite with a long blue face. "Too many ships needing repair, too few parts, too many interruptions in supply and manufacturing—it's all quite difficult."

"If I don't get in there to talk to her pretty soon, it's going to be even *more* difficult," vowed Riker.

At that moment, the door to Commander Winslow's office slid open, and four engineers walked out and brushed past him with stricken expressions on their faces. They looked like men who had just been chewed out. Riker straightened his uniform and tried to be calm. *Honey instead of vinegar,* he told himself.

He stared expectantly at the Benzite, who took his sweet time in looking up and saying, "You may go in, Commander."

"Thank you." Riker stode through the door from the anteroom to Commander Winslow's inner office. The first thing that struck him was the size of the office: it wasn't ready-room-size but more like a miniature auditorium with several rows of seats and a large viewscreen. Either Commander Winslow conducted classes here, or she liked to chew people out en masse.

The second thing that struck him was Commander Winslow herself. She was a striking brunette about his own age, with dark eyes that drilled into him as he approached her. She was also partly bionic, with a prosthetic left arm and left leg, which he glimpsed before she limped behind her desk.

Commander Winslow gave him a businesslike smile as she sat down and punched her computer terminal. "Commander Riker of the *Enterprise,*" she read aloud. "I thought that ship was still under the command of Jean-Luc Picard. I trust that Captain Picard is all right?"

"So do I," answered Riker, mustering a smile. "I'm acting captain, and I hope we can return to active duty soon. We've got to support Captain Picard and several of our senior officers who are on a mission into Cardassian space."

"Sounds risky," replied Winslow with extreme understatement. She folded her hands and drilled him again with those dark eyes. "Commander Riker, I know you want to leave right now, but the *Enterprise* has failed almost every readiness test. You've got leakage from the warp coil, stress failure on the outer hull, burned-out circuitry on every deck, and dozens of patchwork field repairs that are holding, somehow, but can't for long."

Riker winced, then held out his hands. "But she's still in one piece. We flew in here, didn't we? La Forge has kept her in top shape——."

Shana Winslow gave him a sympathetic smile. "Despite the redoubtable Mr. La Forge, your ship is in no condition to go back into action. I would be remiss in my duties if I released her now."

Riker's shoulders drooped. "How long?"

"The *Enterprise* is a top priority, Commander, but the best I can promise is a week."

"A week!" blurted Riker, not meaning to. He was shocked that it would take that long—in a week, Captain Picard could be dead.

She fixed him with her disconcerting eyes. "I'm sorry, but if I release you before we complete all the necessary repairs, Starfleet's most advanced starship—and most experienced crew—could be lost to us. It's my job to make sure that ships are ready to do the job for which they were intended, and your ship is not."

Back off, Riker told himself. *Honey, not vinegar.*

He stepped away from her desk and sighed. "I suppose I should welcome a few days of liberty for my crew, but it's difficult when we've got comrades out there."

"Believe me, I know." Winslow lifted her prosthetic arm and set it on her desk. "I was once a ship's engineer—I'm still not used to flying a desk."

He glanced at her arm and wondered why Starfleet hadn't provided her with a more natural looking prosthetic. "How did you get injured?"

"On board the *Budapest* last year, defending Earth from the Borg. We let them get past us—thanks for saving our hides."

She paused, apparently noting his stare. Smiling gently she said "Your ship and I have something in common." She pointed to her clumsy artificial limb. "We both have to wait out the war shortages to be properly refitted."

Riker grinned. "The *Enterprise* spent a month on 413 after that battle, while we cleaned all the Borg technology out of her."

Commander Winslow leaned forward eagerly. "Oh, I wish I could've been there to see that, to be able to study it firsthand. I've always had tremendous interest in the Borg, which was only heightened when they almost killed me. Their efficiency is amazing—if I could only get a crew of them working for me."

"I've had them on board, and I don't recommend it." Riker stepped closer and flashed a boyish smile. "If you were to have dinner with me tonight, I could tell you all about the Borg."

"Hmmm," she replied thoughtfully, checking her computer screen. "Yes, that would be acceptable at, say, nineteen hundred hours. And I can explain to you about our procurement problems, which have delayed everything. We've got to end this war soon, or the infrastructure is going to break down."

"Right," said Riker. "That's why I'm trying to get back into it."

"I know." Winslow stood and motioned to the door. "We'll meet here again at nineteen hundred hours."

Riker started to the door, then turned nervously. "The *Enterprise,* you are—"

"Yes, we're working on it. See you later, Commander."

Captain Picard steeled himself as he felt the tingle of the transporter beam, although Ro gave him an encouraging nod at the last second. He admired her élan—she seemed more at ease around scoundrels than most, though he wasn't entirely sure she would regard the sentiment as a compliment if he gave voice to it.

They materialized inside a sumptuous dining hall festooned with pastel-colored banners and golden tinsel draped from the ceilings. In one sunken corner were plush pillows and chaise longues that overlooked a stage upon which torches burned brightly. To the rear of the hall was a beautiful table of pure amber, set for four. A Ferengi harpist sat in another corner, playing a sweet melody on his golden instrument.

"'Song for Solitude,'" said Ro with a faint smile. "It's a well-known Bajoran piece. We'll have to thank our hosts."

Picard tried to imagine himself as someone else, a kindly vedek perhaps. Ro was the captain, so she could play the tough one. He needed to appear serene and spiritual, above the baser, petty aspects of life.

Double doors at the far end of the hall swept open, and Shek, the Ferengi, swept into the room, with luxurious satiny robes trailing behind him. Towering over him, looking like a bodyguard, came the hulking Orion, Rolf.

"Welcome!" gushed Shek, rushing toward Ro and taking her hand. He gazed lasciviously into her sullen eyes. "It's a pleasure to have you aboard my humble vessel, the *Success*. This is Rolf, captain of our consort, the *Swift*. Excuse us for firing upon you, Captain Ro, but you can never be sure who you will meet in these trying times."

"Understood," said Ro with a polite bow. "This is my first mate."

"We are enjoying the music," said Picard with a polite bow. " 'Song for Solitude' always reminds me of childhood. Thank you."

"You're welcome. And may I say, that is a very nice earring you're wearing. That stone comes from Jerrado, doesn't it?"

"Yes," answered Picard with a smile. "Not many people realize that."

"We recognize items of value. Since no one can visit Jerrado anymore, that earring is a real collector's item. Are you hungry?" Dwarfed by his oversized robes, Shek shuffled toward the table. "We don't know much about Bajoran cooking, although it looks less exotic than our own. It's certainly less exotic than Orion cooking, what with all those tear-inducing spices."

"Bah," grumbled Rolf. "He likes everything bland."

"I do not," countered Shek. "It's just that we have to respect other people's tastes. Therefore, we are having roasted hornbill, a type of local fowl."

"Yes, we saw some at a Cardassian farming colony on our way here," said Ro. "The Cardassians stole half our cargo; they said it was contraband."

Rolf laughed heartily. "Yes, they'll do that. If you don't have a ship that can outrun them, what do you expect?"

Shek pulled out a chair for Ro. "Please sit here, Captain."

"Thank you," said the Bajoran, taking the proffered chair.

Shek quickly sat on one side of her, and Rolf sat on the other, leaving Picard to take the outermost chair. He didn't like the way the two pirates were sandwiched on each side of Ro, but his persona didn't allow him to do much about it. With a pleasant smile on his face, Picard had to watch them fawn over her.

"You can't possibly expect to find any terrorists alive after all this time," said their host. "Would you like some Trakian ale?"

"Thank you," answered Ro, folding her hands in front of her. "Whether we expect to find them alive or not, we have to look."

"Have you ever considered dancing?" asked the Orion, admiring her slim physique.

"I'm a ship's captain," she replied, "the same as you. Have you considered dancing?"

"Eldra!" shouted Shek, waving toward the door. A short, blubbery Ferengi woman rushed in with a pitcher full of dark ale, bubbling at its narrow neck. Picard had to admit that his throat was dry, and the beverage looked good. There was a pause in conversation as glasses were poured and drinks were hoisted.

"To hell with the Dominion!" cheerfully toasted the

Orion before downing his entire glass. Picard and Ro drank along with him as they exchanged glances.

"You don't care for the Dominion?" asked Picard.

"Who could like those Denebian slime devils?" grumbled the Orion. "The Cardassians were fine before they came—they were corrupt; they could be bought. The Dominion just wants to take over everything. They don't want any competition. What fun is that?"

"And they're trying to kill our best customers," sniffed the Ferengi. "The Dominion is bad for business. A Ferengi will take a monopoly if he can get one, but he still knows it's unnatural. These people think it's all right for a puddle of shapeshifters to rule the galaxy, and skim off everybody."

The Orion snorted with laughter. "We hope the Federation wins, but we hope the war goes on for a long time, don't we?"

"Of course," answered the Ferengi. "War is good for the black market. It's chaos, and chaos is always good for those of us who work in the shadows. But not this war—too much killing."

The guests nodded, unable to add much to that sentiment. Fortunately, the food arrived shortly thereafter, delivered by the rotund Eldra, who encouraged them to eat. So zealous were her entreaties that Picard assumed she had prepared the meal. He hoped she hadn't also prechewed it.

It was good food and decent company, with discussion on all sorts of matters, ranging from the price of antimatter to Bajoran neutrality. Picard wanted to casually slip the idea of an artificial wormhole into the conversation, but it seemed premature. They had just now struck a civil discourse with one another, and even the Orion was behaving like a gentleman.

After the dishes were removed, Shek clapped his hands and rose to his feet. "It's time for the evening's entertainment."

They retired to the cushions and lounges of the sunken den in front of the stage. Picard was a little light-headed after all the ale, although he had tried to pace himself. He had to admit that the food had been excellent, very similar to squab, and he had eaten more than his share. Thus far, this respite with the pirates had proven to be surprisingly enjoyable.

Once they had settled into the upholstered lair, Shek tugged on his ear and gave them a snaggle-toothed grin. "Tonight's entertainment is furnished by my good friend, Rolf. Ah, here is the Saurian brandy."

When Eldra appeared with a carafe and small glasses, Picard felt like declining, but he saw a warning look in Rolf's eyes. When the green giant took a glass of brandy, he held it up for all to see, and Picard knew that he had better do the same.

"We toast to your health and your gods," said the Orion.

"To the Prophets," said Ro, drinking.

"To the Prophets," echoed Picard, taking a sip.

"To the dancing girls!" crowed Shek.

A drumroll crashed and thundered behind them, and Picard was about to turn around when three lithe figures leaped from the curtain behind the stage. They landed in the flickering pool of light given off by the torches and began to sway. As the drums increased their frenzy, the green-skinned Orion women undulated to the pulsing beat. Picard had heard of these famed entertainers, but he had never thought he would actually see them . . . in the flesh, so to speak. There was a great deal of green flesh exhibited by the filmy costumes.

He felt so relaxed and content as he snuggled in the oversized cushions, watching the acrobatic and suggestive dancing of the Orion women. It was hard not to imagine that this dinner party was really a gathering of pirate chieftains in some remote tropical harbor, participating in the drunken debaucheries of yore.

Picard looked over at Ro Laren, and she was asleep, curled peacefully among the pillows. *So rare for her to look so peaceful,* thought the captain. He looked back at the dancing women—so animalistic, so exotic, so voluptuous. He could almost smell their pungent scent and taste their sweet green skin. Sweat was breaking out on the back of his neck. Enough was enough, he decided. It was time to get some air.

As Picard staggered to his knees, he heard Rolf laughing uproariously in his ear, and a big arm reached out and dragged him back into the cushions. "Settle down, my good man. What about the girl you came in with?"

The captain looked again at Ro Laren, and he realized that she shouldn't be sleeping. A spark in the back of his brain cut through the fog and told him that this shouldn't be happening. He was in some kind of trouble. He started to reach for his communicator to give it two quick taps—the signal—but his limbs felt as leaden as tree trunks.

A hand came from nowhere, slapped his chest, and ripped the comm badge off. He touched the hole in the fabric where it used to be, gazed bewilderedly at the big ears of the Ferengi, then slumped back onto the pillows.

"All right," said Shek, leaning over him, "why don't you tell us where you really came from. And what you're really doing here."

"My . . . my ship!" gasped Picard helplessly.

"Yes, let's not forget about your ship," agreed Shek. He tapped his comm badge. "Captain to bridge: activate tractor beam. Prepare to board."

Chapter Ten

LYING SUPPINE ON CUSHIONS in the dining hall of the Ferengi ship, Captain Picard had a strong sense of déjà vu. He felt the way he had when he was going through emergency heart surgery—conscious but unable to feel anything or control his limbs. He didn't exactly float over his body, but he wasn't inside of it either. He felt oddly apart, like an observer, shunted off to the side.

The Orion dancing girls kept undulating suggestively to the throbbing drumbeat, but there was something wrong with them, too. They seemed to be nothing but moving bodies, devoid of consciousness.

The Ferengi, Shek, clapped his hands. "Computer, end program."

At once, the green-skinned women disappeared, and so did most of the furnishings and decorations in the sumptuous dining hall. Glasses of brandy dropped to the floor and shattered, and Picard's body collapsed onto a hard floor as well. He struggled to sit up—but couldn't.

"It's a nerve conditioner," said Shek. "You have no control over what you do or say. Oddly, you and Captain Ro reacted completely differently to the drug. She fell asleep."

"And you?" asked Picard in a hollow, raspy voice.

Shek smiled and pointed to Rolf, the big green Orion. "Oh, we took the antidote before dinner."

Rolf scowled. "I miss the days when we used to torture people to get information."

"Yes, but you must admit, these new species-specific drugs are faster and more efficient." Shek patted his large partner on the shoulder, then turned back to Picard. "All right, what is your real name and position?"

He tried to make his mouth form the words "Lieutenant Tom Smith," or "Chief Ray Jones," or anything but the truth. But to his horror he heard his own voice say "Captain Jean-Luc Picard of the *Starship Enterprise.*"

"Really?" said Shek, obviously impressed. "And your friend, Captain Ro?"

"She is Captain Ro Laren of the *Orb of Peace,* formerly of my command."

"What are you doing in Cardassian space?"

"We are looking for the Dominion's artificial wormhole."

Rolf burst out laughing. "And what are they going to do with it when they find it? The Federation is more desperate than I thought."

Perhaps he could pretend to be as feebleminded as

he felt and change the subject to something a bit less controversial. "The dancers?" asked Picard reaching toward the empty space where they had been.

"Alas, they're holograms," replied Shek. "In this day and age, who can afford real Orion slave girls? But you're more interesting, anyway, Captain. What *were* you planning to do with the artificial wormhole, should it exist?" Change the subject, indeed. Perhaps he *was* as feebleminded as he felt, Picard thought bitterly.

"Destroy it," he whispered.

The Ferengi and the Orion looked at one another and laughed, slapping their thighs. "Do you know how big that thing is?" asked Shek.

"How big?"

Shek pushed him back onto the hard floor. "We need to confer now, Captain. Your eyes are getting heavy, and you're very tired. All you want to do is sleep, like your comrade. Go to sleep, Captain Picard, you've earned the rest."

With that the captain closed his eyes and drifted into unconsciousness.

"When the reactor exploded and the concussion hit me, I went unconscious," said Commander Shana Winslow as she stirred her Mai Tai with a swizzle stick held in the mechanical fingers of her left hand. She and Will Riker were sitting at a back table in a place called the Bolian Bistro, reputed to be the best restaurant on Starbase 209, although it served a limited menu. All of the eateries on the starbase were suffering from shortages.

"For all intents and purposes, I was dead," she went on. "I never knew they beamed me out until I woke up in a bed on a medical ship. And when I looked down and saw how much of me was missing, I cursed the hell out of them."

Will Riker smiled and shook the ice in his glass. "I can imagine you did. How long did your recovery take?"

"It's still going on," answered Winslow. "The physical therapy, the counseling sessions—I don't think it will ever end. As I said, I long to be out there as much as you do, but I've got to be realistic. This is my job now; it's a job for which I'm suited."

"And you don't have any family to worry about?"

The engineer shook her head sadly. "Not now. I had a husband, but he died aboard the *Budapest* in the same action against the Borg."

"I'm sorry," said Riker, regretting his glib comment.

Winslow managed a bittersweet smile. "Don't worry about it. Talking about it is part of my recovery. In some respects, it was a marriage of convenience, since we were both so wrapped up in our careers. We had finally gotten assigned to the same ship, and we were going to work on the marriage. Instead, we nearly died together in our first action."

She stirred her drink and looked at him coyly. "What about you?"

"Confirmed bachelor," answered Riker, leaning back in his chair and grinning. "Although I won't say that I haven't come close to marriage—but only once, seriously."

"And what happened to her?"

"She's my best friend," answered Riker, taking a sip of his drink. "She understands me better than anybody—well enough to know that she wouldn't want to be married to me."

"Yes, that's what I miss most about Jack being gone. It's good to have at least one person who really knows you, around whom you don't have to pretend." Shana Winslow gave him a melancholy smile.

Riker reached for her hand. "Listen, you were spared for a reason. We've all been spared this long for a reason—maybe it's to fight this lousy war."

"Ah, now you're getting back to the subject of your ship," said Winslow. "It's still seven days—six if we can get the EPS couplings we need by tomorrow."

Riker smiled. "Who do I have to rob to get those couplings?"

"Just hope for the supply convoy to get through."

Riker quickly lifted his glass. "Here's to the supply convoy. And also to good company."

"To good company," echoed Shana Winslow, hefting her glass and peering at him over the rim with her intense dark eyes.

"I hope my crew is enjoying their liberty as much as I am," said Riker.

Ro Laren awoke with shooting pains in her arms, legs, and head. She quickly determined that the cause of the pain in her extremities was from the ropes binding her to a stiff, hard chair. But the pain in her head was like the worst hangover she'd ever gotten from drinking's Derek's homemade wine.

She looked around the empty room, which had a grid on the walls but nothing else, and she saw Captain Picard sitting about five meters away. He was also bound tightly to his chair. The captain looked more disheveled and beaten than she did, although he managed a wan smile. "Good morning."

"What happened?" she asked with a groan.

"We were drugged by our hosts."

"But they ate and drank the same things we did."

"Yes, but they took an antidote first." Picard struggled against his bonds for a moment, but it was useless.

"Where are we?"

"Same place we were before," answered the captain, "only now you can tell it's a holodeck. Listen, my memory is hazy, but I believe they know everything."

"Everything?" she asked in horror.

He nodded grimly. "I don't know what they intend to do to us."

Ro shivered, not wanting to think about all the gruesome options they had.

Picard continued, "I believe they know they have a valuable prize. If I were them, I might go to both the Federation and the Dominion, seeing who will bid more to get a starship captain."

"The ship—" began Ro.

"Your ship is all right," said a snide voice. With difficulty and pain, Ro twisted her head around enough to see Shek and Rolf stride through the doors into the holodeck. The Orion was holding a padd, a handheld computing device, which looked out of place in his big green hands. The Ferengi had a pulse whip tied to his belt in a serpentine coil.

"We've just interrogated your crew and searched your ship," said Shek glumly. "As I suspected, you have nothing of value. Why are patriots always so broke?"

"There are some young Bajoran females." Rolf smiled lasciviously at the prisoners.

"They aren't really Bajoran," countered Ro.

"We know," muttered Shek, "and that is problematic. If they ever found out we sold them fake merchandise . . . well, that's not a good way to conduct business. So the only thing of value is Captain Jean-Luc Picard."

"I'm not valuable," answered Picard. "I would be just one of thousands of prisoners of war."

"At least that way you might get to see your artificial wormhole," joked Rolf.

Both Ro and Picard stared at the Orion. "Then it does exist?" asked the captain.

Rolf nodded. "Oh, yes. It's a gigantic thing, bigger than several moons I've seen. If it were up to Shek here, you would never see it, because he wanted to sell you to the Dominion. But I convinced him not to."

Ro and Picard looked accusingly at the scrawny Ferengi, who gave them an apologetic shrug. "Hey, a fellow has to make a profit."

"I convinced him that we should let you carry out your mission," said the muscular Orion with a note of pride in his voice. "With a little help from us."

Ro gaped at him. "You're going to join us with your ships?"

The Orion burst out laughing. "Hardly! Do we look like fools? We can't be seen having anything to do with this."

Shek pointed a bony finger at them. "And we hope you have the good sense not to get captured again! Next time, have the decency to get killed, will you?"

Picard ignored the last part of Shek's request. "We

have no intentions of being captured by the Dominion," he said.

"Good." The Orion held out the computer padd. "We've done some calculations, and we don't see how you could ever destroy the verteron collider, even if you had the *Enterprise* with you. But maybe you don't have to destroy it to keep it from working."

Ro and Picard glanced puzzledly at one another, then back at their captors. "What do you have in mind?" asked Ro.

Even though they were all alone on the Ferengi vessel, Shek glanced around nervously and lowered his voice. "I received a nice bit of intelligence the other day. The Dominion has had a hard time finishing the mouth of the wormhole, because they need a rather exotic material to withstand the pressure. They blew up a tanker trying to off-load a sub-quark compound, and now they're getting desperate."

Shek tapped his fingertips together. "My spies tell me that they've sent a mining vessel to a black hole called the Eye of Talek. They're trying to extract some Corzanium to use for the building material. Does this sound plausible to you?"

"Very," answered Picard.

"So," concluded Rolf, "you don't have to destroy the whole thing to stop them. You just have to keep them from mining the Corzanium—destroy the mining vessel."

"Do you know the location of the Eye of Talek?" asked Ro. "I've heard of it, but I don't know where it is."

"Right here," answered Rolf, pointing to his computer padd.

"Then why are we still tied up?" demanded Ro. "We need to get moving!"

The Orion and the Ferengi glanced at one another, and the Orion shrugged and pulled a curved knife out of the gold sash around his waist. Ro winced as the sharp blade ran down the skin of her forearms and sawed the rope tying her wrists. When her arms finally dropped to her sides, Ro never thought she could feel such relief. She watched intently as he cut the rope around her ankles, then she stood and stretched, trying to ignore the screams of her cramped muscles.

Picard sat stoically as the Orion cut away his bonds; then he stood and rubbed the chafed skin on his wrists. "You know, we could have reached the same conclusion without so much trouble."

"Ah," said the Ferengi, grabbing the handle of his whip, "where is the fun in that? Frankly, if you had told us that a little Bajoran transport with two torpedoes was going to take out a verteron collider that is ten kilometers long and protected by a Dominion fleet, we wouldn't have believed you. Would we have, Rolf?"

"I'm still not sure I believe them," grumbled the Orion. "But the truth potion never lies, which means they are simply deluded—so let's give them a chance to die for their cause! Besides, we want to keep the war going, don't we, Shek?"

"Yes, we do," answered the Ferengi, "but if I find out that you've been captured—when I could have *sold* you to them—I'll be very angry."

"You won't have to worry about that," vowed Picard. "Can we go back to our ship now?"

Rolf nodded and shoved the padd into the captain's

hands. "Use this information well—we hate to give it away for free."

"Is it going to be hard to reach the Eye of Talek?" asked Ro.

"In your ship, it's a journey of two days," answered Rolf. "But you have made it past the front, where most of the Dominion ships are deployed, so you shouldn't encounter many of them."

"Thank you," said Picard. He reached for his comm badge and found a torn patch of fabric where it should have been.

"Oh!" exclaimed Shek, producing two Bajoran comm badges from a pocket on his vest. With an apologetic smile, he handed them over.

"Thank you." Picard tapped his badge and said, "Away team to the *Orb of Peace.*"

"Captain!" answered La Forge's breathless voice. "Are you all right? We thought you were dead . . . or worse."

"We're fine, Geordi. Our hosts are letting us go."

"They hit us with a tractor beam," said La Forge, "and we had no choice but to let them board and search us."

"Yes, they're very thorough when it comes to digging for information," agreed Picard. "But they've given us some news that could prove to be invaluable. Two to transport back."

"Yes, sir."

"We never had this conversation," insisted Shek as the tingle of the transporter beam gripped Ro's spine. "You don't know us!"

"Nevertheless," said the Bajoran, "we won't forget your help."

After they were gone, the two pirate captains looked at one another and shook their heads in amazement.

"Do you think they stand a chance?" asked Shek.

"None!" scoffed the Orion. "A tiny transport against the entire Dominion? They'll have to get very lucky."

"Something tells me that Captain Picard knows a thing or two about luck." Shek tugged on an oversized earlobe. "Maybe they will disrupt the Dominion long enough for us to pull off a caper or two. Let's go to the chart room and plan it."

The Orion slapped his scrawny partner on the shoulder. "Now you're thinking. Lead the way!"

Before the two scurvy captains could exit the holodeck, the Ferengi's comm badge chirped. With a scowl, he tapped it and answered, "This is Captain Shek. What is it?"

"Captain," said a quavering voice, "that ship which just left—three men beamed over from transporter room two when the others beamed back. *Desert* they did, sir!"

"The scoundrels!" growled the Ferengi, reaching for the handle of his whip. "Listen, hail the Bajorans and tell them they've got stowaways!"

"We tried that, sir, and there's too much interference. The plasma storms are really bad out there—they'll be lucky if they make it through. Should we go after them, sir?"

"No," growled Shek, "not if the storms are bad. Plus, we've got to meet the Plektaks here. Who did we lose?"

"The three Romulans."

"Good riddance," muttered Shek. "Out."

Rolf chuckled. "I *told* you not to take them on. Now they've decided to grab their own ship and go freelance. Pretty good timing."

"Captain Picard's luck just turned the other way," muttered the Ferengi, shuffling out the door.

Will Riker stood at the door of Shana Winslow's quarters, wondering how far he should go in the pursuit of special treatment for the *Enterprise*. Logic told him that no matter what he did, it wouldn't make any difference. Maybe in the field, under fire, Winslow would be willing to make quick and dirty repairs; but in her current post, she was determined to follow procedures. He didn't think she would make any exceptions for an amiable dinner date.

Then why was he here, paused to follow Shana into her private chambers? He had to answer that he was interested in the woman, not what she could do for him. She had lost her family and her ship, and his heart went out to her. Will knew how many people doubted his sanity over his refusal to leave the *Enterprise* to take command of another ship. But the *Enterprise* and her crew were like no other ship. They were family, and the *Enterprise* was home.

"A penny for your thoughts," said Winslow as her door slid open.

He smiled wistfully. "I'm afraid I was thinking about my ship and her crew. I can be awfully single-minded."

"Me, too." She motioned toward her small but tastefully appointed cabin, standard issue, as if she hadn't really moved in yet. "Would you like to come in for a drink?"

"Yes, I would."

She led the way. "I have to warn you that even the replicators are offering reduced selections these days. We have to ration both raw materials and power consumption."

"Do you still have cold water?"

"I think so," she answered with a smile, moving toward the food slot. "One cold water. Please, have a seat."

"On the ship, our biggest problem is a lack of experienced personnel," said Riker, dropping into a cushy sofa. "It doesn't do any good to throw bodies at a problem unless they have the experience to deal with it."

"Tell me about it." Winslow brought him a glass of water, carrying it in her natural hand. "How would you like to have to compete with ships of the line for good people? The admirals just want to throw everybody into the front, forgetting all about the support services. We've shut down two wings of the station—nobody to do maintenance."

"I noticed." Riker sipped his water and looked quizzically at her. "You're not drinking anything?"

"I'm going back now. I have a hard time carrying more than one glass at a time."

Riker fought the temptation to jump up and fetch her a drink. Instead he watched her laboriously get herself a cup of tea and return to the sofa. He was flattered when she sat down close beside him.

"Ah," said Winslow with a sigh. "Now, where were we?"

"We were complaining about how we don't have enough good people."

"These are extraordinary times," said the engineer. "Starfleet has fought plenty of conflicts before, but we've never been stretched so thin, over such a long period of time—with no end in sight."

Riker sighed. "There is an end in sight, but it's not one we want to think about."

"That bad, huh?" She shook her head. "I know the shortages and pressure we're under, but I don't really get a feel for it. I wish I were out there—with you people."

"We're holding our own," he lied. "Even without you."

Winslow smiled sweetly at him, her dark eyes glimmering. "I suppose we have to make the most of every moment we're alive. That's something I really haven't learned to do since the *Budapest* went down. Sometimes it's just so easy to get caught up in your work."

"I know," said Riker, his arm curling around her shoulder. "Maybe this is a good time to start."

She snuggled back into the crook of his arm and closed her eyes. "Can I just sit here for a moment? Human contact, and all that. There's one thing you don't get much in Starfleet—a hug. They ought to have a couple of people in charge of hugs, just to dispense them randomly."

Riker settled back, too, his arm around this very agreeable women, not in any rush himself. In his younger years, he would have been all over Shana, but now the simple contact felt good. He hadn't had much time for hugs either.

When she finally opened her eyes, they sparkled like two black opals, faraway and dreamy. Her face had beauty, ruggedness, and character—the face of a woman who worked too hard for too little in return. Looking surprised, she touched his other arm, as if trying to make sure he was real. That was when he knew he had to kiss her.

Riker bent low, and she angled her chin upward, closing her eyes again. As his mouth was about to taste her honey and tea-scented lips and her hand gripped his bicep, an urgent beep sounded on a nearby comm panel.

"I'm sorry, Will," said Winslow apologetically as she rose to her feet. "I told them not to call me unless it's an emergency."

"I understand," said Riker.

She tapped the panel and said, "Winslow here."

"This is Lieutenant Harflon, work detail three on the *Seleya,*" came a crisp voice. "The energy fluctuations in the IPS are still affecting the grid. Lorimar said you had an undocumented fix for this, and the work orders say to call you."

"Yes, yes," she answered. "Is the test flight still scheduled for oh-eight-hundred?"

"Yes, Commander."

"I'll be right there. Out." Winslow winced at Riker as she headed toward the door. "Sorry, Will. But you know, this might not take long. You're welcome to make yourself at home . . . relax."

"How come the *Seleya* is getting special treatment?" asked Riker, following her out into the corridor. "Because it's the admiral's ship?"

"Could be, except that it's been in my shop for a week already, and the admiral is like you—impatient." She headed determinedly toward the turbolift.

"Well, then . . . what about enjoying life?"

Winslow waved as she entered the turbolift. "In case you hadn't heard, there's a *war* on! Dinner tomorrow, same time?"

"Sure."

The turbolift door shut, leaving Riker to shake his head in amazement. He turned and headed back the other way, curious to see if any of his crew were still at the Bolian Bistro.

On a large moon where the atmosphere was so thin that day looked like night, Data sat in the powdery dust, watching his portable instruments. They were attached by wires to a small sensor array which he had mounted on the roof of his shuttlecraft. Doing so had helped him target the Badlands.

In his short stay on the nameless moon, Data had monitored considerable traffic in Dominion ships moving to and from the front. He kept diligent notes on the enemy ship movement, thinking that someday the information might be important. But he hadn't found the *Orb of Peace,* nor had he detected the return of the *Enterprise.* Even concentrating long-range sensors on the Badlands, he had yet to locate any ship that could possibly be the Bajoran transport or its emergency beacon.

As far as he could tell with the shifting borders, this moon was located well into Cardassian space, and he dared not go any deeper. Going farther would only endanger his mission without substantially increasing his odds of success, which were not good to begin with. Data calculated that the odds of the *Enterprise* or another Starfleet vessel finding *him* were less than one in four. He preferred not to calculate the odds of recovering Picard, Geordi, Ro, and the *Orb of Peace.*

In this instance, the android couldn't be sure that patience would have the desired effect, but he counseled himself to be patient anyway. Nevertheless,

Data had recurring thoughts about Japanese soldiers in World War II stranded at their jungle posts years after their war was over. He thought about not ever seeing his friends again, and he academically considered the grief and worry he would be experiencing if his emotion chip were turned on.

No, Data decided, war required a level head, good judgment, and that ethereal commodity known as good fortune. Unfortunately, it appeared as if he would have to wait for the good fortune part.

Chapter Eleven

THE EYE OF TALEK LOOMED before them like a hole punctured in the fabric of space, notable for an absence of stars and a golden halo of gas and dust streaming into it. The black hole was the size of a saucer section on a big starship, but almost brilliantly black, like the sun as seen in a photographic negative.

Sam turned away from the viewscreen and looked at Grof, who was beaming with pleasure. "Isn't it magnificent?" asked the Trill with a grand sweep of his arms.

"'Scary' is the word I would use," replied Sam. "I thought you said this was a *small* black hole."

"It is. If it were a large one, we couldn't have come this close."

"What's on the other side?" asked Jozarnay Woil, the Antosian material handler.

Grof laughed. "There is no other side—it's a celestial body with gravity so strong that not even light particles can escape. An old professor of mine used to call this singularity a 'gravity graveyard.' The smaller the black hole, the older it is. Over time, some material will escape through natural quantum stepping, so in ten billion years, maybe this black hole will shrink to nothing. For now, it's the only place where Corzanium can be found."

"However," said Taurik, seated at the conn, "the main reason our task is so difficult is that gravity warps space. At a distance directly proportional to the mass of the collapsed object, an event horizon occurs. In essence, the material making up the black hole exists in a different space-time continuum, which is why the gas and debris seem to disappear when they enter. This is also why we must quantum-step the Corzanium out, particle by particle."

"Have you and Horik made the adjustments to the tractor beam?" asked Grof.

The Vulcan nodded. "The metaphasic shield enhancer is on-line and has been integrated with tractor-beam operations."

"Excellent!"

Sam's mind wandered while Grof and Taurik engaged in a rapid-fire discussion of various scientific aspects of their mission. He was more concerned about the Jem'Hadar attack ship that had trailed them halfway across Cardassian space, just to make sure they attended to business and didn't try to escape. Sam was determined to disappoint them and escape anyway.

Since they didn't have any weapons and couldn't run fast enough from the small warship, the only plausible plan was to escape in the attack craft itself.

Either that, or they had to use their transporters to damage the Jem'Hadar ship—in effect, tossing a monkey wrench into their engine.

While Grof, Taurik, and Woil continued their discussion, Sam used the ops console to locate the Jem'Hadar ship. The small but deadly craft had assumed an outer orbit around the Eye of Talek at a distance that was a hundred kilometers beyond their transporter range. The trick would be to lure it closer with some kind of catastrophe or emergency. But what?

The Jem'Hadar were undoubtedly prepared for an escape attempt, and they were certainly under orders to make sure the prisoners perished rather than escaped. As prisoners and crew, they were expendable, but their cargo was not. The tanker would soon be very important to the Dominion and the war.

That meant they would have to extract a large amount of the exotic ore before they could make their move—probably by making the tanker appear to be threatened. If they weren't careful, they could all die in an accident before they had a chance to make a break for it. Reluctantly, Sam tuned back in to ongoing conversation, figuring he had better concentrate on their mission for the time being.

Jozarnay Woil still looked confused as he scratched the bun of tight black hair atop his head. "Professor, can you go through the high points one more time? Listening to you and Taurik is over my head."

Grof thrust his finger into the air. "To begin with, the Corzanium is extremely volatile until we quantum-step it beyond the event horizon and recombine it in the chamber. The sequence goes like this: Using the tractor beam, we lower the mining probe into the black hole just above the event horizon. Then we bombard the hole with tachyons, which changes the terms of probability and quantum-steps the particles, expelling them in the process. You might compare this to drilling in a typical mining operation. Now we have escaping matter which we can guide into the probe with the tractor beam. Then we beam the probe on board and put it in stasis.

"After that, Mr. Woil, you work your magic and transfer the orc from the stasis field into the recom chamber. Then it's just like any other metal, except that it has a unique resistance to gravity."

The Antosian shook his head. "No wonder it's so rare."

"We wouldn't be here if it weren't," muttered the Trill.

"Remember, we only have three probes," said Sam, trying to sound interested. "We can't afford to lose any."

"That will be plenty," countered Grof.

"When do we start?" asked Woil.

"There's no time like the present!" The Trill clapped his hands together.

"I would take issue with that," replied Taurik. "While some of us have been sleeping, others like myself have been on duty for twenty-five hours straight. Although you make the extraction process sound relatively simple, it is anything but. A mistake by any one of us could destroy this ship and all aboard."

"But we could get a start," countered Grof. "Take some readings, prepare the equipment."

"A mistake in any of those tasks would be equally disastrous," answered Taurik.

"He's right," said Sam, putting a friendly hand on Grof's beefy shoulder. "Let's get some rest. Do you think our shadow would mind?"

"Forget them," said Grof irritably. "They're merely an escort—*I* am in charge of this mission."

"But they have the weapons," Sam reminded him.

"Oh-six-hundred hours," grumbled the Trill, checking his chronometer. "No later than that."

"Okay, no later," Sam assured him. "Woil, can you tell the others?"

"Sure, Captain." The Antosian climbed down the ladder, and the last thing to disappear was the bun of black hair atop his head.

"I want this to go smoothly," warned Grof,

"And if it doesn't," said Sam, "you can harangue me about it in the next life."

The Trill shot him a look of disgust. "Remember, I'm an unjoined Trill—I only get one life." Then his glower changed into a tepid smile before he clomped down the ladder, pulling the hatch lid shut behind him.

"Is he mellowing, or is he crazy?" asked Sam rhetorically.

"I think a bit of both," answered Woil. "The question is, what are *we?*"

"We're biding our time," said Sam, biting off the wrapper of a rations bar.

"All instruments and systems back on-line," said the young man at the ops panel with obvious relief. On the viewscreen of the *Orb of Peace,* the murky but alluring dust cloud called the Badlands faded from view. The rectangular transport finally escaped into open star-studded space.

Ro Laren looked up from her conn and turned to see a dozen young pseudo-Bajorans gathered on the cramped bridge, beaming at her. The final leg through the Badlands had been extremely tense, with plasma storms rippling all around them, and most of the crew had peeked into the bridge to offer support or look for camaraderie.

Ro gave them a smile and said, "Well done."

"Well done to you," declared Captain Picard, who then leaned back in his seat at the tactical station and took a deep breath. "There aren't many people who could have made it through there."

"Nobody else was foolish enough to try," answered Ro. She stood and stretched, thinking that she was more stiff now than she had been when she was tied to a chair on the pirates' ship.

"Captain Ro, I think you deserve some relief, and some rest." Picard motioned to one of the young bystanders to take her place at the conn, and Ro didn't resist. She stepped aside and let the blond woman have her seat.

"Our course is laid in," Ro told her. "Just take her to maximum warp, when ready."

"Yes, sir."

The Bajoran turned to Picard and asked, "Any sign of enemy ships?"

"There are a few possible ships on long-range scans, but none of them are headed to intercept us. I think we're finally clear of the border patrol."

Ro let out a sharp breath. At last, they were behind enemy lines.

Picard squinted at his board and reported, "I'm picking up something that might be the artificial wormhole. It's where our friends said it was."

"Can you put it on screen?"

"Yes, but it won't be very clear. These aren't the most accurate scanners and screens."

A large, gleaming cylinder appeared on the view-screen, floating in the blackness of space. It might have been mistaken for some kind of space probe or satellite, except for the bright blips that surrounded it like fireflies swarming around a log in the woods. Ro knew these insignificant blips were in reality mighty warships, tankers, and troop transports.

"Boy, up close, it must be the eighth wonder of the universe," said the officer on ops.

"I'm glad we don't have to take it out," answered Ro.

But she wondered if this terrible threat could be resolved as easily as all that—by just destroying a mining vessel outside a black hole. Thus far, the pirates' information had proven correct, so perhaps this incredible structure did have a weak spot. Still, it was hard to imagine that the Dominion's most important project in the Alpha Quadrant would turn out to be nothing but a white elephant, useless for lack of the right building material. But now they had seen it—the artificial wormhole really existed.

"Can we take a holoscan of it for Will Riker?" she asked.

Picard smiled. "I don't believe that will be necessary. He'll be more than happy to apologize when we get back."

"I'm not sure I'll be going back," said Ro. "I'm not that fond of prison."

Picard's jaw tightened. "I'll do everything I can to get your situation squared away, I promise. In fact, I can even see about getting you your commission back."

"One step at a time. First, let's make sure there's a Starfleet to go back to." Ro started toward the rear of the bridge and paused in the doorway. "If you want to talk about it, Captain, I'll buy you a drink."

"All right. I think things are under control here." Picard rose from the tactical station and motioned to a junior officer to relieve him. The young crew members were all too eager to resume their stations now that they were away from the unpredictable dangers of the Badlands.

"We should have someone check on those fruits and vegetables in the hold," suggested Picard. "Let's dispense them to the crew before they start going bad."

"Good idea," replied Ro. "Henderson, you have the bridge. Send a detail to the cargo bay—we'll be in the mess hall."

"Yes, sir."

Ro followed Picard out, and the Bajoran felt a weary sense of satisfaction as they strolled down the corridor. She finally felt as if she had earned the trust of her unfamiliar crew. She'd had Captain Picard's trust all along, but the others didn't know her and what she could do. Now they did.

Picard stopped at the turbolift and smiled at her. "Do you mind if we ask Mr. La Forge to join us? He could probably use a break, too."

"That's fine," answered Ro. In reality, she was too weary to make much small talk, and she knew the gregarious engineer would fill in the gaps in the conversation. Also she wasn't ready to commit to going back to Starfleet, even if they would have her. Ro knew she ought to sleep, but she was too wired for that. Just a chair, a glass of juice, and nothing to do for a few minutes—that sounded manageable.

Picard tapped his comm badge. "Boothby to La Forge: can you meet us in the mess hall?"

"Sure," answered the engineer. "Let me assign my relief, and I'll be right there. Out."

Picard and Ro wended their way down a spiral staircase to the lower level, then strolled along a deserted corridor.

"I was serious about what I said," began Picard, "about getting you back into Starfleet."

"I know you were," answered the Bajoran, "and I appreciate it. But if my people really are neutral in the war, perhaps I should be, too. That would be a change of pace for me—I'm always partisan."

"I know," said Picard with a smile. "Well, you have our gratitude. Without you, we wouldn't have known about the Dominion's plans until it was too late. Apparently we're here in time to stop them."

Ro led the way into the mess hall. "Let's hope so."

A moment later, they sat down in a small, austere dining room, decorated in tasteful beige colors and subdued lighting. All the rest of the young crew were either working or taking their sleep shift.

"What would you like to do when this is over?" asked Picard. "Providing it ends the way we hope it will."

"Maybe I'll help refugees. There are bound to be millions of them." She held up her hand, cutting him off, she hoped not too abruptly. "I know, there are positions like that in Starfleet, but I have a hard time thinking that far ahead. Whenever I make plans to have a normal life, things go haywire."

"I know that feeling," replied the captain wistfully. "You think you can escape from the pressures, but they always come after you."

La Forge strolled jauntily through the door, still looking rather roguish with his earring, nose ridges, and pilot's goggles. "Hello, Captain Picard, Captain Ro," he said cheerfully, stopping at the food replicator. "What's your pleasure?"

"Hello, Geordi," said Picard with an uncharacteristic yawn. "Tea, Earl Grey, hot."

"Knowing that replicator, I think you might have to settle for Bajoran tea," said Ro. "I'll have the juice cocktail."

La Forge repeated their orders a few times into the recalcitrant replicator until it was finally able to produce their beverages. He delivered their drinks to the table, then went back to get his glass of milk.

"So, is it clear sailing from here?" asked the engineer, pulling up a chair.

"Theoretically," answered Picard. "If we can delay them by destroying the shipment of Corzanium—and we can get back to our lines and tell everyone what we've seen—maybe we can mount an attack against this thing. A few distractions here and there along the line, and a sizable attack force could slip through to the Badlands. At least we found the wormhole before it's operational."

"I wouldn't mind playing with a verteron collider that huge," said La Forge wistfully. "It's really too bad that we've got to destroy it, or at least make sure it never works. A completely stable artificial wormhole that we have total control over—it sounds like a dream come true."

"Or a nightmare, depending on which side you're on," muttered Picard. He took a sip of tea.

The Bajoran's comm badge beeped, and she answered, "Ro here."

"This is Ensign Owlswing outside the cargo bay," responded a female voice. "Henderson sent us down to check on those vegetables and fruits in the hold, but something's wrong with the cargo-bay hatch. We can't get it open—it's locked and won't respond to the controls."

Ro started to rise wearily from her seat. "We can override the lock, take it off the computer, and open it manually."

"I know, sir," said Owlswing, "I just wanted your permission to try it."

Ro sunk back into her seat and saw Picard smiling at her. "Yes, go ahead. Ro out."

"See, it really is your ship," said Picard, "and your crew."

"For a young crew, they've been relatively calm and levelheaded," conceded Ro. "Let's hope they stay that way, because we're not done yet."

Picard sat forward and folded his hands in front of him. "That's true, and we've got to decide how we're going to destroy this mining vessel with our limited firepower."

"If they're working in the vicinity of a black hole," offered Geordi, "it should be fairly simple to cause them to have an accident and get sucked inside. Maybe it's something we can do from a distance, with a minimum of risk."

From somewhere in the ship, they heard a muffled

shout. Picard turned around at looked at the open door and the empty corridor beyond. "What was that?"

Geordi shook his head. "I think it was just the welds groaning. No offense, Ro, but this ship is kind of a bucket of bolts."

"No offense taken," answered Ro. "We're all aboard the *Orb of Peace* because we didn't have a lot of choice."

Suddenly, they heard frantic footsteps on the spiral ladder, followed by a loud shout. A young female officer paused in the doorway, a stricken look on her face, as a beam of red light shot from behind her and drilled into her back. As she stood transfixed in the doorway, her eyes wide with horror, a glowing red splotch appeared on her chest, and she collapsed in a heap on the deck, her eyes staring straight upward.

Picard jumped instantly to his feet and rushed for the door as another young officer ran past. He, too, was consumed in the beam of a sloppy shot, which scattered sparks off the bulkhead. Before Picard could reach the wounded man, the doors slid shut on their own, blocking out the scene of carnage in the hallway. The captain started to pound on the wall panel to open the portal when caution got the better of him. They didn't have a weapon among them, and to rush into the line of fire was foolish, no matter what the horror.

Ro slapped her comm badge. "Captain to bridge! What's going on?"

A harried voice came on, "Intruder alert! Intruder on the bridge . . . aaggh!" His voice dissolved into a strangled scream.

Ro looked at Geordi, who ripped his goggles off and

stared at her with alarmed, pale eyes. He tapped his comm badge. "La Forge to Engineering—respond! Engineering, come in!" No one answered his frantic call.

"It doesn't mean they're dead because they didn't answer," said Ro. "Communications may be down."

"Then again," said Picard grimly, "if they hit the bridge and Engineering on this ship, they've hit it all."

The *Orb of Peace* was indeed a tiny ship, which a small, determined party of armed intruders could capture from stem to stern in a matter of seconds. But who? Where had they come from? Ro didn't want to think that someone on their own crew could have mutinied against them, but she read that very thought in Picard's face.

Only a few seconds had passed since the attack started, but it was now deathly quiet on the transport. The mess hall was about the most useless place to be during an emergency, as it contained no weapons, no equipment, and no computer terminals, except for the food replicator. There was also no escape, except for the door that Picard stood ready to open. Or perhaps he intended to keep it shut, in case the intruders tried to break in.

"I've got to go out there," said the captain.

"We'll all go," offered La Forge.

"No. You two stay in hiding. If worse comes to worse, you may have to take back the ship."

"Sir, it's *my* ship," said Ro, brushing past the captain. "It's my place to see what's going on."

He looked as if he wanted to argue with her, then thought better of it. "I'll give you a few seconds' lead, then I'm going to see if they found the weapons storage in the dormitory. Geordi, we have to keep you in reserve. You've got the mess hall—see what you can do with it."

"Yes, sir."

"Let's hope it's not what we think it is," muttered the Bajoran as she slapped the panel and opened the door.

Ro stepped out into the corridor to see three dead bodies. The woman was slumped in front of the door, the man was crumpled against a bulkhead a few meters away, and another officer was sprawled across the top of the spiral staircase. Whoever the intruders were, they shot to kill.

She walked cautiously toward the stairs, knowing that she had to go to the bridge to find out who was behind this massacre. On the deck was a lump of silvery metal, which Ro recognized as one of their Bajoran phasers, melted by a blast from the intruders' weapon.

After stopping to remove her shoes, she started up the stairs in her stocking feet, hopeful not to unduly surprise whoever was on the bridge—whoever was now in command of her ship. Ro didn't enjoy walking into death, but she and death were old friends by this time. He had brushed awfully close to her lately, especially when he took Derek. Ro didn't fear death, but she was awfully angry about the way he toyed with her, and the way he exulted in this insane war.

After climbing the staircase, she found another dead body, this one blasted almost in two by beamed weapons. The destruction was so horrible that Ro wanted to look away, but she had to search the body for weapons, on the off chance that the assailants had missed collecting them.

After searching unsuccessfully for a handheld phaser, Ro strode down the corridor toward the open door to the bridge. She could hear muffled voices. On the bulkhead walls, storage cabinets had been pulled open and rifled through, and a pile of bandages lay strewn across the hallway. Another body—this one Henderson's—blocked the doorway. His petrified face gazed up at her, no longer looking so arrogant.

Ro steeled herself for an odious job. In essence, she was poised to surrender her ship—her first command—to whomever was in charge of the bridge. Considering the ruthlessness of the attack, she would probably join her shipmates in death, but she had to meet the new masters of the *Orb of Peace* first. She had lost the ship in the blink of an eye, while she had been relaxing, negligent in her duties. That was the most galling part.

Captain Picard jumped up from a crouch and dashed across the expanse of the dormitory room, where several score of hammocks hung from the ceiling like old moss. It was dark, and he dared not turn on any lights for fear of being spotted. As he neared the last row of hammocks, he stumbled over the dead body of a young ensign. By her loose clothing, he concluded that she had been ruthlessly cut down while she slept.

The war and a life fraught with danger had inured him somewhat to death, but it was still difficult to accept when the victim was a young person with so many years ahead of her. To see her cut down unexpectedly, for no reason, was a sinful waste. Even so, thought Picard, he had been willing to kill this same young woman instead of letting her be taken prisoner by the Dominion. He had killed and was prepared to do it again.

He tried to concentrate on the task at hand. Why had someone wanted this ordinary little ship so badly they had to kill for it? Their assailants seemed to know their way around the ship fairly well; they knew exactly where to strike. So Picard wasn't optimistic about finding their cache of hand phasers intact as he reached the rear bulkhead in the dormitory.

Sure enough, the cabinet had been stripped of its weapons. He heard a groan, and he whirled around to see a lump in the corner, twitching, groping for him. "Help me!" rasped the figure.

Picard ran to the wounded man and tried not to gape at his wretched condition. "I'm right here," he told the dying man. "Please stop trying to talk. Save your strength."

The man gripped Picard's shoulder, and the captain could feel him shivering, growing weaker. Both of them were obscured by shadows. "No warning," croaked the officer.

"Who was it?" asked Picard as he tried to straighten the man's limbs and make him comfortable.

"Romulans!" wheezed the officer with a violent shudder. Suddenly his shivering and twitching stopped, and he went limp in the captain's arms.

"Rest in peace," whispered the captain, setting the man gently onto the deck. His jaw set determinedly, Picard rose to his feet and looked around the dormitory for any object he could use as a weapon. He spotted a toolbox and quickly opened it. Among the tools was a heavy spanner, which he hefted in his hand with grim satisfaction.

What his plan was, Picard didn't yet know. He was in reaction mode, thinking of other ships, other times when intruders had taken over and forced him into guerrilla warfare on his own decks. Every time, his foe had been so ruthless as to leave him no choice.

Picard pounded the spanner into the palm of his hand, jumped up, and dashed back through the dormitory. It was deserted except for the ghosts.

Ro paused outside the door of the bridge. Still in her stocking feet, she had approached the hijackers unseen and unheard, and she could see them hovering over the consoles, oblivious of the butchered bodies that littered the deck. The streaked image on the viewscreen led her to believe that they were still in warp drive, probably still on course for the Eye of Talek.

She saw two of the victors and heard the voice of a third, all men and dressed in civilian clothing—not the Bajoran uniforms of her crew. At least it hadn't been a mutiny. To know so much about the ship, these intruders had to be connected to the pirates. Maybe they had boarded during the search of the ship, while she had been drugged. Chuckling and congratulating each other, they sounded elated over the success of their murderous assault.

At that moment, when she had intended to surrender to them, Ro knew she couldn't do it. Her fury at losing her ship and her instincts for survival forced her to back slowly away from the door. Suddenly she heard angry voices, and one of the intruders turned around and strode toward her. Although his uniform was unfamiliar, she identified his straight black hair and imperious bearing.

A Romulan!

He stared at her, scowled, and reached for a Klingon disruptor in his belt. Ro darted down the hall and
vaulted over a body and into the spiral staircase. She
plunged several steps as a disruptor beam vaporized
the hand railing, scattering droplets of molten metal
down on her.

Chapter Twelve

Ro CHARGED DOWN THE STAIRS, listening to the shouts and footsteps of her pursuer. She had no intent but to run like hell, which she did as soon as she hit the lower deck. Glancing behind her, Ro didn't see the first body sprawled across the corridor, and she stumbled over it. She crashed to the deck just as heavy footsteps bounded onto the deck behind her.

"Need help?" shouted a distant voice from above.

"No, no!" answered the grinning Romulan as he leveled his disruptor at Ro. "I've got matters in control."

Expecting to be vaporized, Ro flinched, and she nearly missed seeing Captain Picard spring from behind the staircase and hit the Romulan across the back of his skull. His features contorted for a second before he collapsed onto the deck, sending the disruptor skittering across the floor toward Ro. She instantly pounced upon the weapon and aimed it at the top of the staircase, waiting for more of them to descend.

Picard searched the fallen Romulan but found nothing worth keeping. He motioned to Ro, and she picked herself up and scurried over. Picard pointed to the body and back down the corridor; then he gripped the prisoner's closest armpit. Keeping her weapon aimed at the Romulan, Ro gripped the other armpit, and together they dragged their prisoner back down the corridor toward the mess hall.

Seeing the bodies of their comrades was no easier this time, but she struggled on, helping Picard drag the unconscious Romulan to the door of the dining hall. When the door didn't open, Picard pushed the panel beside it. When that failed, he rapped on the door.

"Geordi! It's us!"

The door slid open, and they dragged the Romulan inside, as Ro stole a glance down the corridor. The other two were still above deck, thinking their friend was in control.

La Forge gaped at them. "You caught a Romulan?"

"Yes," answered Picard breathlessly. "I see you have the door rigged?"

"For now," answered La Forge, gingerly sticking a fork back into the open wall compartment and making an adjustment. "These aren't heavy-duty doors— they could bust through fairly easily. How many are there?"

"Three," answered Ro. "Him and two others, all Romulans."

"And there were Romulans in that bunch of pirates who boarded us," recalled Geordi. "I guess they had a look around and liked what they saw."

Picard's jaw tightened. "We've got a weapon, and we've lowered the odds. But I really don't want to try a direct assault on the bridge."

Their prisoner groaned and began to move his limbs. Ro looked at the disruptor and scowled. "This is the cheap model, the one with no stun setting."

"Don't hesitate to kill him if necessary," ordered Picard. "Mr. La Forge, have we got anything to tie him up?"

The engineer reached into the open panel and yanked out several long strands of electrical wiring, which he tossed to Picard. "Use this, because I've disabled the door's circuitry."

When the Romulan groaned some more and tried to open his eyes, Ro's finger encircled the trigger of the disruptor and aimed the weapon at his chest. La Forge jumped down and helped Picard tie the captive's wrists together. They were working on his feet when he came to and gaped at them with startling clarity.

"What?" he gasped. "What is—"

"Quiet," ordered Picard. "Kill him if he breathes another word."

"With pleasure," answered Ro.

The Romulan's darting eyes took in Picard's stern visage, then the disruptor in Ro's hands, and finally the intense look on Ro's face. She didn't need to do anything to put the fear into him, because her determination to kill him was etched into her gaunt features. He stopped his movements and stared at them, wide-eyed.

"Why did you kill so many of us?" demanded Picard.

"We wanted your ship," said the Romulan evenly. "Would you have given it to us?"

"Why did you want *this* ship?" he pressed the captive.

"It was the only one which presented itself to us." The Romulan winced as he shifted position. "You don't know what it was like, serving under Rolf and Shek! We were virtual *prisoners*—allowed none of the luxuries they got. And all the things we were forced to do—well, we learned how to take over a ship from *them.*"

"Did they have anything to do with this?" asked Picard.

"No, Rolf would torture and kill us, if he knew. We had been talking about deserting, if we could get a ship. After we returned from searching your vessel, we put our plan into action. We're Romulans. We were born to rule, not serve."

"We're recapturing this ship," vowed Picard.

"There's no need for bloodshed," offered the Romulan, struggling against his bonds. "Turn me loose. Let me talk to them."

Ro glanced at Picard and La Forge, and it was obvious from their grim expressions that the Romulan was not getting his freedom any time soon.

"On your feet," ordered Picard.

"You're going to let me go?" asked the Romulan in amazement.

"Yes, and you're going to march straight to the bridge. Only I'll be right behind you, with the disruptor in your back."

When the Romulan struggled to stand up, La Forge tried to help him. With a sullen expression, he bumped Geordi with his shoulder and knocked him away. "I can do it!" snarled the Romulan. He strode resolutely toward the door, staring straight ahead.

Something is wrong, thought Ro. None of this seemed right to her—not the hijacking, not the senseless killings, not the piratical Romulans.

"Wait a minute," she said, moving toward to the prisoner with the disruptor leveled at his stomach. "What are you doing here—in Cardassian space— with a war going on?"

It was the same question she had been asked a day earlier, and like her, the Romulan did not have a satisfactory answer. He looked evasive as he replied, "We were young and foolish, out for adventure."

"They're Romulan spies," concluded Ro. "Perhaps they're even here for the same reason we're here."

Picard and La Forge glanced at each other, while the puzzled Romulan turned abruptly to Ro. "I thought you were Bajoran merchants."

"No," answered Ro with a clenched jaw. "You murdered a dozen Starfleet officers who were disguised to *look* like Bajorans. Now I'll ask again: Why are you here?"

The Romulan licked his lips, as if tasting the truth for the first time in his life. "We may be neutral in this war, but it's only natural to gather intelligence."

La Forge frowned. "And what better way to see what's happening than to enlist on a Ferengi ship that prowls back and forth across the lines. So what have you found out?"

The Romulan smirked. "I know you're losing the war, but I don't suppose that's news."

"Hakron!" shouted a voice that was distant, but not distant enough.

When the Romulan looked as if he wanted to respond, Ro jabbed him sharply in the ribs with the disruptor and glared at him. "What else?"

"Let's make a deal," he whispered. "Let me talk to my comrades. The chances are, we both want the same thing."

"You wanted our ship," said Ro testily. "Why? What do you know about the Dominion's artificial wormhole?"

"Hakron!" shouted the voice, sounding closer.

"You haven't got a chance," said Hakron smugly.

Picard promptly grabbed their captive and shoved him toward the door. "Be quiet and don't say a word." He nodded to La Forge, who went to the doctored door panel and awaited his orders. Then he held out his hand to Ro, who gave him the disruptor.

Picard grabbed the Romulan by his collar and pressed the barrel of the weapon against his neck. "We're going out. Tell them to hold their fire. Don't try to get away, or you're dead. Understand?"

The Romulan nodded languorously.

The captain looked at Ro. "Can you be the eyes in the back of my head?"

"Yes, sir."

Picard nodded to La Forge, and the engineer applied his fork to the circuitry. With a jolt, the door slid open, and the captain pushed his captive out ahead of him. Ro immediately peered around the edge of the door, looking in the direction where Picard's back was turned. To her relief, she didn't see anything but a corridor littered with bodies.

Her relief was short-lived, because Hakron suddenly whirled around with his foot and caught Picard in the knee. The captain started to fall, but he kept his grip on the Romulan's collar and dragged his prisoner to the deck with him.

"T'ar'Fe:" cursed the Romulan.

At the end of the corridor, his confederate leaped out of the dormitory, saw them, and aimed his weapon. Picard hoisted the Romulan to his knees and ducked behind his torso just as a red disruptor beam streaked down the length of the hallway.

"No!" screamed Hakron as the beam struck him in the chest, setting it aglow. Using the slumping Romulan as cover, Picard fired his own disruptor. The deadly beam pulsed down the corridor and sliced his foe's left arm off at the shoulder. His screams echoed throughout the ship as he staggered for cover inside the dormitory.

Ro suddenly realized that she was neglecting her duty by watching the melee, so she turned to look at the spiral staircase. When she saw the body on the top step move slightly, she shouted, "Watch out!"

Picard whirled around to shoot blindly at the top of the stairs. The disruptor beam blew the corpse off the steps and forced their adversary to retreat; they heard his scurrying footsteps. Now they were in the difficult position of having to defend both ends of the corridor, although it wasn't certain that the Romulan on their level could still mount an attack. Picard motioned to Ro and La Forge to follow him as he led the way toward the dormitory.

"Captain," whispered La Forge, "if I could get up one level to the transporter room, I could fix the guy on the bridge—without risking more disruptor fire."

Picard stopped to consider the problem. "But the only way up is that staircase."

"He might be changing course, taking us into

Romulan space," added Ro. "We've got to get the bridge under control."

The captain nodded. "Let me see if we have another weapon." He moved cautiously down the hallway and inspected the deck in front of the dormitory door, which was closed. Ro could see the severed arm, but apparently their foe hadn't dropped his weapon.

Looking sickened by the violence, the captain returned to his comrades. "All right, I'll cover the stairs and the door to the bridge. Mr. La Forge, you go to the transporter room."

"What are you going to do, beam him into space?" asked Ro.

"Is that a problem?"

"Not under these circumstances," she replied without hesitation. She knew that Picard cringed at the thought of fighting to the death, but the enemy hadn't left them much choice. With Ro keeping an eye on their rear, they began moving toward the spiral staircase.

Startling them, a voice crackled over the ship's intercom. "To those who are resisting—you must stop! We have control of the ship. You must *surrender!* We won't harm you."

Picard never stopped moving, and he was already halfway up the stairs, with La Forge behind him and Ro bringing up the rear. She assumed that if he was speaking to them on the ship's comm, he had to be on the bridge, probably with the door shut. When they reached the top of the stairs, she found her assumption to be true, and Picard covered them while La Forge and Ro dashed down the corridor to the safety of the transporter room.

Ro watched the door while La Forge rushed to the

transporter controls. A moment later, Picard joined them, as a voice continued to plead over the intercom:

"Lay your weapons down, and we will talk. We are reasonable people, and we have all your weapons. I have control of the bridge. You *must* deal with me!"

"Not necessarily," said La Forge as he skillfully plied the transporter console. "I've locked on to the only life sign on the bridge. That's an outer bulkhead behind the transporter. Ro, will you pace it off for me?"

"Sure." She leaped upon the raised platform and quickly paced off the rough distance to the wall behind it. "Five meters," she reported.

"All right," said La Forge with a sigh. "Do we give him a chance to surrender?"

"No!" snapped Ro. "They didn't give our crew a chance."

Keeping watch at the door with his disruptor, Picard shook his head concurring with Ro's assessment. "Energize."

La Forge slid an old-fashioned lever forward, and a almost melodic noise sounded in the air. But nothing appeared on the transporter platform.

"It's done," said La Forge heavily. "What about the one in the dormitory?"

"No," answered Picard, "he's probably in shock. We should be able to deal with him. All of our weapons must be on the bridge—let's go get them."

Cautiously, they made their way down the corridor, following Picard and his disruptor. The small bridge of the *Orb of Peace,* which usually looked so serene, now looked like a chamber of horrors. There were dead bodies everywhere, and an impressive pile of weapons in front of the viewscreen. Ro and La Forge each grabbed a Bajoran hand phaser, and Ro checked the readings on the conn.

"We're still on course to the black hole," she reported. "Still at warp three."

"I want to question the last Romulan," said Picard, "if he's still alive."

Once again, they wound their way down the spiral staircase, past the familiar dead bodies. When they reached the dormitory, Picard motioned them away from the door as he pressed the wall panel. When the door slid open, they flung themselves out of the way, expecting fire to erupt from the room—but none came. Cautiously Picard reached around the edge of the door and felt for the panel that would turn on the lights. When he found it, the shadowy chambers were suddenly illuminated by cheerful lighting.

Once again, they pinned themselves against the bulkhead in the corridor, expecting enemy fire to pulse through the doorway. Picard picked up a piece of nearby battle debris. He tossed the debris into the room, and it hit the deck with a loud clunk.

"Unnh!" groaned a voice with surprise, as if they had awakened him from a nap. Suddenly wild disruptor fire streaked out the door and raked the opposite bulkhead.

"Hold your fire!" shouted Picard, backing away from the door. "Your confederates are dead, and we've recaptured the ship! If you throw your weapon toward the door, we'll come in and give you medical attention."

The scattered beams stopped, and they waited in tense silence, punctuated only by their own rapid breathing. Finally, there came a skittering sound as a disruptor bounced across the deck and out the doorway. Ro instantly scooped it up.

"Mr. La Forge, see if you can find a med kit," ordered the captain. "Let's go."

Still keeping his weapon leveled in front of him, Picard led the way into the hammock-filled dormitory. Ro tried to ignore the sight of more young officers, pointlessly slain in the cowardly attack; she concentrated on searching the room for the wounded Romulan.

"Here!" called Picard.

She caught up with the captain as he knelt down beside a shivering humanoid who was clutching the burned stump of his arm. Sweat and grime smeared his once-proud face, and he blinked at them with terror and shock.

"La Forge!" called Ro.

"Coming!" The engineer reached them a moment later. He popped open a white case and took out a hypospray.

After they injected the hypo into the Romulan's neck, he calmed down considerably and stopped shivering. Ro figured that they had only a few seconds before he lost consciousness . . . probably forever.

She bent over him, her face inches away from his. "The Dominion is building an artificial wormhole. What do you know about it?"

"Must see if it works—" he answered dazedly.

"Why?" He was losing consciousness, and she had to shake him to get his attention. "Why?"

"If it works," he rasped, "we become their allies . . . we join the Dominion."

Then he was out, unconscious but still breathing roughly. She looked gravely at Picard and La Forge.

224

None of them needed to say what it would mean if the Romulan Star Empire turned against them, too. They would be caught in a vise.

"It's not going to work," vowed Picard. "It's never going to work." He slumped back on his haunches, weary and shell-shocked. The raw struggle for survival had been won, leaving Ro with a sense of failure and a dread of the killing to come.

His fingers twitchy and nervous, Sam Lavelle sat at the conn of the *Tag Garwal,* waiting for his crewmates to finish their last-minute preparations. In the hold was a mining probe that would soon be dangled over a black hole. He didn't know why he was so nervous, because theoretically he had the easiest job of the lot of them—to simply maintain their position. Of course, he was captain as well as helmsman, and he knew it would be up to him to take over in an emergency. At the same time, he had to look out for providential opportunities to escape.

He glanced at the viewscreen, knowing it was the Eye of Talek that made him nervous. Although small as black holes went, it looked like a stealth moon—an alien world within the endless void. In some strange way, it made space seem vulnerable. Although Grof had said that matter escaped from it, the flow of dust, debris, and gas seemed to be all one way.

"Beautiful, isn't it?" said Grof, settling into the seat at the ops console.

"It's still scary to me," answered Sam. "Maybe that's because I don't trust it."

"When the Cardassians discovered it," said Grof, "they only had telescopes, no space travel, and they didn't know what it was. But they had a myth about a large monster with one eye which consumed everything it saw. That was Talek."

"That makes me feel so much better," murmured Sam. "I take it your main job is to shoot the tachyons?"

"That, and to monitor everything that goes on. I'd like to observe *you*, for instance, and learn your job."

"I'm sure you would," Sam replied snidely.

"In a positive sense," said the Trill defensively. "We have a small crew, so the more efficiently we can relieve each other, the better off we'll be."

"Just do your job," ordered Sam, "and let everybody else worry about theirs." In truth, he would rather have had Taurik on the bridge with him, but the consensus was that Taurik was needed at the airlock with the mining probe, which was too heavy for anyone else to lift. Then Taurik would assist the material handlers in the transporter room and the recombination chambers.

Footsteps on the ladder made Sam jump, and he whirled around to see Tamla Horik, the tractor-beam specialist, emerge from the hatch. The Deltan looked contented and relaxed these days, just glad to be free. This was Sam's first command, he thought to himself, and he couldn't even enjoy it.

The Deltan took her seat at the tactical station and reported, "The others are all set. Commence when ready."

"Thank you," said Grof testily. He punched the communications panel, and his voice echoed throughout the ship. "Crew of the *Tag Garwal*, we are ready to begin our historic mission. Release the mining probe."

Sam shook his head at the pomposity of the Trill.

He talked as if he were running the operation when, in reality, the only one in charge was the Jem'Hadar attack ship. It continued to scrutinize from afar, with the power to destroy them at any second.

Knowing he had to forget about them and concentrate on the job, Sam put the mining probe on the viewscreen. The small unmanned craft looked ungainly with its array of robotic arms, sensors, and reflector dishes. And it looked helpless as it cruised inexorably toward the deep emptiness of the Eye of Talek.

Sam tried not to think how much was riding on all this Cardassian equipment, but he knew that Grof, Taurik, and the others had checked every piece a dozen times. He had to rely on their judgment about the equipment, as they relied on his about the ship.

"Tractor beam," ordered Grof.

"Tractor beam on," replied the Deltan at the tactical station.

The escaping probe was engulfed in an invisible beam that registered only on their instrument panels. Nevertheless, the probe now had a leash which, theoretically, would keep it from plunging into the black hole.

"Distance to event horizon: three hundred kilometers," reported Horik. "Tractor beam holding steady."

"Don't let it cross that horizon," warned Grof.

"Or what will happen?" asked Sam.

"If the tractor beam held, we could retrieve it," answered the Trill, "but that's a big 'if.' And I don't know what kind of shape it would be in. More than likely, we'd be down to two probes."

"Two hundred kilometers," said the Deltan. "I'm slowing speed to one-quarter impulse."

"It's looking good," said Grof, his eyes intent upon his readouts.

Sam looked at his own readouts to make sure they hadn't drifted in their orbit, which was matched to the slight rotation of the black hole. It seemed odd to be orbiting nothing, but this nothing had a lot of gravity for its size.

"One hundred kilometers," reported Horik. "Thrusters stopped. We're now coasting into position one-half kilometer in front of the event horizon."

"We're sure about those calculations, are't we?" asked Grof, sounding nervous for the first time.

"Yes," answered the Deltan, "unless this black hole doesn't obey the known laws of physics, which is always possible with a singularity."

Sam didn't like the way Grof gnawed on his lower lip as the probe completed its final approach to the black hole. He tried not to think about the incredible gravitational pull on the small probe, counteracted only by their souped-up tractor beam. Sam increased the magnification on the viewscreen to get a better look at the probe . . . perhaps the last look at it.

"Approaching one kilometer," said the calm, contented Deltan. She plied her console. "All right, it's stopped."

The three of them stared at the viewscreen, half-expecting the awkward probe to vanish forever into the gaping blackness. But the probe was stopped, hanging on the lip of the abyss.

Grof let out a loud sigh, and then he rubbed his hands together, ready for his part in the drama. First he made a shipwide announcement. "Attention, crew: the probe is in place. I'm bombarding the black hole with tachyons—stand by tractor beam, remote control, and transporter room."

Sam hoped that soon they would get proficient enough at this operation to do it without Grof's melodramatics; but for the moment, he was glad that someone was calling every shot. On the viewscreen, they watched an impossibly long strand of tachyons stretch from their ship, past the probe, into the blackness of the singularity. Sam knew this was a crucial step, the one that would actually quantum-step the particles and force them outward. The tractor beam would capture and guide them into the probe.

"Extend tractor beam," ordered Grof.

"Extending," said the Deltan.

"Start extraction."

Leni Shonsui's voice came over the comm. "Extraction in progress."

Again there was a tense silence as they watched the timers and their readouts. Sam noticed that some force was slightly altering their orbit, and he compensated without comment. There would be time later to point this out to the others and make a correction for the next shot. Right now, they were all absorbed in their own tasks.

"Load full!" announced Shonsui's voice. "Let's reel it in."

Now everyone breathed a sigh of relief, although they weren't out of the woods yet. Sam knew that they had to perfectly coordinate cutting the tractor beam at the same moment that they transported the probe back to the ship.

Grof held up his finger. "Transport on my mark. Three, two, one . . . mark!"

The Deltan punched her board. They waited for confirmation.

"Masserelli here," came a voice from below. "We've got her, and the stasis field is holding!"

"At last." Grof slumped back in his seat and turned apologetically toward Sam. "I've got to go down and see it."

"Go ahead. I wouldn't mind seeing the next step myself." Sam didn't mention it, but the ship was in extreme danger at this point, with a highly volatile material in stasis.

"You two go on," said Horik at her tactical station. "I can watch things here."

With Grof eagerly leading the way, they tromped down the ladder to the lower level and dashed along the corridor to the transporter room. The glow of the stasis field in the center of the transporter pad captured their attention and forced them to halt in the doorway. Woil, Shonsui, and Masserelli were wearing protective gear that covered them from head to foot, and Sam and Grof sunk back from the danger.

Jozarnay Woil grabbed a flexible tube that hung from a mass of pipes in the ceiling and checked its fittings. As if he did this every day of the week, he calmly walked up to the glowing stasis field, stuck the tube in, and clamped it to the elevated mining probe. Woil stepped back, motioning to Enrique Masserelli, who manipulated the stasis field and the probe with a handheld remote. Shonsui stood at the transporter console, keeping a close watch on an array of readouts. Soon the tube was bulging as the contents of the probe were being evacuated to the recom chambers in the hold.

Grof nudged Sam with an elbow. "Come on."

The human followed the Trill to the stern of the ship. From there, large double doors opened into the two-story-high cargo hold. As an antimatter tanker, the *Tag Garwal*'s hold was by far her most impressive feature. Antimatter was the most volatile cargo in the galaxy, and it had to be stored in special forcefield containers and transported in special conduits, which snaked all over the ceiling and walls of the hold.

The upright containers looked like massive African drums. Having been used strictly for storage, now their forcefields were being used to recombine particles that had, until a few moments ago, existed in another space-time continuum. Despite Sam's misgivings, it was exciting to think that they could fill these drums with material dredged from a black hole.

They heard footsteps, and they turned to see Enrique walking toward them with his headgear and a tricorder in his hands, and a big grin on his face. "How does it look?"

"Like Corzanium!" declared Grof. "Which one is it in?"

Enrique muscled past them in his bulky suit and approached the first upright container. He opened a tricorder and took readings. "Right here. It's all going as planned."

Suddenly there came a loud crashing sound from directly behind them—in the transporter room. Big man though he was, Grof whirled around like a dancer and bolted down the corridor. Sam and Enrique jogged after him.

When they reached the transporter room, they were all horrified to see the mining probe lying on the transporter pad, many of its external components broken and smashed. No one needed to ask what had fallen over.

"What happened?" roared Grof, shaking his fists.

Shonsui looked at Woil, and the Antosian shrugged. "When I cut the stasis field, then it . . . I don't know."

"Cutting the stasis field had nothing to do with it," said Chief Shonsui on the transporter controls. "I take full blame. I didn't have it adjusted for the correct weight of the empty probe, which is something I wouldn't have to do with a Federation transporter. I mean, you don't expect to empty a probe and have it weigh *more.*"

"You idiot! Up to this point, it was going *perfectly!*" Grof stomped around like a little boy denied his dessert at suppertime.

Sam knew he should keep his mouth shut, but he couldn't help himself. "I wouldn't say it was perfect. I had to compensate to hold our position, and *that* wasn't in any of the models."

Now the Trill glared at him. "And you didn't say anything? Imbeciles! I'm surrounded by *imbeciles!*" Grof stormed out of the transporter room, and they could hear him shouting all the way down the corridor.

Sam looked at his crew and shook his head. "I'm personally proud of you that you managed to pull that off so well. In one day, we've collected more Corzanium than anybody else in two quadrants, and that's using Cardassian equipment, with a *gun* pointed at our heads! Screw that old goat."

"Yeah, so we had a few minor glitches," said Enrique. "That's to be expected." Still, there was no way to look at the damaged probe without thinking they had made a grave error—one that might cost them their lives.

Taurik appeared in the doorway, looking nonplussed by the mess on the transporter pad. "I will prepare another probe."

As the Vulcan hurried off, Sam sank against the bulkhead. He was disheartened by the realization that they would have to go through that tense procedure again and again until they had collected a hoard of Corzanium. He looked around and could tell by the stark faces that his crew knew the truth: they were still slaves, even with a ship at their disposal. This tanker was nothing but a floating jail, with a lunatic as the jailer.

"Get another probe out there," said Sam. "But don't worry, we're getting out."

Chapter Thirteen

RO LAREN, GEORDI LA FORGE, AND JEAN-LUC PICARD stood in the transporter room of the *Orb of Peace*, with La Forge at the transporter controls. The room's nonthreatening, welcoming atmosphere was severely tested by the sight of four bodies piled like firewood on the transporter pad. Picard tried not to think of the other three piles of corpses which had lain there in the last hour. Very badly, he wanted to wash his hands, but he wasn't done yet.

This pile of bodies was a mixture of two of his crew and two dead Romulans. Whether they would appreciate the burial rites, he didn't know. The captain's face drew tight as he performed his least favorite duty.

"We commit these bodies of our comrades—and our enemies—to the void of space, to which they dedicated their lives. I only wish they could have experienced more of the joyful, awe-inspiring aspect of space exploration, rather than the senseless destruction of war. But no matter how advanced the races of the galaxy, we still suffer from greed and bloodlust."

The captain sighed, bereft of words to explain what had happened to these young people—and so many other young people who were dying at that very moment in the far-flung theater of war. He knew why they fought, and what they fought to preserve, but excuses for killing were beyond Picard at that moment.

"May their beliefs in the afterlife be fulfilled," concluded the captain.

He nodded to La Forge, who turned the pile of corpses into a glittering funeral pyre for a few brief seconds until they disappeared entirely.

Picard strode to the door. "I wish there were time to reflect and mourn, but there's not. Since there's only three of us, we have to conserve our resources. One of us must be sleeping while the other two are on duty—one in the engine room and one on the bridge."

As they followed the captain down the corridor, Ro asked, "What about the one-armed Romulan?"

Picard stopped to consider the question. Against all odds, their prisoner hadn't died . . . yet. When it came to first aid, none of them were Beverly Crusher, but they had apparently done a satisfactory job of patching him up. It helped that he was a fit, young Romulan. But if he kept recovering, he would soon become a problem.

"Lock him in the captain's quarters," said Picard.

"Whoever is stationed in Engineering will pay periodic visits and keep him sedated."

"I volunteer—" began Ro.

"No," answered Picard with a smile. "You steered us through the Badlands, and you must be exhausted. I'll take the bridge, La Forge Engineering, and Ro—you get the bunk. And that's an order."

"Aye, Captain," she answered with weary resignation. "Do you think we can do this by ourselves?"

"We have to," said Picard with determination. "There's no one else."

Collecting three more loads of Corzanium without incident had mollified Enrak Grof somewhat. The Trill sat in the mess hall, playing with his newest toy, a fist-sized chunk of Corzanium, while Sam drank a cup of coffee. Although Grof hadn't liked it, he had agreed to give them a rest break for two hours. Everyone needed it.

Grof hefted his golden rock, then removed his hand, letting it float in the air. "This is amazing stuff," he told Sam. "If we had enough of it, we could build shuttlecraft that required only a slight push to get them off a planet. We could shoot probes into the largest sun and have them come out again on their own power. In fact, gravity-resistant probes would make mining Corzanium itself a snap."

He squinted at the floating rock. "I wonder if it will ever be possible to replicate this stuff?"

Sam yawned. "Grof, do you ever stop thinking about getting ahead?"

"No, as a matter of fact, I don't. Progress is my business. The rest of the universe may be content with the status quo, but I never am. Most of our greatest achievements are only beginnings, halfway measures until the real thing comes along. I'm going to be famous someday, Sam. You'll be able to brag to your grandchildren that you knew me."

"Only if we escape from here," said the human, staring pointedly at the Trill.

For once, Grof met his gaze. "What do you want from me? Some pointless act of patriotism that won't stop the juggernaut of the Dominion for one second? You think I don't hear your little whispered conversations and plots? I do. Of course, Sam, I've heard you talking about escape for several days now, and I think it's just talk. Just by doing your job, you're getting closer to freedom—by *earning* it instead of being stupid. If there's such a big difference between us, I'd like to know what it is."

"You think it's just talk," murmured Sam, worried that the Trill could be right.

"Let me put it this way: I'm a man who looks for options, and thus far, you haven't presented me with any." Grof snatched his floating rock from the air and stalked out of the mess hall.

Sam watched the collaborator go, thinking that, for once, he was right. The time for talking and waiting was over.

Commander Shana Winslow led the way through the aquarium, which was part of the Natural History Exhibit on Starbase 209. Will Riker followed behind her, marveling at what had been done in such a small space to give the feeling of an aquatic world. There were magnified tanks of starfish, seahorses, and neon-orange coral fish, letting a few aquatic animals stand in for many. He paused in a round anteroom, where a school of hundreds of glinting sardines swam around the amazed visitors, moving like electrons in their circular tank.

"Beautiful, aren't they?" asked Winslow. "At one time, they were a staple food source for our ancestors."

"Seems like it would take a lot of them to make a meal," observed Riker.

A cacophony of excited voices diverted his attention, and he and his date stepped out of the way as a gaggle of schoolchildren walked through, talking and pointing excitedly at the whirl of sardines. Since he was taller than them, his view was unobstructed; still Riker found himself watching the school of children instead of the school of fish. Some of them looked distracted, sad.

When the group had moved on, he turned to see a melancholy look on Winslow's face. "What's the matter?" he asked.

She sighed and shifted her weight onto her natural leg. "Most of those kids are war orphans whose parents are not coming back. This base isn't really at the front lines, yet we're filling up with war refugees, orphans, and the like. You brought us almost a hundred of them. I don't know how much longer we can go on before we start busting at the seams."

"Aren't there any transports out?" asked Riker.

"Not very many of them. The commercial space routes are all shut down, and Starfleet's ships are all too busy. There was a time when we could ask a ship like the *Enterprise* to ferry some of these folks for us. I don't suppose you'd like to take a side jaunt to Earth or Bajor before you go back into action?"

"No," admitted Riker, studying the woman's honest face and large brown eyes. "In truth, we probably couldn't make it to Bajor."

"Then the Bajorans may be stuck on this starbase . . . for the duration." Winslow left the school of sardines and wandered toward a wall tank of swaying seaweed and skittery octopus. Riker silently followed her between the soothing tanks of fish.

When he reached her, she mustered a smile and said, "You haven't asked me about your ship all evening. I don't know whether to thank you or be offended."

"I know you and everyone else on 209 are doing all you can." He reached out and brushed a strand of dark hair off her pronounced cheekbone, as he gazed into her wide, sultry eyes. "It's funny. When we first got here, I was in a big hurry to leave. But now I'm not in such a big hurry. I'd be a fool not to enjoy these last few days . . . with you."

"You don't expect to come back either?" asked Winslow hoarsely.

"To tell you the truth, Shana, I don't know what to expect. I'm scared. But I'll keep doing my duty and trying to protect my crew until . . . until there's no point. All I'm trying to say is that you've made these few days better than I had any reason to expect—"

Before he could finish, Captain Winslow pulled him toward her with surprising strength. Her mouth met his in a kiss that was fierce and demanding, only becoming tender after they tasted each other. She gripped his broad shoulders as if hanging on for her life, and he pulled her slight frame into his chest.

They heard giggling, and they turned to see two of the schoolgirls watching them intently. "Shoo!" said Riker with a good-natured grin. The girls ran off, joining the larger pack of children as they wound their way out of the aquarium.

Winslow stepped away from him and pushed a few strands of hair back into place. "I should think twice about public displays of affection, or the other captains will think you have the inside track."

"Well, don't I?" asked Riker with a grin.

"I mean, for getting your ship serviced faster."

"Ah." His hands encircled her waist. "That's not on my mind anymore."

Winslow gently pushed him away. "We need to be more discreet. Shall we return to my quarters?"

"It's your call," said Will, giving her a graceful way to escape his clutches. Under the best of circumstances, he knew he could be something of a wolf, and these weren't the best of times. He only knew that Shana Winslow filled some empty spot within him, and he hoped he did the same for her. These weren't good times to be alone.

"I'm inviting you," she answered, taking his hand and squeezing it. "But, Will, I want you to know that I . . . my body is—"

"You're an oasis of beauty," insisted Riker. "I've got a few scars, too—we can compare them. The Klingons gave me a dandy one when I served aboard the *Pagh,* and it's in a place few people get to see. Then this Borg scratched me across the back with a drill bit—"

Winslow snuggled into the crook of his arm. "I look forward to exploring all of them."

They walked slowly through the suddenly quiet aquarium, and Riker asked, "Are you going to get any emergency calls?"

"Not tonight. The admiral's ship is gone." She gave

him a worried smile and gripped his forearm tighter. "Unless all hell breaks loose—"

"It won't tonight," Riker assured her. "Maybe tomorrow, but tonight the galaxy is going to stand still for us."

After several shifts and a dozen loads of Corzanium, a professional level of confidence was creeping into the work of the tanker crew. No longer was every extraction from the black hole into the recom chambers a white-knuckled dance with death. More and more, the process was like a slow-motion relay race, where the baton kept getting handed off until it crossed the finish line. The flaky Cardassian equipment began to seem stable, even adequate.

They began to think of the Eye of Talek as a deep mining shaft instead of a black hole, and they called it simply "the Hole." It was still dangerous, to be sure, but the Hole was no longer the ominous mystery it had been when they had first seen it. For good or evil, they began to see the black hole as a resource to be plundered.

Grof was still bossy, but he was in a fairly good mood over their progress. The best result of their latest fight was that Grof was now keeping away from the bridge entirely, which suited Sam just fine. Most of the others were good company on the bridge, whenever they filled in at relief or simply stopped by to hang out. But even his best friend, Taurik, wasn't around very much. In the pecking order, it was beginning to seem as if the real action was below-decks in the cargo hold, and Sam was just an afterthought, like the shuttlecraft pilot on the company picnic.

Nobody thought much about the Jem'Hadar ship off starboard, except for Sam. He watched it every spare moment and thought about it constantly. After all this time, he still didn't have a plan to capture the attack craft or disable it. He didn't know whether the Jem'Hadar were getting cocky and overconfident at all, but they deserved to be. So far, everything had gone their way. *Patience,* Sam told himself, *a good idea will come. An opportunity will present itself—be ready to act.*

Perhaps his troubled thoughts were distracting him that first shift of the day, when he should have been at his most alert. But why was Enrique so unobservant at the tactical station? Why was nobody even at the ops station? Were the Jem'Hadar groggy from their white stuff? It probably wouldn't have made any difference, but *somebody* should have seen that meteoroid come streaking out of nowhere, headed straight toward the Eye of Talek.

The meteoroid caught them at the most critical juncture of the extraction, when they had just extended the tractor beam into the black hole to attract the escaping Corzanium. The probe hung on the edge of the event horizon, centimeters from plunging into another realm of space and time. It couldn't have appeared at a worse time.

"Oh, my God!" muttered Enrique when he saw the thing on his readouts.

Both he and Sam stared up at the viewscreen in time to see a monstrous rock as big as a house come hurtling past them. As if that near miss wasn't bad enough, the meteoroid crossed the tractor beam, breaking the seal with the probe. The delicate piece of machinery, which they had babied since dropping the first one, was sucked into the blackness in a microsecond. It disappeared from Sam's readouts like a phantom blip.

"What's going on?" demanded Grof over the ship's comm.

There was no time for Sam to reply, because the meteoroid's path was altered by the tractor beam. It passed through the beam again, caught hold, and jolted the ship. Having much greater mass than the probe, the meteoroid abruptly dragged the tanker toward the Eye of Talek.

"Cut the tractor beam," ordered Sam, but it was too late. Angry footsteps sounded on the ladder behind him.

"We're falling into the hole!" yelled Enrique.

Sam threw every forward thruster into full reverse, and they were tossed out of their seats by the opposing forces. He heard Grof roar with rage as he was dumped off the ladder, but Sam was totally preoccupied with his job now. With every reflex, instinct, and sliver of experience he had, Sam worked the controls in a desperate attempt to save the *Tag Garwal* and themselves.

But the response was sluggish—it was as if the ship were under water, a submarine. Sam realized it was the gravity from the Eye of Talek and possibly some unknown effect of the event horizon. They were too low—on a reentry course with something they couldn't possibly reenter.

Finally Grof stomped up the ladder and stormed out of the hatch, his face purple with rage. "What are you doing, you *idiot?* You're wrecking my ship!"

"Shut up," growled Enrique. "He's trying to save it. Look at the viewscreen—it's a huge meteoroid!"

Sam heard gasps as the giant rock disappeared into the hole, which had come close enough to fill the entire viewscreen with blackness. All of this was on the periphery of Sam's senses, as he struggled with the helm. Perhaps a first-class shuttlecraft with a slew of thrusters would have survived this descent, but not the awkward antimatter tanker, which was not a terrestrial craft. It didn't have enough power to fight this kind of gravity.

"Pull out!" bellowed Grof. "Before we hit the event horizon."

"I'm going into warp drive," declared Sam.

"No!" said Grof. "They . . . they'll kill us."

"Not if we're already dead." He was about to apply an emergency procedure that would probably tear them apart, when something else jolted the *Tag Garwal.* Sam looked at his controls and was amazed to see that their plunge into the hole had been slowed by eighty percent.

"The Jem'Hadar ship," said Enrique. "They've got us in their tractor beam."

Sam changed the viewscreen immediately, putting up the pulsing blue vessel, which was closer than it had ever been before. It was even in transporter range! Although they had just saved his life, his first instinct was to disable them. But he wasn't prepared—it was too sudden.

He again jammed on the jets and finally began to pull away from the gaping singularity, which had swallowed a gigantic meteoroid and a probe without so much as a burp. The Jem'Hadar ship backed away quickly, but Sam was already counting in his head how many seconds they had stayed within his transporter range. They didn't release his ship and return to their former position until the tanker was well out of danger. For almost a minute, they had been vulnerable.

Sam didn't relax until the *Tag Garwal* was safely parked in her former orbit. He felt an odd mixture of anger, fear, and elation. They had almost gotten killed, but they had learned a valuable lesson: the Jem'Hadar were willing to risk their ship and their lives to save the tanker from disaster.

He flicked on the comm. "Captain here. We're okay now, but we lost that probe. Start looking for damage." He tapped it off.

Grof breathed a raspy sigh of relief. "You see, Sam. *Now* what do you think about the Jem'Hadar?"

"I think the damned idiots should have shot down that meteoroid before it got to us!" growled Sam. "Enrique, open a channel to them."

"Belay that order," said the Trill. "Sam, I beg you, don't do anything foolish."

"I'm the captain of this star-crossed ship," muttered Sam. "Enrique, do it."

After a brief pause, the dark-haired human punched his panel. "Opening hailing frequencies. Audio and visual."

Sam stood up and whispered to Grof. "Have some faith in me, will you."

"You're on," said Enrique.

Sam straightened his jumpsuit and stared resolutely at the viewscreen. "I wish to thank our escort for their quick action in saving the *Tag Garwal*. Our entire crew is in your debt, because we would have been lost, along with our valuable cargo.

"However, that meteoroid should not have been allowed to get so close to us. I know you consider that your primary mission is to watch *us*, but you've also got to watch the sky. That meteoroid must have had a trajectory that could be tracked. You have to be our shield and look out for us. If you do that, it will make our job easier." Sam put his hands on his hips and waited.

"They're responding!" said Enrique nervously.

"On screen."

A spiny, cracked, gray face appeared on the screen. The Jem'Hadar lowered his heavy lids and nodded. "Message acknowledged. We will add the service you requested to our duties."

"Thank you." Sam allowed them a polite smile, although he didn't get one in return.

"Out," said the Jem'Hadar before the screen went blank.

Sam turned to look at Grof, who appeared relieved, terrified, and amazed at the same time. "You got them to change their mission."

"To help us stay alive," Sam added. "I guess they think that's a good idea. Don't you?"

"Yes, yes," answered Grof. "I'm sorry I yelled at you, Sam. I didn't know what had happened."

"Yeah, but you're awfully quick to blame your coworkers for everything that goes wrong, when sometimes it's just a matter of Murphy's Law."

"Murphy's Law?" asked Grof. "I'm unfamiliar with that concept."

"Anything that can go wrong *will* go wrong."

Grof nodded sagely. "Yes, I can see the wisdom in thinking along those lines. And I must take responsibility for only bringing three probes, which I thought would be sufficient."

"Let's take a look at the one we dropped," Sam

suggested. "Maybe there are some parts we can replicate."

They heard footsteps on the ladder, and Taurik emerged from the hatch. "We have secured the cargo and the equipment, but we did suffer minor damage. I suggest we suspend operations for the rest of this shift to make repairs and review our procedures."

"Absolutely," said Grof. "We can't be too careful. From now on, we follow the maxim called Murphy's Law. We learned a valuable lesson today."

"Yes, we did," agreed Sam, although he wasn't talking about the same lesson. He had learned the chink in the Jem'Hadar's armor, but it would require a great deal of courage to exploit it.

There was really only one person he would need to take into his confidence—Leni Shonsui, the transporter operator. For the time being, the fewer people who knew, the better; plus Shonsui disliked Grof and wouldn't be inclined to talk to him. The Trill had to be kept in the dark and neutralized, when the time came.

He looked up to see the professor giving him a warm smile, which he found rather unsettling while he was scheming to murder the man. "You did a superb job during the crisis, Sam, and I was wrong— it was a good idea to contact our escort. From now on, I'm going to temper my criticism."

"Good idea, Grof." Sam patted the Trill on the back and steered him toward the ladder. "We might as well get along, because we're all going to hang together."

Chapter Fourteen

SAM COLLAPSED INTO HIS BUNK in the alcove off the bridge of the *Tag Garwal*. He was vaguely aware of the lowered voices of Taurik and Woil as they held down the bridge and monitored shipwide systems. It was downtime on the tanker while they licked their wounds after the near-fatal accident. Apart from the shaken nerves, the major effect was obvious: they were down to one probe with only about a fourth of their projected cargo in the hold.

Unfortunately, this meant that Sam would have to put his plans into effect before they accidentally destroyed the third and last probe. He had no doubt that they would head back to base with half a load rather than none, and he knew he might never get another opportunity to escape like this one, with a ship.

Sam struggled to push all these conflicting concerns and details out of his mind. He had always been a worrier, even when he was a little kid. In the last couple of years, he had learned not to let it show so much, but it hadn't gone away entirely. Since developing more faith in himself, Sam now made quicker decisions and backed them up more forcefully. He guessed he was learning to command, although most of the time he felt helpless and frustrated.

Of all the commands in the galaxy, this had to be the worst: in charge of both the ship and the mutineers, perched on the edge of a black hole with phasers breathing down his neck. That realization didn't console Sam as he struggled to clear his mind and fall asleep.

Finally the lieutenant succumbed to exhaustion and slipped into an agreeable dream. In this dream, he was a lowly ensign back on the *Enterprise* with Ogawa, Sito, Taurik, and those veteran officers like Riker and Worf, who seemed so wise and calm. Now he knew they must have been sweating out every crisis along with the rest of the crew, but it was their job not to show it.

Even Riker was nice to him in this dream, which was like an endless party in the Ten-Forward lounge. Promotions, recommendations, congratulations, and salutations all around! It was like graduation from high school. In fact, some of his old high-school chums were there, too, which struck Sam as odd for a few seconds, until he remembered that this was the *Enterprise.* Anything was possible on the *Enterprise!*

He danced with Jenny, his high-school flame, on the dance floor of the Ten-Forward lounge in his dress uniform. *Hot dog! Does it get any better than this?*

After they danced, they walked off to a dark corner where they could study the serene starscape together and hold hands, while listening to the soft jazz of Riker's quartet. He could feel her hands in his, caressing his chest, stroking his face—

Real hands shook him forcefully. "Captain, wake up!" insisted the Antosian, Jozarnay Woil.

Sam bolted upright, disappointed to find his dream replaced by stark reality. "What now?"

"Another ship has just arrived."

Sam rolled off the bed and pulled his shoes on. He dashed out to the bridge and gazed at the viewscreen, rubbing the sleep from his eyes. Sure enough, another ship had approached the Jem'Hadar craft at a respectful distance, and the two seemed to be parlaying. He didn't recognize the ship or its origins; it was an inelegant craft, possibly even uglier than the *Tug Garwal*.

"Is that another tanker?" he asked Taurik on the conn.

"Negative," answered the Vulcan. "The warp signature identifies it as Bajoran. I would say it is a transport, perhaps a scientific vessel."

"Bajoran?" muttered Woil, shaking his head. "This war just gets weirder and weirder."

Sam's sleepy vision and foggy mind cleared as he studied the strange craft, wondering if he dared to hail them. That would depend, he supposed, on how the Jem'Hadar treated the new arrivals. Unless they were part of the club, he sincerely doubted that their guard would let them hang around the prison work party. Still there might be some way to use their presence to his advantage, and this could be an opportunity waiting to be snatched.

"Should we tell the others?" asked Taurik.

"No," answered Sam. "Look, they're leaving. Track them, Taurik."

"Yes, sir."

The bridge crew watched silently as the boxy ship made an awkward turn and retreated. "Maintain long-range view," ordered Sam.

Observing the Bajoran vessel proved worthwhile. She hadn't gone very far before she stopped and turned around to watch *them*. Sam wondered if the strangers could provoke the Jem'Hadar enough to chase them and desert the tanker, even for a few seconds.

"They have moved outside weapons range," reported Taurik. "Although I can hardly believe they would be any match for the Jem'Hadar craft."

"Maybe it's the Eye of Talek they're interested in," said Woil. "You know, tourists."

"Or a scientific team," suggested Taurik.

Whatever the ship was doing here, Sam didn't want to lose an opportunity. If the Bajorans could be coerced into playing a role in their escape, he had to find a way to do it.

"How close are we to first shift?" asked Sam.

"Twenty-nine," answered Taurik.

"I think we should get everyone up and get an early start on the day's work," declared Sam, rubbing his hands together as if he were Grof. "Let's put that probe out there and grab some more Corzanium."

Taurik gave him a raised eyebrow, but he still rose from his seat and headed for the ladder, ready to carry out the orders.

Woil looked at him point-blank and smiled. "You've got something planned, don't you?"

"Just don't get too attached to your job," cautioned Sam.

Ro Laren stood on the bridge of the *Orb of Peace*, flanked by Captain Picard and Commander La Forge, who was seated at the conn. According to their shorthanded work regimen, one of them should have been in Engineering and the other one asleep in his bunk, but all three had come to the bridge to survey their target:

The Cardassian mining vessel floated in space, looking like a glint in the Eye of Talek. To Ro, it seemed incredible that they could deal a crippling blow to the Dominion's plans merely by destroying this insignificant craft. Thus far, all of the Ferengi's intelligence had been correct, even though they had paid a high price for it. The mining ship had to be destroyed.

As with most of the objectives on this foolhardy mission, this one wasn't going to come easily, because sitting between them and their target was a Jem'Hadar attack ship. They had seen enough of these craft in the last few days to know exactly her capabilities and strengths. Making a frontal attack on the mining ship would be suicide, especially with two torpedoes.

They had already tried stealth and guile, by telling the Jem'Hadar that they were a Bajoran scientific mission sent to study the Eye of Talek. The Jem'Hadar had told them to go away. Now they were just outside weapons range, knowing that the Jem'Hadar had undoubtedly meant for them to go farther away than this. Would the watchdogs feel threatened by the small transport, or would they leave them alone?

Picard frowned at the enemy ships on the viewscreen. "We have to act quickly. Mr. La Forge, can we shoot a torpedo from this range and know that it will eventually make it to the black hole?"

"We could," answered the engineer, "but it would have to be sublight speed, and they would have time to take evasive maneuvers. Then the black hole's gravity would throw off the torpedo's guidance system."

"And we'd be dead thirty seconds later," added Ro.

"Is there something we could do which would be undetectable?" the captain asked hopefully. "Can we make use of the black hole and its side effects?"

With his ocular implants, La Forge scanned quickly between the screen and his readouts. "Maybe there is something we could do. What if we caused a rock slide?"

"A rock slide?" asked Picard.

"Yes. We passed an asteroid belt about three hundred thousand kilometers back. In a bunch of years, those asteroids will find their way into the black hole, anyway, but we could speed up the process."

Ro leaned over him. "How?"

"Collect as many as we can in a tractor beam," answered La Forge, "then take off at low warp speed. We cut the tractor beam and come out of warp, leaving the rocks to go on their way. Sort of like a giant slingshot. At near-warp speed, they won't know what hit them."

"I used to throw rocks at Cardassians as a kid," said Ro. "Sometimes they can be very effective."

"It's the shotgun approach," admitted La Forge with a shrug. "We might miss, but we won't have to use any of our torpedoes. There's nothing that will divert those rocks from that black hole—no shields, no phasers. You can blast them into smaller bits, but they'll just keep coming."

Picard tugged thoughtfully on his earring, then he nodded. "Make it so."

Leni Shonsui was probably the oldest member of the *Tag Garwal* crew, and the Terran had a tough, no-nonsense attitude about life. She had taken the accident with the first probe personally and had withdrawn from the rest of the crew. She was of Asian extraction, thought Sam, and she might have been very beautiful in her youth. Now she was attractive but much embittered by captivity. Nevertheless, what she had managed to do with the Cardassian technology was quite impressive, despite her one lapse.

Sam didn't want to leave seeing her alone to chance, so he purposely called a shipwide meeting in the mess hall for everyone to discuss the probe situation, only he summoned Shonsui to the bridge one minute beforehand.

After the small woman had climbed out of the hatch, he quickly locked it shut behind her. "Leni," he said, "I won't waste time. You know what we have to do—we have to escape. Now we know that the Jem'Hadar will come into transporter range and lower their shields to save us, and *you* have to disable them so that we can get away. Any ideas."

The woman took a sharp breath. "What about Grof?"

"We'll get somebody to neutralize him."

"Okay." She lowered her voice and stood on tiptoes to reach his ear. Her trembling hands gripped his forearm. "Let me beam some of that Corzanium into their warp coil. I grabbed a chunk for myself. Anywhere I put it is bound to cause a problem, even if I miss a bit. We must have schematics of an attack ship on board."

"Yes, I've already located them," answered Sam, pointing to his console. "You take over here on the bridge while I go to the meeting. We'll use the notification icon on your readouts. When I give you the signal, that means we're within transporter range. You have about a minute to do your part. Don't worry about how I get them within range."

"But we won't go into the hole?" asked Shonsui with concern.

"No. Leave that to me. I'm counting on you, Leni, and not a word to anybody. Basically, you and I can make this happen."

"Okay, Captain," she answered with a grin. "And we get to kill a lot of the enemy in the bargain."

"Yeah," answered Sam with somewhat less enthusiasm. Sometimes when he looked at his fellow prisoners, he forgot that they were damaged goods, driven beyond endurance by their captors. He tried to remember all the details he had to attend to.

"We'll fix them," promised Leni, sitting at the conn. "I'll be ready when I get your signal."

"Thank you," breathed Sam as he backed toward the hatch. Now he was certain that he would really have to go through with it. The one person who might have talked him out of it had embraced his foolish plan wholeheartedly.

Sam stepped down the ladder with a feeling of dread. In a short while, he was either going to escape this hell, or he was going to commit suicide and take his fellow prisoners with him.

Will Riker was jolted out of a deep, contented sleep by a piercing, frightened scream. He rolled out of bed, momentarily uncertain where he was.

Turning, he saw Shana Winslow thrashing her fists in the air, sobbing pitifully. With her eyes screwed shut, she still seemed to be asleep, but she was also in some kind of torment. Riker felt he had to wake her up.

"Shana! Shana," he said, gently shaking her. "Wake up."

With a gasp she opened her dark eyes and stared at him. For a moment, she didn't seem to know where she was either. Finally she focused on Riker's face; then she gave him a desperate hug, gripping him as if he were the only real thing in her life.

"Oh, Will! Am I crazy? I see my death every night—the one that didn't happen. I was supposed to die on the *Budapest*—I know it—but they pulled me back from death."

Her fingernails dug into the flesh of Riker's back, and she stared past him. "I see them *all*—the ones who *did* die! My husband, the captain, the first officer—"

"Hey, it's all right to see them," said Riker soothingly. "It's just survivor's guilt. Your dreams may take you back to the past, but you're really here in the present—with me. We're alive. I don't know for how much longer, but we're alive now . . . and we're together."

"That's right," she breathed. "We're alive, and they're dead. Don't know how long—"

In the darkness of a modest cabin on Starbase 209, surrounded by war, refugees, damaged ships, and cold space, the acting captain held the grieving woman in his arms. Riker knew all about survivor's guilt; he was feeling it himself, certain that the captain, La Forge, Data, Ro, and all the rest were dead. He gripped Winslow's fragile body until her shaking stopped.

"Let's do it!" said Sam over the ship's comm. "Prepare to launch the probe."

"That's the spirit," bellowed Grof, standing behind him. He looked uncertainly at Taurik, who was now on tactical. They had gotten used to having the Vulcan belowdeck, filling in where needed, but Sam wanted him here—for this run.

"Whatever happened to that other ship?" asked Grof, sounding as if he were making nervous small talk.

"They left," replied Taurik, "approximately one hour ago."

"Probe ready," announced Woil from below.

"You're on ops, Grof," ordered Sam, slipping casually into his seat at the conn.

"No, wait a minute," blustered the Trill. "With Taurik up here, I'm needed below—we're short-handed."

"Nonsense," answered Sam. "Lately the problems have been up here, not in the hold. I'll let you shoot the tachyons. Please, I want the crack team on the bridge, just for a while."

He thought that appealing to Grof's ego would win

him over. The large Trill sunk into the seat at ops and mustered a put-upon smile. Sam nodded gratefully.

"Captain to crew," he announced. "Launch probe when ready. Stand by on tractor beam."

Despite the disaster of the last probe and the bizarre circumstances, they knew the routine after a dozen successful runs. They were professionals, doing the jobs for which they had trained and lived. The probes may have taken a beating, but the tanker and her crew were still in prime condition, a fact which Sam was counting on. This ignoble craft had to make due as their escape pod back to the Federation.

Without incident, they captured the probe with the tractor beam and lowered it to the brink of the black hole. With a halo of dust flowing into its unquenchable emptiness, the Eye of Talek looked aptly named—a window into the soul of a monster. Its primitive force made the war, the Dominion, and a handful of prisoners seem like plankton to a whale. Worst of all, the hole still looked hungry.

"Beginning tachyon bombardment," said Grof softly, as if taken by the solemnity of the occasion. They were very close to the moment when they had been ambushed by fate the last time.

"Extending tractor beam," reported Taurik.

"Extracting Corzanium," came Tamla Horik's voice from below.

With his heart beginning to race, Sam turned slightly in his seat so that Grof couldn't see his movements. The Trill appeared to be fixated on his own console, as did Taurik, although he would need the Vulcan's attention very soon. After yesterday,

Sam knew enough not to cause a problem while the tractor beam was still extended into the hole. But afterward, when they began to withdraw the probe back to a place where it could be safely transported—that was the time to strike. Now it was time to plant the seeds.

"Grof," cut in Sam, "I'm still having to compensate for slight shifts in our trajectory. That anomaly has never been corrected." He leaned back and pointed to his display.

"Just compensate," growled Grof. "I believe you. There must be spikes in the gravity or something. Someday you can come back and figure it out. For now, just keep us on course."

"If you say so," replied Sam pleasantly, doing as he was told.

Taurik cocked his head thoughtfully. "Perhaps this effect is caused by minute differences in the probes themselves. They may look identical, but they are not."

"Could be," allowed Sam, silently thanking his friend for buttressing his claim. "Like the professor says, nothing to get upset about."

After a few seconds more, Tomla Horik announced, "You were shaking things up in the cockpit, but it's full now. Reel her in."

"Retracting tractor beam," said Taurik. "Stand by to—"

Without warning, the *Tag Garwal* was slammed by a series of sudden jolts, like machine-gun bullets raking their hull. Luckily, Sam's eyes were on his controls, because he immediately fired thrusters to get them away from the black hole.

Sparks and acrid smoke spewed from a wall panel

to his left, and Grof was shouting, "What's going on? *We've lost the probe!*"

"Damage on level two," reported Taurik evenly. "Hull breach, losing atmosphere—"

Sam tuned out the noise, the voices, and the panic as he struggled with the helm, visions of yesterday's disaster swimming in his head. He had a slight jump, more distance, and no tractor beam to contend with, and his reflexes were poised for action. Sam stopped their descent at a safe distance from the event horizon, but he tried not to make it appear too safe. Maybe this was the chance he had been waiting for.

Almost as an afterthought, he glanced at the status of the Jem'Hadar ship, and what he saw made him gasp. He put it on the viewscreen to make sure he was seeing it correctly. The attack ship was listing badly, with gases escaping from half a dozen breaches in her hull. Whatever had hit them, she had taken the brunt of it. Her sensors must have been malfunctioning; normally a Jem'Hadar ship could deflect just about anything. Her thrusters burned brightly, trying to escape the inevitable gravity, but she was on a slow descent straight toward the Eye of Talek.

"Shields up!" he ordered Taurik, thinking they might be hit by more of the invisible missiles, whatever they were.

Sam watched the crippled Jem'Hadar ship drift closer, until she was nearly in transporter range. His finger moved to the corner of his panel, where a special icon awaited his touch: it was the signal to alert Shonsui in the transporter room.

"Hold it right there!" barked Enrak Grof. Sam

looked up to see the Trill glaring at him with hatred and suspicion in his piggish eyes—and a small hand phaser trembling in his hand.

"Where did you get *that?*" Sam demanded.

"Never mind! I don't know how you did it, but I know *you're* behind this. You're insane! Back away from the conn."

"Professor," said Taurik evenly. "We are likely to die unless you allow Sam to pilot the ship. Now please excuse me, there are wounded below, and I am going to attend to them."

While Grof was momentarily distracted by the departure of the Vulcan, Sam pressed his panel and sent the signal to the transporter room. Now it was a moot point. They might all die, but the Jem'Hadar would die first.

The burly Trill looked so angry that his spots were pulsing on his forehead. "Sam, I swear I'll shoot you!"

"Then *shoot* me already! I was going to knock you out before we made a move, but then this happened. You want options, Grof? Here are two: shoot me and die, or escape with us to freedom!"

Stricken by indecision, the Trill looked up at the viewscreen and the damaged attack ship. Now its thrusters weren't even firing, and the vibrant blue glow along its hull was gone, replaced by a dull, lifeless gray—like the skin of a Jem'Hadar.

Grof wailed, "They'll think *we* did this! They'll hunt us down from one end of the galaxy to the other. You could *save* them, Sam—lock the tractor beam on to the Jem'Hadar. Do it, or I shoot!"

Sam flinched, certain that in the next instant he

would feel the phaser beam rip into his skin. But he ignored Grof and maintained steady impulse power away from the attack ship and the black hole which was about to claim it.

"I warned you," muttered Grof, aiming his phaser.

Chapter Fifteen

IGNORING THE PHASER pointed at his skull, Sam Lavelle gazed at the viewscreen and saw the Jem'Hadar attack craft go into a slow spiral in its inexorable descent into the Eye of Talek. He wondered if those stoic warriors showed any panic when confronted with imminent death. Sam himself was surprisingly calm, considering that death was all around him. The destruction of the Jem'Hadar ship had seemed like an act of God, and Sam was willing to believe that nothing would stop their dash to freedom.

"Grof," he said slowly, not turning around, "am I to assume you're not going to kill me?"

Glumly, the Trill lowered his phaser. "I should, but I'm not going to."

"Welcome back to the Federation," said Sam, mustering a wan smile. "And wave good-bye to your friends."

The two crewmates, prisoners, and former enemies watched in stunned silence as the Dominion warship sank into the blackness of the Eye of Talek and disappeared. It was a terrible ending for any starship, thought Sam, as if space had consumed one of its own children.

"Now to set course," said the pilot, shaking off the willies and turning back to his controls. "Any ideas?"

"We could—"

Before he got a chance to finish his sentence, they were struck again by an unseen object. This time, the impact knocked Grof to his feet and threw Sam out of his chair, while sparks and smoke engulfed the tiny bridge. Sam glanced at the viewscreen long enough to see the crate-like Bajoran transport heading toward them, coming in for the kill!

Coughing from the acrid smoke, Sam staggered to his feet, vaulted over the unconscious Trill, and collapsed on top of the tactical station. With his last shred of consciousness, he opened the hailing frequencies.

"Their shields are gone," reported La Forge at the conn of the *Orb of Peace*. "The next one will finish them."

"Target the last torpedo," ordered Picard grimly. "Fire when ready."

When he didn't hear his order repeated back to him after a suitable time, Picard turned to glare at Ro on tactical. "I said fire when ready."

The Bajoran squinted puzzledly as she held an

earphone closer to her head. "I know, sir, but . . . I'm getting a message from one of them. He says they're Federation *prisoners.*"

"Prisoners?" echoed Picard in amazement. "Ask him to identify himself."

Ro gaped at the captain. "It sounds familiar— Lieutenant Sam Lavelle?"

"Lavelle!" The captain strode to Geordi's station and gazed over the engineer's shoulder. "Are we in any danger? Can they fire weapons?"

"No, sir, they're unarmed." La Forge looked at him and frowned. "They're drifting into that black hole. Unless we do something to help them, they're finished, anyway."

"Very well, get down to the transporter room, and lock on to whoever's on that bridge. Beam one over, and if he's really one of ours, get them all."

"Yes, sir." La Forge bolted to his feet and dashed off the bridge.

Ro hefted a phaser and checked the settings. "I'd better help him out."

"Go ahead, I'll take over the conn. Ro, we've already got one prisoner, and I don't want to take any more, unless it's necessary."

"Understood, sir." Her jaw set determinedly, the lanky Bajoran strode off the bridge, leaving the captain alone.

He slumped into the seat at the conn, watching the Cardassian mining vessel drift toward the same monstrous end as the Jem'Hadar ship. Now that he had seen the awesome black hole up close—and witnessed its dangers—he had no problem believing that the Dominion was using slave labor for this sort of work.

Would a person who had free will plant himself at the edge of a black hole? Could a sane person look into that opaque abyss every day?

Picard wasn't surprised when he heard from Ro a few moments later. "Captain," she said breathlessly, "it's true. They're Starfleet, all but one Trill civilian. There are seven in all, and a few are wounded. But they're alive."

"Make them comfortable," ordered the captain. "Send La Forge to Engineering, because we're getting out of here. I'm concerned that the Jem'Hadar may have sent out a distress call. I'm pulling back to maximum torpedo range."

Had he more than one torpedo, the captain would have blasted the Cardassian tanker right then and there. But with only one, he had to be content to sneak away to a safe distance and watch the crippled vessel drift closer to its doom. If he ever had to destroy a starship without leaving a trace, now he knew where to bring it. Finally, the ship disappeared like a candle flame being blown out.

At least they had rescued a handful of prisoners, prisoners who might have a great deal of firsthand intelligence. Most importantly, they had stopped work on the artificial wormhole. Feeling a measure of relief, Picard set course for the Badlands at maximum warp.

Captain Picard and Ro Laren sat in the mess hall of the *Orb of Peace* with the three healthiest of the rescued prisoners. Two of them had served aboard the *Enterprise,* Sam Lavelle and the Vulcan, Taurik— Picard remembered them as friends of Sito Jaxa. The other man was a Trill scientist named Enrak Grof, who had been captured during the fall of Deep Space Nine.

After the preliminaries, they got down to important matters. "Have we really managed to deal a serious setback to the enemy's artificial wormhole?" asked Picard.

Sam, who was still dazed over their rescue, nodded slowly. "I think we have. They can't finish it without the Corzanium you sent back into the hole. Thanks to you, I think we've stopped them."

Taurik and Grof looked less convinced. A show of enthusiastic confidence was not expected from the Vulcan, but the Trill's gloomy expression was troubling.

"What's the matter, Professor Grof?" asked Picard. "You don't share Sam's opinion?"

The Trill sighed heavily. "I wish I could, but I know something they don't know." He looked glumly at Sam, whose smile slowly melted from his face.

"Sam, I . . . I made it sound as if we were the only team sent to extract Corzanium, but that isn't true. At least one other team of Cardassians was sent secretly to another black hole. I fully expected *us* to be the ones who succeeded when they failed."

"Why am I not surprsied?" muttered Sam, rising to his feet. "Just one more lie you had to tell us, huh, Grof?"

"Come on." The Trill scowled. "You didn't expect the Dominion to put all their eggs in one basket. We were an important experiment, but they were prepared for our failure . . . or attempted escape."

Ro Laren slumped back in her chair. "So what you're saying is—we've still got to take out that verteron collider."

Grof nodded wearily. "Yes, it's a shame, too, because it's a triumph of engineering and construction. It would have worked."

"It will work, if we don't destroy it," concluded Taurik. "The Dominion has the resources and the resolve to complete the work. Before the accident which necessitated our mission, I believe they were nearly ready to begin tests."

"And they'll probably use prisoners for that," said Sam gloomily.

Tight-lipped, Picard turned to Ro and said, "Put the subspace beacon away. We're not going home for a while."

Boredom was an abstract term to an android, but Data knew very well what it meant: the absence of something to do. He had a duty, of course—monitoring the scanner array he had set up on the barren moon—but it required less than one percent of his attention. Staring at the starlit sky had never impressed him as being an entertaining activity, as it was for many humanoids, but he found himself doing just that for hour after hour.

Finally, in the interest of experimentation, Data turned on his emotion chip. At once, a shock wave of worry, fear, guilt, and war sickness slammed into him, making him feel more despondent than he had ever felt in his entire existence. The horror, tragedy, and destruction of the war was too much to contemplate, even for his positronic brain, and Data could only stare at the dust at his feet. He fretted over his lost comrades, all of whom were afraid, lonely, grieving, and bored.

Realizing it had been a mistake to activate his

emotion chip, Data reluctantly turned it off. After returning to normal, he still felt weakened and so-bered by the assault of heartrending emotions. Now Data had an interesting question to contemplate as he sat on his barren outpost: How did humans and other sensitive races deal with war, knowing its horrors? How could they possibly maintain their sanity?

Look for STAR TREK Fiction from Pocket Books

Star Trek®: The Original Series

Star Trek: The Next Generation®

Star Trek: Deep Space Nine®

Star Trek®: Voyager™

Star Trek®: New Frontier

Star Trek®: Day of Honor

Star Trek®: The Captain's Table

Star Trek®: The Dominion War